I0618717

# LEPAN'S SHADOW

Non-fiction by Douglas Pearce

*Tourist Destinations: structure and synthesis*
*Frameworks for Tourism Research*
*Tourist Organizations*
*Tourism Today: a geographical analysis*
*Tourist Development*

An International Mystery

# LEPAN'S SHADOW

# DOUGLAS PEARCE

WELLINGTON

Copyright © Douglas Pearce 2025

First published 2025 by Opihi

All rights reserved

No part of this book may be reproduced or transmitted in any form or by any means, electronic or mechanical, including photocopying, recording or by any information storage and retrieval system, without prior permission in writing from the publisher.

This is a work of fiction. Any references to historical events, real people, real companies or real places are used fictitiously. Other names, characters, companies and events are products of the author's imagination and any resemblance to actual persons, living or dead, is entirely coincidental.

A catalogue record for this book is available from the National Library of New Zealand.

Soft cover ISBN 978-0-473-75194-4
Epub ISBN 978-0-473-75195-1
Kindle ISBN 978-0-473-75196-8

Cover design by Amanda Sutcliffe
Design & layout www.yourbooks.co.nz
Author's photo by C. Pearce

For Chantal

# CHAPTER 1

Antoine Lepan lowered his long-lensed camera and gesticulated wildly, as only an agitated Frenchman can. '*Merde*! I had those flamingos perfectly framed. Now look what you've done, you spoilt little brat. You've scared them all away. Young kids shouldn't be allowed on these tours. We're not on holiday here, you know.'

Rico had raced to the head of our tour party, busting to get as close to the birds as possible.

'Steady on, Antoine,' I said, 'the boy meant no harm. And look, the flamingos have settled down again. You can take your photo now.'

He gave me a mind-your-own-business look and stomped off uttering Gallic imprecations. I smiled; I hadn't heard some of those for a while.

'Antoine hasn't mellowed much, has he, Cliff?' said Viviana Arévalo. She had quickened her pace to catch up with me after being buttonholed on the bus by one of the contributors to the book she was editing. Her hazel eyes twinkled under her fashionable gaucho-style sunhat.

I gave her a hug. 'Not one bit. He's as self-centred as ever. But you're looking radiant as always.'

'Must be the sun reflecting off the salar,' she said with a laugh.

Chile's Salar de Atacama, that is. The shimmering white of the salt-encrusted surface of the salar contrasted with the blue waters of the Chaxa Laguna where wading flamingos breakfasted on small crustaceans and micro-organisms or stretched out overhead in graceful flight.

We walked on, admiring the flamingos and chatting with the ease of old friends, as if it had been only a couple of weeks, not eighteen months, since we had last met at a workshop in Brussels.

'I don't know how flamingos manage to do that,' Viviana said and pointed to a couple of the magnificent birds unmoved by the constant stream of tourists.

'Do what?'

'Stand on one leg so easily. Looks like they could do that for hours. Our Pilates instructor gets us doing that, or at least trying to. I lose my balance after ten seconds.'

Pilates. So that's how she kept so trim and fit-looking, a sixty-something going on fifty.

'I didn't know you were into Pilates, Viviana.'

'We all have our secrets, Cliff,' she replied.

•••

Lepan was right about one thing, we weren't on holiday. Well, not entirely. We were due to attend the 2018 Latin American Conference on Tourism and Development being held in Santiago under the auspices of the Tourism and Development Studies Association International (TADSAI). A group of academics, from young researchers to elderly professors, all with an interest in tourism. With us, there was often a blurred line between touring for pleasure and taking a professional interest in what we were seeing, how it was managed, who the visitors were and so on. I had given up trying to explain that to envious colleagues and neighbours. On this tour Lepan was to lead a workshop on co-governance, on how the Atacameño communities, the indigenous inhabitants of the Atacama, might become more involved with government agencies in managing natural attractions in the region.

Even though we all spoke Spanish, not much inter-mingling had occurred yet. Our tour group consisted of five Chileans, four Argentinians (Viviana, Rico Toledo and his parents, Pablo and Alba), two Mexicans, a Brazilian couple, and what I thought of as the Rest-of-the-World contingent: Maria Paz Casals (Spain), Pat Mason and Rory O'Connor (Ireland), Antoine Lepan (France) and myself, Cliff West (New Zealand).

In her early thirties, Maria Paz was making a name for herself studying tourist movements in rural destinations using GPS. Her sharp facial features were framed by her long black hair; distinctive green eyes typical of her Alicante ancestry revealed a keen intellect.

I had met Pat Mason, an amiable, if at times cynical, red-bearded bear-like Irishman, at various conferences over the years. His research was invariably original, carried out with meticulous care and presented in his delightful brogue.

I did not take to his younger colleague, Rory. His shifty look gave the impression he was continually weighing up how to take advantage of you. Rory must have known his stuff; Pat did not tolerate fools.

Emeritus Professor Antoine Lepan was the big name in the group. A widely published anthropologist and distinguished professor of development studies at the University of Bordeaux, Lepan was the keynote speaker at the conference. In my experience, big names tended to fall into two categories: collegial, down-to-earth types who mixed freely and did not expect their reputations and positions to confer any special treatment; and arrogant, aloof personalities with huge egos and a massive sense of entitlement. Lepan led the latter pack by a country mile.

In his early seventies, Lepan was not a physically imposing figure. Short and slightly built, he had a bluish birthmark the size of a bantam's egg below his right eye, like a half-back left with a permanent reminder of being clobbered by a large lock cleaning out a ruck. Lepan did not stand tall but dressed to stand out in his trademark brown leather vest and peaked mariner's hat. Very *m'as-tu vu*.

Like Lepan, I am an emeritus professor. In my case, of tourism management at Victoria University of Wellington. I remained active by being reactive. I accepted invitations that came my way to join a research project, be a visiting professor or give a keynote address, providing the activities were interesting and enabled me to indulge my passion for international travel. My research was widely recognised, I did not want for opportunities and wasn't troubled yet by my carbon footprint.

•••

The afternoon visit to the Valle de la Luna (Moon Valley) was much more arduous than watching the flamingos in the relative cool of the morning. We followed a track up a giant dune, then up another, and another one still, clambering over sunbaked rocks now and again for good measure. My feet kept slipping and sliding in the sand. I was soon sweating profusely and reached for my water bottle at the top of each dune. The Atacama experiences the highest levels of solar radiation in the world according to our guide, Marisela. I was more grateful for the breather while she explained this than for the actual information that she imparted. The younger ones in our party, and even Lepan, were not troubled by the climb or the heat. I was out of shape. I had eaten too many empanadas and drunk too much carmenere during my recent stint as a visiting professor at the Universidad Austral de Chile (UACh) in Valdivia.

The view compensated for the sweat and my complaining legs. The weird and other-worldly landscape around me was how I envisaged the moon. Barren and desolate, sand dunes rippled between jagged rocky outcrops of every imaginable shade of brown, sprinkled salt white, sulphuric yellow or some other mineral hue. The purplish cone of the Licancabur volcano loomed large in the clear blue sky. This was what I had come for. The Atacama was living up to my expectations.

Rico had not learnt his lesson and his parents were still having difficulty keeping him in check. He tripped in his haste to be the first to the top of one track and would have tumbled down a sandy slope if Maria Paz hadn't reached out and grabbed his arm as he sailed past.

Rico almost bowled Lepan over, causing the Frenchman to let rip. 'Can't you keep that unruly kid of yours under control? We had enough trouble this morning at the flamingos, but here someone could get hurt the way you let him run loose. And tomorrow we're going to the geysers. You have to watch your step there. Discipline the boy or stay back at the hotel.'

Lepan had a point. Kids can be disruptive, but he did not need to be that hard on Pablo and Alba. Rico reminded me a lot of our son Rod. We had taken him on similar tours at that age and often had to curb his enthusiasm at all the new and exciting things he experienced. Once, on a field trip up Mount Etna, I turned round to find him perched on a rock, peering over the crater's rim. My heart skipped a beat. Or two. Rod looked up with a big grin and said, 'Dad, I can see the molten lava down there.'

Later in the afternoon Rico's energy ebbed and he joined me in the rear-guard as we descended. At one bend in the track, I had to stretch from one rock to another. Rico jumped across, turned and said, 'One small step for man, one giant leap for mankind.'

'Who said that?' I asked, surprised by this quote from a ten-year old half a century after the event.

'Neil Armstrong, the first man on the moon?'

'How do you know that?'

'I've got some cousins in a town called Armstrong, not too far from where we live in Rosario. They brag that it is named after Neil Armstrong, but my dad says it's actually because of some railway pioneer.'

'Well, now you will be able to tell them you've been on the moon,' I said. 'Valle de la Luna. I can take your photo to prove it. Stand there.' I snapped a couple of shots with the most lunar-looking landscape in the background.

'Boy, that will make them jealous.' He eyed me up and down. 'You must be really old. I bet you can even remember when Armstrong and Aldrin landed on the moon.'

I could. My second year at university. I told him all about that time in July 1969 when I had stood in a crowded quad after a late tutorial and looked up into the night sky wondering how in hell the Americans had pulled it off. The moon had seemed so impossibly far away.

We carried on down, deep in a discussion of stars and planets and the moon.

'That's a bright boy you've got,' I said to Pablo when I delivered Rico back to his dad in the car park.

'But he can be a bit of a rascal at times, can't you, Rico?' He tousled his son's mop of curly brown hair.

'Do try and keep out of Professor Lepan's way, Rico.'

He grinned.

•••

Day Two of the tour would reveal another face of the Atacama. Marisela assured us that our 4am start was essential if we were to see the El Tatio geysers at their best. We wound our way out of San Pedro de Atacama, the second in an informal convoy of tourist vehicles, and arrived at our destination still half asleep. Despite the early hour and the countless trips she must have made, Marisela, a buxom extrovert in her forties, exuded enthusiasm.

'Here we are at the world's third largest geothermal field,' she announced. 'You have an hour and a half to look around and appreciate the awe-inspiring beauty of Mother Nature, or Pachamama as the Atacameños call her. You are free to wander around at your own pace—I will be staying behind with Jorge to prepare breakfast for when you get back.'

'Do we need a map?' one of the Chileans asked. 'It's still quite dark.'

Marisela looked out the door. 'It does seem exceptionally steamy this morning but the sun is starting to peek through. Stick to the marked paths and you will be fine. The surface crust is thin in places, and we don't want you breaking through it or falling into any of the hot pools. The water is boiling hot. So, be careful. No misadventures.'

Was it at all dangerous or were we being left to wander round on our own to heighten our sense of awe and discovery?

'It looks cold out there,' the Brazilian woman said. She shivered in anticipation.

'It will be freezing outside because of the time of the day and the altitude—we're at over four thousand metres above sea level,' Marisela said. 'Make sure you put on your woolly hats and scarves, zip up those jackets and keep your gloves on.'

Lepan had commandeered the front seat next to the driver and made sure he was first off the bus again. Why the rush? Did he want his photos Rico-free? I prefer to have a few tourists in my photos—tourist attractions, after all, are not tourist attractions without tourists.

Maria Paz, Pat and I had been sitting at the back and were last off. We instinctively hunched our shoulders against the freezing temperature and tugged the drawstrings of the hoods of our puffer jackets tighter. Pat had gone ethnic and sported the colourful woolly hat which he had bought in San Pedro. 'Those Incas knew a thing or two about living in this environment,' he

7

said, unconcerned by the incongruous sight he presented after he had pulled the flaps over his ears. Practicality trumped style every time with Pat.

'I need my scarf after all,' Maria Paz said and stepped back into the bus. She was gone a couple of minutes. 'Sorry, I couldn't find it right away, it had fallen under the back seat.'

We made our way from the car park towards the hot pools. What had happened to the convoy of vehicles whose lights I had seen behind us earlier? The only other vehicle in the car park was a ute. Whoever had come in it, along with the rest of our group, had already been swallowed up in the steamy darkness ahead.

An ethereal silence and stillness descended upon us. Once alongside the pools the steam thickened. Hissing vents and gurgling waters broke the silence. So did Rico as he ran up and down shouting 'Spooky, spooky', his long red scarf streaming out behind him.

'Hey, slow down, Rico,' I called as the steam engulfed him again.

'It's like a giant outdoor sauna,' Maria Paz said. 'Where does all that steam come from?'

'From those vents on your left. They're called fumaroles. The steam dissipates as the air temperature rises later in the morning and the place becomes much less spectacular. That's why we had to come at this ungodly hour.'

'Where are the geysers?'

'There's one, right in front of you.'

'That?' She pointed to a spurt of hot water spouting a metre into the air from a silica-covered mound. 'I expected geysers to be much higher, like the ones at Yellowstone I've seen pictures of.'

'Hey, there's a bigger one,' Maria Paz cried a couple of minutes later. 'The sun's breaking through. Let me get some photos while it's spouting. Cliff, could you stand there to give some perspective. And you too, Pat.' But Pat had drifted off.

Maria Paz clicked away and waited without success for the geysers to erupt even higher. I took a few photos with my phone to validate Maria Paz's expectations. I wasn't all that impressed. The Pohutu geyser in Rotorua shoots 30 metres into the air—and at visitor-friendly times throughout the day.

A loud wailing pierced the steam.

'That's Rico. Something's happened to him.' Maria Paz raced off along the path that began to curve around the pool.

I followed, afraid the boy had charged off the path.

We came across him sunk to his knees in the middle of the path, his head buried in his hands. His wailing reduced to a whimper. He was being comforted by Ana, one of the Chilean women. Maria Paz crouched to help calm him down.

The steam cleared briefly. A few metres further along, Pat knelt at the pool's edge trying to catch hold of the boot of a body spread-eagled in the boiling water. I knew from the distinctive green jacket that Antoine Lepan would not be delivering his keynote address.

'Cliff, give me a hand to pull the poor bugger in,' Pat shouted.

I grabbed Pat by his belt so that he could stretch out further and grip Lepan's boot without toppling into the cauldron himself. I leaned back and heaved. Pat grunted with effort. On our third attempt we managed to drag his body up onto the path and put him in the recovery position.

I couldn't see his breath coalescing in the chilly air. I reached in under the collar of his heavy jacket but found no pulse on the side of his neck. I grimaced and shook my head. 'Nothing. We're too late, he's had it,' I said, thankful that I did not have to try and revive him. I practically threw up at the thought of doing mouth-to-mouth on that blotched and blistered face, the colour and texture of freshly boiled corned beef.

Pat appeared to be taking it all in his stride, as if he hauled bodies from hot pools every day. Maybe he had experienced much worse growing up in Belfast during the Troubles.

'What happened?' I asked.

'Didn't see. I was wandering back wondering where you and Maria Paz had got to. The track forks not far from here and I thought you might have gone the other way. I couldn't see much in all this steam. It cleared for a moment with a breath of wind and I saw Lepan lying in the water. I tried to pull him in but he was just out of reach.'

Pat had been kneeling on a red scarf to protect his knees from the row of stones that fringed the path. Lepan's hands were bare, and his camera hung on a strap around his neck.

'Looks like he's tripped on one of those stones or on that scarf while he was taking a photo and fell in,' I said. I looked again. That's Rico's scarf, I realised with dismay. The poor kid's seen the body in the water and thinks it's his fault, that it's his scarf Lepan has tripped on.

I looked around for the boy but couldn't see or hear him. Thank God for that. Maria Paz and Ana had already taken him away from the gruesome scene.

'What do we do now, Cliff?'

'I suppose we should leave him here. We shouldn't disturb anything in case the police or coroner need to be involved. I don't know how they handle fatal accidents in Chile.'

'We can't just leave him on the track,' butted in Felipe, one of the Mexicans who had just happened upon us. 'It's undignified. Other tourists will be arriving soon. The nearest police are back in San Pedro. Rodrigo, run back and tell Marisela that Lepan has had an accident, that he's dead,' he ordered his colleague. 'And see if they have a stretcher at that visitor centre.' Rodrigo rushed off.

Felipe bent and rested Lepan's head on the scarf. As if the corpse on the cold ground would derive any comfort from the gesture. The excitable Mexican started prattling on. How Lepan was such a good man. A fine scholar. What a loss he would be to academia. How could he die like that? A tragedy.

'Shut the fook up, Felipe,' Pat growled. That silenced the Mexican. We were left with the intermittent hissing of the fumaroles and the gurgling of the hot pool as we waited for somebody to come and take charge.

I stood staring through the steam out across the pool, determined to ignore the corpse on the track. Lepan's hat drifted away on the rippling waters and gradually sank.

Pat turned to me, touched my arm and asked if I was OK. 'You've gone all white,' he said.

'A bit shocked, that's all. Tourism management doesn't expose you to a lot of raw death.'

To be honest, I was completely shaken. I felt faint. My heart thumped. Not because of Lepan—I scarcely knew the man, except by reputation. No, the sight of his grotesque face was overshadowed by the memories that came flooding back to me of the only other dead body I had ever seen, Rod's.

•••

It had been two long decades since the young constable in Hanmer Springs knocked on my motel door. He informed me that my son had had a fatal accident and asked me to accompany him. Rod lay entangled in his mountain bike amongst the rocks in the stream bed twelve metres below the trail. He looked at peace. No external signs that Rod had broken his neck in the fall, the cause of death later confirmed by the coroner.

Another biker who had pulled off the trail because his gears had jammed had seen it all unfold. Rather than brake as he came down the trail, Rod was pedalling faster and faster. He did not try to take the bend. Rod had deliberately gone straight ahead, full speed. We found his helmet a couple of hundred metres back along the trail. It was no accident. Rod had taken his own life. He was fourteen years old.

•••

We waited with Lepan's body for the centre's staff to turn up before we joined the rest of the group back at the bus. By now everyone knew of Lepan's fate. The ham and cheese rolls which Marisela and Jorge had prepared lay untouched on the folding table. We all needed a strong coffee. Pat produced a flask of Irish whisky from inside his jacket and slipped a generous measure in my mug. It helped me to regain some colour and recover my composure. Maria Paz did not hesitate to hold her mug out for some whisky too. Her face was as pale as her jacket.

The incident brought us closer together; no longer separated by nationality but united by the death of one of our party. Gone was the animated chatter of the previous day when we had been fascinated by the flamingos and thrilled by lunar landscapes. In other circumstances my fellow travellers would have been comparing selfies shot in the steam, trying to outdo each other in describing the largest geyser they had seen. Not this morning. We stood around as a group, trying to make sense of what had happened. Everyone offered an opinion.

'He spent all his time peering through that camera of his. When you are trying for a long distance shot you can easily lose sight of where your feet are.'

'Or he might have been trying to take a selfie. Lots of accidents happen like that.'

'What a horrible way to go.'

'Makes you think, it could have happened to any of us, with all that steam and the darkness.' Heads nodded at the realisation. Some were visibly shaken by the possibility.

'Marisela should have come with us.'

'Well, she did warn us to be careful.'

'Didn't he trip on that boy's scarf?'

'Could have been a heart attack. He would have been the oldest one in our group, wouldn't he?' Sideways glances at me.

It was all speculation. No one had been on the spot and seen him fall.

I kept my thoughts to myself.

Ana stepped down from the bus where she and Viviana had been comforting Rico and his parents and joined the group. I added three spoons of sugar to a mug of coffee and handed it to her.

'How's Rico?'

'He's badly shaken up but has quietened down a little. He keeps saying it wasn't his fault. We've all been assuring him that Lepan had an accident.'

'Why is he so upset?' Pat asked. Pat was a childless bachelor.

'His scarf came off when he was running along the track,' Ana said. 'He was coming back looking for it when he saw Lepan's body in the pool. Right by his scarf. He was racing off to tell someone when I came across him. He was bawling his eyes out. Seeing Lepan like that was awful for such a young kid. He thinks it's all his fault, that Lepan tripped on his scarf. Later he overheard one of the Mexicans say so too. That only made matters much worse.' She glared at Rodrigo.

Yesterday's incidents at the flamingos and Valle de la Luna wouldn't have helped either.

'How are Pablo and Alba?' I asked.

'Alba's clinging on to Rico. Pablo's feeling terrible, blaming himself for letting Rico run loose again. Viviana's doing a good job trying to console them,' Ana said. Viviana always looked out for others.

Marisela, who had been standing to one side, put away her phone and came over. 'Jorge, start clearing everything up. Everyone, please get back on the bus, we will be leaving in ten minutes.'

We needed no urging and clambered aboard. Viviana and the Toledos were sitting at the back of the bus so they would not have to put up with everyone else filing past and looking at them. Nor could they see Lepan's empty seat from the back. The rest of the group could not help but look at it, some openly, others more discreetly.

Jorge stalled the bus twice turning around in the empty carpark and clipped a sign near the exit as we left.

Marisela explained what was happening in a composed and professional manner. 'Señor Alvarez, our managing director, extends his sympathies to you all regarding this unfortunate incident, particularly those who were close colleagues of Professor Lepan.'

Did any of us fall into that camp? Lepan had kept to himself. His behaviour yesterday would not have endeared him to anyone. He had nodded when I first boarded the bus—we had shared a table at a conference dinner a couple of years ago—but that was the limit of our exchanges on this tour other than me telling him to go easy on Rico at the flamingos. However horrific the sight of his corpse, I was more shaken by the memories of Rod's death which it had triggered than by grief for Lepan.

Viviana had been too busy caring for her compatriots for me to have had a chance to talk to her. She would have been familiar with Lepan's research in South America and two of his articles had appeared in her journal. She had witnessed his egoistical behaviour at other conferences and was not enamoured of him.

Pat had not appeared unnerved when we pulled the body from the hot pool nor showed any emotion afterwards. He had taken more than one swig from his whisky flask. Was I underestimating the effect of Lepan's death on him? Or was the whisky just to ward off the cold?

I could not understand why Felipe Montoya had become so upset and had insisted that Lepan's body be removed from the track. I hadn't noticed the two together beforehand. Basic human decency? Perhaps.

The Brazilians and Chileans were in their thirties and early forties and were less likely to have been familiar with much of Lepan's earlier work. They probably knew he was a prominent scholar but would not have had much, if any, exposure to him personally. None of them had approached him the previous day that I saw. Ana was concerned for Rico, not worried about Lepan.

Maria Paz had helped her calm the boy and take him back to the bus. The unsettling sight of Lepan's corpse in the steaming hot pool did not sink in until later. Little wonder she needed a nip of Pat's whisky in her coffee.

Jorge kept looking over at the empty seat previously occupied by the Frenchman. Not surprising, Lepan had been sitting right alongside him yesterday and on the way out to the geysers. Now he had one passenger less.

'Let's not dwell on what has happened,' Marisela said. 'The authorities will look into Professor Lepan's accident. We need to return to San Pedro immediately. The local police will want to take statements from everyone this afternoon and you will all need to stay in the hotel until you've been interviewed.'

'What about this afternoon's workshop with the Atacameño representatives?' Pat asked. 'I was looking forward to that.' I cringed. Sensitivity was not Pat's strongest suit.

'That won't be possible now, Pat. But I will see if the coordinator can join us tomorrow.'

'Marisela, are we still stopping at Machuca?' one of the Chileans asked.

'No, we need to head straight back in case of delays along the way. Two old cars driven by young Australians crashed into each other at one of the bends twenty kilometres back and blocked the road right after we came through. Some people don't realise how tricky it can be driving in the Atacama, especially in the dark.

'Now, if you look out the window, you will see the steam has cleared away and the place is not as awesome as when we first arrived. So, it was well worth getting up so early for, wouldn't you agree?'

'I don't think Antoine Lepan would,' Pat said. With irony, not compassion.

We travelled back in silence, lost in our thoughts.

I tried to put aside my memories of Rod and the sight of Lepan's corpse and to think about his death objectively wearing my visitor management hat. Seeing the geysers, the hot pools, the steam, and all the hissing and bubbling would be an adventure for most visitors. However, they would not be in any real danger provided they used their common sense and stayed on the paths. The paths were wide, level, well-formed and clearly marked. From a safety point of view, there was no need for Marisela to have accompanied us.

From what I could make out, it did appear as if Lepan had tripped, either on the marker stones or on Rico's scarf. That was surprising for such a veteran international traveller. He would have been in far more dangerous places. He looked as agile and sure-footed as a mountain goat the way he had managed the dunes, skipped around the rocks, and side-stepped Rico at the Valle de la Luna.

What other explanation could there be?

As we gradually encountered vehicles coming the other way, I wondered about the Australians' crash. That must have been why we had the geysers to ourselves. Apart from the occupants of the ute, that is. Strange that we had never come across them at any stage. They would surely have done something or told someone in our group if they had seen Lepan fall in. Wouldn't they?

# CHAPTER 2

After lunch I did a quick online search to see what I could find about the local Carabineros de Chile before being interviewed. San Pedro de Atacama, I discovered, was not a tourist oasis free of major crimes. Over recent months there had been reports of people smuggling, seizures of substantial amounts of drugs and a couple of drug related murders. I should not have been surprised considering San Pedro is not that far from Bolivia and Peru. Monitoring the desert borders would be a challenging task. One of the murders had occurred only ten days earlier. The accidental death of a tourist would not warrant much attention or draw heavily on San Pedro's police resources.

It was a relief to be called into the manager's office where the air conditioner functioned perfectly. Sergeant Figueroa sat back in the executive chair behind the manager's tidy desk, complete with potted plant and family photo. This was a place where business was done and complaining guests were pacified, a much more dignified setting in which to interview international guests about what had happened to their unfortunate colleague than the police station. The interviews were being recorded to save us the inconvenience of making formal written statements.

Figueroa motioned for me to take a chair. He was fiftyish,

portly and his initial demeanour suggested he was assigned the commissariat's more banal duties on a regular basis. The sergeant surprised me when he began by asking what exactly an emeritus professor was. 'You and the deceased are the only ones in the group with that title.'

'It's an honorary title which a university awards to a full professor with a distinguished career when they retire. We're no longer on the university payroll but we're expected to continue to contribute to its academic life and reputation. Most of us go on researching and writing.'

'No longer on the payroll. Then you emeritus professors must be devoted to what you do. How do you manage? Travel to Chile and accommodation in hotels like this does not come cheaply.' He looked out the window towards the swimming pool where other guests enjoyed relief from the afternoon heat.

'In my case, I'm working my passage. I completed a spell as a visiting professor in Valdivia last week.'

'And Professor Lepan?'

'An eminent scholar. He wouldn't have had any trouble getting cost-covered invitations to conferences, visiting professorships, consultancies, research grants and so on. He spoke several languages, so that helps.'

'How would he have supported his…his activism?' Figueroa had difficulty with the word, as if it tasted unpleasant on his palate.

'I've no idea. I'm not an activist.' Where was Figueroa going with his questions?

'How well did you know him?'

'Some of his research on tourism overlapped with my interests. I had heard him speak and met him at several conferences. That was the limit of my personal contact.'

'You weren't acquainted with him in France?' How did he know about my French connections, my doctorate from Aix-en-Provence, my visiting professorship at the Sorbonne?

'No. We never met there.'

Figueroa moved on to the questions I expected. He took me step by step through what I did from the time Lepan got off the bus until I saw his body in the hot pool.

'So, you were the first to reach him?'

'No, Dr Mason was there already, trying to drag his body out of the pool. The two of us were able to pull him out of the water and onto the track.'

'What did you do next?'

'I thought we should leave Lepan there. The Mexicans had other ideas.'

'Where did they come from?'

'I don't know, I was checking Lepan for a pulse. We hadn't passed them so they must have come from the other direction.'

'What did you think had happened to Lepan, Professor?' He swivelled from side to side in the manager's chair—not standard commissariat issue—without taking his eyes off mine.

'It looks like he tripped while taking a photo. Maybe on those red stones that line the edge of the path. I also saw a scarf on the ground. But who knows?'

'While you were waiting, did you notice anything unusual, out of place?'

I had been too shaken by memories of Rod's death to take in much else. 'I wondered what had distracted Lepan. That hot pool didn't seem any different from the others.'

'Anything else?'

'Lepan usually had a heavy black camera bag slung over his shoulder. He was forever switching cameras and changing lenses.'

The manager rapped loudly and burst into the room. 'Sergeant, come quickly, someone has been searching Professor Lepan's room.'

'Professor, wait here,' Figueroa ordered and followed the manager out.

Was this the moment when the cop or FBI agent conveniently leaves the room to provide our hero the opportunity to go through files he should not have access to? That's what happens in the books I read. Unlikely; the manager looked too flustered when he barged in for his interruption to be anything other than spontaneous. Anyway, I was no hero.

I got up to stretch my legs. On the desk I recognised the orange TADSAI conference booklet with which Figueroa had covered his note pad. He must have got it from Marisela whose parent company were the event organizers for the conference. It contained short bios of Lepan, Viviana, me and the other session chairs. That explained how he had made the French connection. I nudged the booklet aside to see what he had written. Three words: 'emeritus professors  money???' Why was Figueroa so interested in how professors emeriti survived financially? He was doing more than going through the formalities of an accidental death. I was tempted to check and see what else he had written from the earlier interviews. Too much of a risk, he could return at any moment.

When he came back ten minutes later, the sergeant picked up where he had left off.

'So, Professor, no sign of Lepan's camera bag?'

'I didn't see it.'

'Other than members of your group, did you see anybody else at the geysers this morning?'

'No. There was a ute in the car park when I got off the bus, but no one was in it.'.

'Ute?' Figueroa looked puzzled.

'Utility truck, you know, a pickup.'

'What sort of ute?'

'I'm not sure. I'm not good with models and makes of cars. And it was still dark when we arrived.'

'Colour?'

'Darkish with a bit of white on the doors.' He made a note.

'Do you know what Lepan had been investigating recently?'

'He didn't discuss his work in advance. He relished making a big splash with his presentations, especially if it was controversial. All I know is his keynote address was to deal with tourism's contribution to improving the lives of indigenous peoples in Latin America.'

'Would that have been controversial?'

'The topic can generate heated debate, that's for sure.'

'And at the Atacameño workshop this afternoon?'

'He would have been the facilitator and offered some international comparisons.'

The sergeant thanked me and I left.

Rory O'Connor was sitting outside the office like a misbehaving schoolboy waiting to be called in to see the headmaster. He had not been with us at the geysers because he had altitude sickness the night before. 'You're looking more chipper, Rory. What have you been up to now?'

'Nothing, it's just red tape. The sergeant must've been told to take statements from everyone in the group and he's following it to the letter of the law, you might say.' He got up and entered the office.

On my way to the bar where I knew I would find Pat, I crossed the Toledos in the lobby. They were returning from a special outing which Marisela had arranged for Rico to see some of the local animals. Downcast, he clung to Alba's hand.

'*Hola* Rico, what did you see?'

'*Hola* Professor Cliff.' He looked up at me and gave a brave little smile. I could see from the redness around his eyes that he had been crying again. 'We saw seven vicunas and a desert fox with crafty eyes. The guide said we were lucky to see one that close.' He burst into tears and Alba hurried him off to their room.

I told Pablo that I was sorry to see Rico in such a state. I asked what I should do with his scarf which I had picked up after Lepan's body had been taken from the path.

'Just get rid of the damn thing. Rico won't be wearing it again.'

I needed that drink.

•••

Pat was sitting on one of the bar stools, admiring the mural on the wall. It depicted the salty expanse of the Salar de Atacama.

'Smart idea, that,' he said, tilting his glass towards the mural. 'Makes a man want to drink.' Not that Pat usually needed any urging to bend his elbow. He drained his pisco sour, called the young woman tending the bar over and said, 'Give my friend one of these and another for me, would you, my love? These must be the best thing that Chile ever invented, Cliff.'

'Well, I'm not sure the Peruvians would agree with that. They also claim it.'

'Whatever. They go down a treat. How did it go?'

'Pretty straightforward. The sergeant wanted to know what we professors emeriti do. Otherwise, mainly what I expected. What I did from getting off the bus until someone from the visitor centre showed up. What about you?'

'Much the same. Concentrated on whether I had seen Lepan fall in, seeing as how I was first on the scene. Did he ask you about that?'

'Yeah. I explained you wandered ahead when Maria Paz and I stopped to take photos. That we caught up again when we rushed off to see what had happened to Rico. He also wanted to know what Lepan might've been working on recently.'

'What's that got to do with anything?'

'No connection I can see. Lepan's written papers on umpteen topics, I doubt if geothermal activity is one of them.'

Pat finished off his glass. 'They say pisco is good for the health, that's why I made a start waiting for you.' The bartender handed me my pisco sour and Pat his second. 'You were longer with the sergeant than me.'

'Oh, that. The manager barged in on us and said Lepan's room had been searched. Figueroa didn't give anything away when he returned. Maybe that's when he became interested in what Lepan was working on.'

'Well, I don't have any idea or care about that. I'll not be crying into my pisco sour over that fooker,' Pat said, holding his glass tightly. 'If it wasn't for that fooking Frenchman you would be having a drink with Professor Patrick Mason.'

'How come?'

'He's the bugger who put the kibosh on my last application for promotion.'

'How do you know that?'

'Well, and keep this to your good self, my cousin's wife Jean works in HR. In the last promotions round she compiled all the referees' reports for the committee and couldn't help but take a quick peek at my file. One of the external referees was the esteemed *Professeur* Lepan. His report said my research was, and I quote, "utterly pedestrian and extremely limited in its contribution to the literature. Its impact within the profession is minimal; well below the standard of a professor in any reputable university."' Pat snorted. 'Concerned to maintain his institution's good name, our beloved dean had no choice but to follow the recommendation of this internationally renowned scholar and reject my application.'

'I'm sorry to hear that.' Making the jump to full professor is a significant step for an academic. Pat should have had a strong case. His comparative work on rural tourism employment creation in developed and developing countries is cutting edge. He has published a couple of books on the topic and has numerous articles in leading journals.

'Fooker,' repeated the associate professor. He stared into the bottom of his empty glass.

'You're probably not the first he's done that to.' I had witnessed Lepan humiliate senior colleagues with his penetrating questions or arrogant commentaries on their conference presentations. Rumour had it that more than one journal editor refused to send him papers to referee or books to review because of his belittling and unscholarly comments.

Rory spared me any further outbursts from Pat when he came into the bar and perched on a stool beside us.

'You again,' he said. Seeing me sitting alongside Pat, he hesitated to say more.

Pat could not contain his curiosity. 'Get one of these inside you and tell us what the cop wanted with you,' he said. He waggled his glass to catch the bartender's eye.

'He asked me if I had heard anything or seen anyone suspicious lurking in the corridor.' Rory turned to me. 'Lepan's room's opposite mine. I didn't, was in bed all morning. They've only discovered the break-in. Normally housekeeping would have cleaned the room before lunch but someone hung a *No molestar* sign on his door. About an hour ago the manager discovered a mix-up in the bookings for a tour group coming in this evening. He figured Lepan's room could be made up to accommodate the extra guest since he would no longer be needing it. The housekeeper found his stuff strewn everywhere.'

'Bloody hell, that's a bit of a liberty,' Pat said.

'An eventful morning all round,' I said.

'What do you mean, eventful?' Rory asked. He looked at me with narrowed eyes.

'Lepan falling in the hot pool and his room being ransacked. The crash which held up the traffic behind us. Did you see who was in that ute, Pat, the only one at the geysers?'

'No, it was gone by the time I got back to the bus. They didn't have to wait with Lepan's body, lucky sods.'

'I don't need any morbid details,' said Rory. He turned around and gazed at the bar's mural.

I didn't need to be reminded of them either. I got up to leave.

'Not staying for another, Cliff?'

'I'm good for now. I'm catching up with Viviana and Maria Paz for dinner in town later. How about you two?'

'We will stay in and have a steak; it will be safer for Rory's gut.'

I climbed the stairs to my room and enjoyed a refreshing shower. Fragments of the conversation with Pat and Rory and the interview with Figueroa danced round in my mind, coalescing then drifting apart like the streams of cold water running down my back. Lepan's death, the sergeant's interest in the finances of professors emeriti, the mysterious ute, the Australians' crash, the break-in. Coincidence or were these incidents connected? What did it matter to me? It was Figueroa's job to enquire into Lepan's death, not mine. Time for dinner.

# CHAPTER 3

'I was telling Maria Paz that the Toledos are leaving for Santiago in the morning instead of coming with us to the lagunas,' Viviana said when I joined them in the lobby. 'Alba and Rico are flying on to Rosario and Pablo will give her paper at the conference. Pablo is blaming himself for not keeping Rico in hand.'

They must be taking it harder than I thought. Alba had been looking forward to getting some feedback on her paper at the conference.

'Rico is young. I'm sure he will get over it,' Maria Paz said. She was not a mother. Rod's experience made me less certain that Rico would shake off the morning's events. Now was not the time to dwell on that.

Outside the door we met Amalina and Edílson, the Brazilian couple, who were trying to decide on what to do with their evening. We invited them to join us and the five of us headed into the night.

We were staying in one of the newer hotels on the outskirts of the town, a twenty-minute walk to the restaurant recommended by Marisela for its regional dishes. The streets were unpaved, dusty and poorly lit.

'Watch out, Viviana.' I caught her before she stumbled in a

pothole. She clutched my arm until we reached the busier streets. There was something to be said for poor infrastructure.

San Pedro is the hub for day or half-day trips out to the surrounding natural attractions. The rapid growth of tourism has spawned a tourist strip of small travel agencies and tour operators, currency exchange offices, souvenir shops selling handicrafts of dubious local origin, pizzerias, restaurants and noisy bars. Unlike the faux facades of more developed destinations, San Pedro's strip of single storey adobe buildings are mostly original, converted from some earlier use.

The more mature affluent tourists on package tours were resting up back in the comfort of their hotels. The streets throbbed with young backpackers, mainly Europeans or North Americans judging from their accents. Searching for a cheap place to stay, still deciding on which tour to take the following morning or debating the best place to quench their thirst after a hard day's sight-seeing in the desert.

'Larry,' said someone with a broad Australian twang, 'we need another beer to rehydrate and replace those lost fluids.'

'No argument there, mate. You can't be too careful. The Atacama must be drier than out the back of Bourke. Those Swedish chicks can wait.'

The restaurant Marisela had suggested was not yet crowded. We were shown to a quiet table away from the bar. The lighting was modest and the décor simple: a few woven artisanal rugs hung on the wood-panelled walls, succulents in earthenware pots added some desert character. Neither an 'authentic' tourist trap nor the type of place where the locals would eat out, but one where we might enjoy the evening and relax after the day's drama.

Our elderly waiter confirmed they served *pataska*, a traditional spicy stew eaten by Atacameños at festivals to thank Pachamama for the harvest. Amalina and Maria Paz opted for the quinoa risotto when the waiter explained the restaurant's take on *pataska* contained tripe. The bar did not stock a local *vino de desierto* and the waiter recommended a good syrah from the Elqui valley further south.

'And a glass of orange juice for me, please,' Amalina said. She smiled at Edílson, placed her hand on her stomach, turned to the rest of us and announced with pride, 'I'm pregnant. We found out right before we left Curitiba.' Edílson beamed. I leaned over and shook his hand. Viviana and Maria Paz wanted to know if it would be a boy or a girl, had they considered names yet, and would she carry on lecturing. Viviana encouraged her not to give up on her career, universities were more supportive now than they were in her younger days. Maria Paz argued they should do a lot more, considering how few women hold senior academic positions.

'And do you have children, Cliff?' Amalina asked.

'No.' Not anymore. Would there be no escaping memories of Rod today?

Sensing some discomfort in my reply, Maria Paz changed topics and asked about Lepan's room being searched.

I related what I knew. The return of the waiter with our wine and Amalina's orange juice halted fruitless speculation on what the intruder might have been after. We toasted Amalina's and the baby's good health and wished Edílson all the best in his new role as father.

'Speaking of new roles, with Lepan gone I suppose Hector Muñoz Muñoz will now be the next president of TADSAI,' he said.

That had not occurred to me. Subject to confirmation at the forthcoming AGM, Hector would hold the position he had long sought. He had been furious when he had lost to Lepan by such a narrow margin and had to settle for vice-president.

'A pair of academic alpha males,' Viviana said. 'A Frenchman and a Mexican to boot.' Harsh words indeed. Viviana generally saw the best in everyone.

'But is being president of TADSAI such a big deal?' Maria Paz asked.

'Status like that matters in this part of the world,' Edílson said. 'It would boost Hector's international credentials in Mexico. No doubt about that.'

'Hector is also Felipe's father,' Viviana said. 'Felipe doesn't like to be known as Hector's son. He goes by his mother's name, Montoya.'

Interesting. I hadn't made that connection before. But why was Felipe so upset up at the geysers?

'Was Lepan married?' Amalina asked.

'Was,' Viviana said. 'Wife Number Three left him earlier in the year. He was a serial strayer with a seducer's silver tongue, not just the caustic one he used to berate under-performing academics and young boys who got in his way.'

Just gossip, or was Viviana speaking from personal experience? Lepan would not have got far with Viviana; she had been devoted to her husband.

'You would have had to watch out, Maria Paz,' Edílson said.

'No, I just hung closer to Cliff when I saw him coming.' She laughed.

Viviana sent her a look as cold as the 6am temperature at the geysers. Maria Paz did not notice. She was joking. Lepan had kept to himself, preoccupied. Was it with the salar, the workshop or an entirely different issue?

The waiter returned with our meals and gave us something other than Lepan to focus on. The *pataska* was on the heavy side but I prefer rustic dishes to haute cuisine and enjoyed it. Viviana pronounced it 'different'. Amalina and Edílson traded forkfuls from each other's plates and agreed she had made the right choice. The wine matched both dishes. We were well onto our second bottle when I excused myself to answer the call of nature.

Most of the tables were now taken and the restaurant was much noisier. A poncho-clad flute player made his way from table to table. *El Condor Pasa* usually evoked some fond early memories of South America for me, but not this less than melodious version. As I passed the bar, I noticed the two Australians had tracked down the Swedish girls and were busy chatting them up. One of the Australians looked a bit battered and bruised.

On the way back from the *baños* I stopped at the bar to order another bottle of wine. I waited while the barman and our waiter ejected the flute player. Over the noise I caught snatches of the Australians' attempts to persuade the Swedes to accompany them to Cochabamba in Bolivia.

'What, cross the desert in that old car... No way.'

'Nah, nah. We are getting a much better one.'

'Oh yeah. Where…get the money for that?'

'Well, we are not supposed to tell anyone …. says to Larry here, "How would you… accidentally crash…write it off. … quite safe… a ford, on the way out to the geysers where you fellows are going … and a grand, in dollars" …some insurance scam …'

'I don't know, Jase. … block the road… some bigwig up ahead of them wanted to see the geysers without all…. needed to be early.'

'You mean you deliberately caused that crash this morning?' One of the Swedes stared at them in disbelief. 'When we eventually got to the geysers… missed all the steam and stuff we saw on TripAdvisor. So, pay for our drinks and piss off. Come on Berit, we're out of here.'

'Aussie wankers. Go shag a kangaroo,' Berit added. The two girls stormed out.

I admired their command of the Queen's English and their character appraisals. The barman cum bouncer returned, took my order and grumbled his way out the back for another bottle of the Elqui. Before I could ask them about the crash, Larry and Jase slipped out without paying.

Amalina and Edílson were back gazing into each other's eyes when I returned to the table. Viviana and Maria Paz were deep in conversation. '... sensitive about the accident and doesn't like talking about his family,' I heard Viviana saying before she noticed me and greeted me with, 'I see they've got rid of our flute player.'

'That condor has got a lot to answer for,' I said, grateful that she had changed topic.

We finished off our meal and the third bottle of wine, skipped dessert and made our way back to the hotel. The walk seemed longer, the streets darker and the potholes more treacherous. Viviana clutched my arm more tightly, or was that my imagination? We got back without any sprained ankles and in much better spirits than when we had left the hotel. The day's events were temporarily behind us but their impact would remain.

●●●

The following morning, I made a point of catching the Toledos before they left for Calama.

'Here's a little souvenir from New Zealand, Rico.' I handed him a black New Zealand cap with a kiwi on it to help cheer him up. I always take a couple of these caps when I go away. They make good little gifts for children of hosts or serve as a handy thank you for any students or young research assistants who are asked to take care of old farts like me at a conference or when I am a visiting professor. Rico brightened for a moment.

'And thank you for the photo you sent Papa. It shows I really am on the moon. I can't wait to show it to my cousins in Armstrong.' A tiny smile.

Pablo shook my hand, picked up the suitcases and the subdued trio got on the shuttle.

I had breakfast with Pat and Rory, who appeared fully recovered. No news about who had searched Lepan's room.

When we boarded the bus for the trip to the Miscanti and Miñiques lagunas our group was further depleted. Felipe Montoya did not join us. Jorge had been replaced by a younger, more cheerful and less weather-beaten driver named Carlos. Marisela introduced Ximena, the organiser of the workshop with the Atacameños. She was in her early twenties, had long black hair and a bronzed complexion. No traditional dress for her, but fitted jeans, a pale blue blouse and a Universidad de Antofagasta baseball cap.

In a sombre but steady voice, Ximena explained that she regretted that the workshop had to be cancelled and outlined what Lepan had been planning to do. After the Atacameño communities had campaigned for years, they were now involved in the co-management of several protected areas including the flamingo reserve and the Miscanti and Miñiques lagunas. The tour operators had been reined in by better regulation and nature conservation efforts were becoming more effective. Lepan would have shared his experiences in other countries and shown how he had helped indigenous communities take more control of what rightfully belonged to them. He would also have discussed how to resist the mining operations which were damaging her people's water supplies.

The intense dark blue waters of the two lagunas edged white with salt deposits contrasted vividly with the arid landscape and the snow-capped volcanoes, brought closer by the clarity of the air in this high-altitude desert.

'How come there are lagunas in the middle of the desert?' Maria Paz asked Ximena. 'I thought it didn't rain here.'

'It doesn't. We're the driest place in the world outside parts of Antarctica. The water comes from underground streams formed by snow melt percolating down from the mountains and volcanoes that block out moisture-bearing winds from the Pacific and the Atlantic. Water is extremely scarce everywhere in the Atacama. That's one of the issues right there,' Ximena said. She reached for my iPhone.

'What do you mean?' I asked.

'Smart phones are powered by lithium batteries and much of the world's lithium comes from the Salar de Atacama. Lithium mining operations tap into the underground sources and draw down the water table causing a lot of problems for us.'

'How was Lepan going to deal with that?'

'He didn't give any details but said on the phone last week that he had come across some crucial information which he would reveal at the workshop. That's all I know,' she said, before Amalina called her over to ask about the vicunas which grazed undisturbed on sparse tufts of dry grass on the other side of the Miscanti Laguna.

On the way back to San Pedro we stopped and took selfies or each other's photo standing under a large green sign marking the Tropic of Capricorn. What exactly was the Tropic of Capricorn? What was the significance of Latitude 23° 26' 16'? No one could be sure, but we knew that we should record we had crossed it. Marisela asked Carlos to take a group photo, or rather a series of group photos as everyone handed their phone or camera to him. This must have been one of his regular duties for he handled multiple devices easily. When she got her phone back, Ana checked Wikipedia and informed us that the Tropic of Capricorn marked the most southerly position at which the sun can be directly overhead. The significance of that escaped us.

Back in town, we ate a quick lunch at the hotel before leaving for the airport. Sergeant Figueroa took me aside as I came out of the restaurant and said he needed me to sign something. He pulled out a blue-covered book from his satchel, the Spanish edition of *Principles and Practices of Contemporary Tourism Management: international perspectives.*

'Would Emeritus Professor Cliff West be so kind as to autograph his book for my son, Miguel. Your name sounded familiar yesterday. When I got home, I remembered seeing this book in his room. He's studying in Valparaíso, almost finished his degree. He's doing an internship in Santiago at present. I wanted Miguel to be more than a guide or a waiter, that's what he would have become if he had stayed in San Pedro. He will be disappointed he missed you but thrilled to have a signed copy of your book. Perhaps you could include 'study hard Miguel' in your dedication.'

A glimpse of the man as a father, not just a carabinero. I handed the signed book back and enquired how his investigation was going.

'At this stage it appears your unfortunate colleague tripped and died immediately when he fell into the hot pool. We must wait for the inquest to be completed. Oh, I see you should be boarding the shuttle,' he said, closing the conversation.

I sat next to Pat who had been watching this exchange with interest.

'What was all that about, Cliff?'

'Autographing a book for another of my adoring readers.'

'Who? Our good sergeant?'

'Hardly. His son's doing a tourism degree in Valparaíso.'

'Did he mention Lepan?' Rory asked.

'Only that they need to wait for the coroner's report to confirm he tripped and died in the hot pool.'

'What did I tell you, case closed.' Pat pointed to a group of tourists boarding a bus. 'This town is so dependent on tourism that they will quietly bury Lepan's accident. We won't hear anything more.'

As the airport shuttle pulled out of the hotel carpark, I noticed a purple ute drive past. I could just make out the logo with a white background on the front door: Mundial Mining.

# CHAPTER 4

Julio Perez, president of the organising committee, thanked the dignitaries on stage and said that we were all grateful that they had been able to find space in their busy schedules to welcome us to Santiago and set the scene for what undoubtedly would be a very successful TADSAI conference. I checked my watch; their commitments elsewhere had not prevented each of them from overrunning their allocated speaking time.

Once they had left, Perez turned to the chair which had been conspicuously empty. He asked us to stand and observe a minute's silence in memory of Lepan who had lost his life so tragically two days ago. A few gasps from the audience. Puzzled glances were exchanged by those who had come in late and not caught up with the news. In place of Lepan's keynote address, Vinícius de Oliveira Carvalho, the Brazilian chair of the Latin American branch of TADSAI, would say a few words in his honour.

More than a few words, it transpired. Carvalho leant into the podium and lamented in heavily accented Spanish the loss of his dear friend and colleague. A formidable scholar who had contributed immensely to the canon of tourism and development, one who had made countless seminal contributions on diverse topics in various parts of the world. Who could forget that remarkable paper on the effects of tourism on community life among the Iban in Borneo?

Who indeed? Who had even heard of it? Not many, going by the blank faces in the audience.

His unparalleled publications output constituted only part of his legacy. Carvalho praised Lepan for the countless hours he had spent mentoring young researchers from all corners of the globe.

I looked around but saw no proud signs of self-recognition as a Lepan mentee.

Carvalho especially admired Lepan's activism. 'He was no ivory tower academic content to simply theorise and write about the inequities and injustices wrought by colonialists and capitalists on indigenous peoples.' Dramatic pause. 'Lepan did not shy away from personal danger. He stood right alongside our native peoples in Amazonia in their struggles against incursions onto their lands. With Lepan, tradition and technology went hand in hand. He recently engaged one of our bright young lecturers to trial the use of drones to monitor illegal mining there.' And on he droned, detailing Lepan's unceasing efforts around the world for the betterment of his fellow man.

Carvalho wound up his tribute by proposing that TADSAI honour Lepan with a festschrift, a book which would record his legacy and set his scholarship in the context of contemporary issues in development. He would be approaching colleagues who knew Lepan well to contribute a chapter dealing with the great man's work in areas such as anthropology, tourism, development, agriculture and poverty alleviation.

Lepan had been a busy man. How had he managed to fit it all in?

•••

I slipped away to a side street bistro for lunch with Lucas Marchena. Bearded, bespectacled and burly, Lucas was one of the last and brightest PhD students I supervised. Curious, analytical, well-organised and persistent, he had the attributes of an excellent researcher. Unlike me, Lucas never let his work get in the way of a good time. I was not surprised to hear he had become a popular lecturer at the Pontificia Universidad Católica de Valparaíso. It is always rewarding to see one of your students doing well.

We zig-zagged through the bistro's crammed dining room out to a small, paved courtyard and claimed the table beneath an old magnolia tree where the dishes were being cleared away. An ideal place for a quiet catch up.

'So, how was the Atacama? I'm embarrassed to say I've never made it up there yet.'

'Amazing, well worth the trip. What a contrast with the rest of Chile. The landscape is dramatic, a lot more varied than I expected for a desert.'

'I guess what happened to Lepan added to the drama.'

'You could say that.'

The waitress came to take our orders.

'The *pastel de choclo* in this place is always good,' Lucas said, remembering it was one of my favourite Chilean dishes. He opted for an aubergine salad. We settled for mineral water. Even without the soporific effects of a glass of wine, it would be difficult enough not to doze off during some of the duller papers immediately after lunch.

'What did you make of this morning's session?' he asked.

'A bit over the top, to be honest. What Carvalho said about Lepan's activism was interesting. I hadn't realised how engaged Lepan had been.' I recalled Figueroa's question about how Lepan funded his activism. 'Wasn't Lepan involved in some protest here?'

'Yeah, he created a bit of a stir down in Patagonia, eight or ten years ago. I was in Punta Arenas at the time. He joined up with a group of eco-warriors protesting the expansion of salmon farming, claimed it destroyed marine life in the fiords. That's big business down there. Those companies aren't to be trifled with and didn't take kindly to their pens being cut.'

'Was Lepan putting his body on the line?'

'I got the impression he didn't zip around in Zodiacs out on the water himself much. He was more of an agitator and organiser. Then he got into strife siding with the Mapuche in Araucania against the loggers. According to some accounts, one of those huge logging trucks tried to run him run off the road into a ravine. Those salmon companies and the big logging outfits have a lot of clout with the government and Lepan got kicked out of the country soon afterwards.'

'Is that right?'

'Yeah. Rumour has it that he only got a visa for this visit because of his status as the incoming president of TADSAI, coupled with pressure from the French Embassy.' He stroked his beard. 'You don't think there was any funny business up at El Tatio, do you Cliff?'

'Doubt it. Not many salmon or trees in the Atacama.'

Lucas laughed. 'It used to produce a lot of nitrates. And copper, though world prices for that have tumbled. Lithium too, that's becoming important.'

The waitress brought our meals. 'But enough of Lepan,' I said. 'What are you working on at the moment?'

'I'm trying to analyse the factors which influence participation in tourism networks in Chile. There's still a hangover here from Pinochet's time when anything which smacked of being cooperative was viewed as suspect and associated with communists.'

'Context is everything.' I ate a few mouthfuls of my corn pie. 'You're right, this *pastel de choclo* is one of the best I've had. I've tried making it at home but it never tastes the same. Different sort of kernels. A lot of network analysis these days loses touch with local conditions, with what's happening on the ground.'

We tossed around ideas about his research and chatted about PhD students who were contemporaries of his.

On the way back to the conference I asked Lucas if he had a Miguel Figueroa in his class.

'Yeah, I do. He's bright kid. How do you know him?'

'His dad up in San Pedro got me to sign a copy of my tourism management book for him.'

'I've made that compulsory reading in one of my classes. The royalties must be rolling in.'

'I wish! I've just spent all last year's on your lunch.'

'Speaking of publications, I see we're getting a lot of citations of our *Annals* paper. It certainly helped the way you polished up my draft and framed the results.'

'Well, you gave me some pretty good material to work with,'

'Should help when I put in for promotion later in the year, a paper in an A-star journal.'

'Should do, but you can never be sure how those things go. Hang on, I'll buy a copy of *La Tercera* from that kiosk.'

•••

During the inevitable delay for the afternoon session to start, I leafed through *La Tercera* looking for news of Lepan's accident. Not surprisingly, it did not rate a mention in a national paper dominated by politics (Sebastien Pinera's proposals to rebuild public finance and encourage investment during his second term, demonstrations by high school and university students) and sports (the lead up to the 2018 FIFA World Cup).

I had a frustrating afternoon getting to hear the papers that interested me most. As always happens with multiple streams in a programme, many of the papers I wanted to listen to clashed.

Afterwards, I grabbed a glass of carmenere from the drinks table at the welcome cocktail and started to circulate. Participants were catching up with friends and colleagues, discussing the afternoon sessions or engaging in academic gossip. I caught the occasional mention of Lepan's name amidst the growing hubbub as the participants started to relax. They would have known him by reputation, read his papers or heard him speak at some earlier conference, but only a few could claim to have known him personally and would experience any direct loss.

'Interesting paper, Pat. How did the rest of the session go?' I asked my Irish colleague.

'Good. We had more time for discussion at the end. Felipe Montoya wasn't there to give his paper.'

'How come?'

'He had to go back to Mexico last night, some family emergency. Sorry, Cliff, I should have introduced you to Jose and Jorge, my Colombian colleagues. They did a lot of the technical analysis on our paper.' We shook hands.

Statistical technicalities are not my thing. I turned, accepted a mini empanada from a passing waiter and crossed the room to ask Maria Paz how her presentation had gone.

'Lots of interest and no tricky questions. One of the participants from the sub-secretariat came up to me afterwards and talked about applying the same technique in Chile. That drones guy Carvalho mentioned was also in our session. C'mon, Cliff, I'll introduce you to Ramón.'

Ramón Macedo was Black, slim, not far off two metres and had a crew cut. He could have been mistaken for a competitive high jumper. I was curious about his relationship with Lepan and their project in the Amazon.

'I only met him once, a few months back,' Ramón said in his quiet voice. 'We were supposed to meet up here to work out the details. He had found out that one of our mining companies was becoming involved with the independent miners—*garimpeiros* we call them in Brazil— illegally mining for gold somewhere in Pará.'

'How did you fit into that?'

'He was planning on using drones to film the damage they

were causing. He wanted to document the deforestation he had seen and show how the *garimpeiros* were discharging mercury from their mining into the rivers.'

'But can you use drones in the rainforest?'

'You can't in dense vegetation, but mining creates clearings where you could fly one. Of course, we would also have to do it undetected. Those *garimpeiros* and mining companies don't want anyone poking their noses in.'

'Wouldn't that have been dangerous?' Maria Paz asked.

Ramón shrugged. 'It would have been a bit of an adventure.' He grinned. 'Not much happens in Curitiba and I've never been to the Amazon.'

Was Ramón a naïve nerd? Things could cut up rough in those places.

'Besides,' Ramón said, 'Lepan had the funds to buy all the equipment I needed. I can always use another drone or two. Some really advanced ones have come out lately. They're horribly expensive, out of my reach. But that's as far as we got. Without him, the project won't be going ahead.'

A hand on my shoulder. Carvalho nodded at Maria Paz, completely ignored Ramón—the 'bright young lecturer' he had mentioned earlier in the day— and steered me over to a quieter corner of the room. Ill-mannered as well as bombastic.

'Cliff, my friend, such terrible, terrible news about Antoine.' He wrung his hands. 'We absolutely must honour him with a festschrift. Antoine would have appreciated it.'

'I am sure he would have. Moreso if he were alive.'

'Viviana's agreed to write about his work in Latin America. Your chapter would deal with his tourism research in English and French. I'm not sure I could trust anyone in France to be objective. A lot of professional jealousy there.'

My chapter? That's rather presumptuous. 'I can't say I knew him as well as you did, Vinícius.'

41

'I'm counting on you. And include Spain too, all of Europe in fact.' With that he headed off to twist the arm of another potential contributor.

Viviana came and rescued me from an earnest young Peruvian who was haranguing me about his new online tourism journal. She suggested we share a taxi back to the Vegas, the hotel in the Paris Londres *barrio* where we were staying.

We saw an empty table at the cafe next to the hotel. The nibbles at the cocktail had not sated our appetite so we ordered a platter of cheese and chorizo and a cabernet sauvignon from Lolol. At last, some time alone with Viviana.

Viviana tilted her glass against the white tablecloth to examine the colour and clarity of the cabernet sauvignon. She sniffed the wine, stuck her nose into the glass and inhaled deeply. She swirled the wine around, took a sip, then a mouthful. She compared the winemaker's notes on the back of the bottle with her own judgement, a habit she acquired from her late husband, a wine exporter. She nodded, put the bottle down and looked up to see me studying her with equal attention.

'Cliff?'

'Just thinking of Monet's haystacks.'

'What?'

'You know, the effects of changing light.'

'On?'

'On you, of course. On your face, the effect of the light cast by that streetlamp compared to the sunshine radiating off the salar.'

'And?'

'Pretty as a picture in any light, like the haystacks. Oops, forget that last bit.'

'How much did you have to drink at the conference? Here, you need something more to eat.' She passed the platter towards me and sipped her wine.

The spell was broken. We moved on to the presentations we had heard and the people we had met.

I reached for the last of the chorizo. Viviana asked what I thought of Carvalho's tribute.

'He may have been sincere, but he overdid it. Lepan was prolific, but did he produce that many seminal papers? And was he such a generous mentor? I wasn't aware of all that activism Carvalho mentioned. He tells me you've agreed to contribute to his festschrift.'

'Lepan deserves one. It shouldn't take me too long to do, I'm familiar with what he has done in Latin America. How about you?'

'I said I would sleep on it.' I wiped my hands on a serviette. 'How many people read festschrifts nowadays? Anyway, since Lepan's dead it should technically be a gedenkschrift. I wouldn't be surprised if Carvalho is pushing the idea to bolster his own name, to bask in the reflected glory of the great man, so to speak.'

'That's enough for one day, Cliff. Now you're becoming cynical. Finish your wine, we've another long day conferencing tomorrow.'

I paid the bill and stumbled across the cobblestones to the Vegas where we collected our keys at reception.

•••

I found nothing about Lepan in *La Tercera* next morning. I checked the Calama paper online for more regional news. Nothing there either. The crash and delay on the road to the geysers got five lines. As word of Lepan's death spread, a scattering of tributes from former students and colleagues appeared on Trinet, an email distribution list for the international tourism research community.

Viviana chaired an afternoon session devoted to Argentina. The content of Pablo's paper was original, his delivery dispirited. He failed to do justice to Alba's paper which he read out in a monotone. Neither paper generated any questions. Viviana salvaged what she could with her insightful comments. When the session finished, I invited Pablo to join me and a couple of the Cubans for dinner.

'Thanks, Cliff, but I'm heading straight out to the airport. I called Alba at lunchtime. She's not coping and needs me at home. Rico's crying all the time, blaming himself for Lepan's death. It's all my fault. I should have made sure he stuck with us at the geysers and didn't go rushing about all over the place. I'm the one responsible.'

I shook his hand. I knew how he felt.

•••

Self-blame. That's what caused Rod's death. We had given him a new mountain bike for his twelfth birthday. That summer, Mark, his best friend, was on holiday in Hanmer Springs, a cool place to go mountain biking. Rod begged us to go down. Wendy had a refresher course that week and said it would be a good opportunity for the two of us to do some male bonding.

I promised not to take any work with me. However, the day before we left I received the proofs of my latest book to correct. The publisher was running behind schedule and gave me a week to courier the corrected proofs back. I needed the book out before the next promotions round as my previous application had been turned down, judged light on publications.

That first morning in Hanmer I hired a bike and we did the Easy Rider trail a couple of times with Mark. We spent the afternoon at the hot pools and grabbed some fish and chips for dinner. Afterwards, I could not help but reach for the proofs to see what eighteen months of hard work looked like on the printed page. I soon discovered that the column and row totals in most of the tables were inexplicably transposed. It was a nightmare. I decided to start afresh the following day.

Rod, of course, wanted to go riding again with Mark. They

had handled their bikes well so I said he could go if they stuck to Easy Rider. I should have known better. Rod persuaded Mark to show him an intermediate grade trail, steeper, with some trickier bits in places where the track narrowed, had some tight corners and the hillside fell away sharply. The second time round, Rod suggested they time themselves to see who could do it the fastest. He was following Mark and catching him up. Mark pedalled faster. He misjudged a corner, hit a rock, and was thrown over the handlebars to the stream bed below.

Mark severely damaged his spinal cord in the fall. He was a tetraplegic. He would never walk again. Would never be able to dress himself again. Feed himself again. Go on to high school in a class with Rod and his friends.

Rod was devastated. He blamed himself for what happened. We assured him repeatedly that it was not his fault. It was an accident. Mark was more experienced. He knew the trail and had ridden it many times before. It was an accident. Mark had misjudged the corner and hit a rock.

Wendy wanted to know where I was at the time. She hinted the responsibility was mine. Hadn't I promised not to do any work while we were in Hanmer? Why couldn't those damned proofs have waited? She was right.

Rod visited Mark regularly after he was discharged from the spinal unit in Christchurch. Mark's parents were not openly hostile but were not at all subtle about who they believed was to blame. They accepted no responsibility for having let the boys go riding on their own. Mark's father was playing golf that morning, his mother had been enjoying some private spa treatment.

Rod's visits became less and less frequent until they stopped altogether. He could not let it go. He became increasingly withdrawn and spent most of the time in his room. He stopped playing rugby. His schoolwork suffered.

Rod's mountain bike hung in the garage for two years. Then

one day he announced he was going to start mountain biking again. We thought this a good sign, that he was at last getting over what had happened to Mark. We agreed that he could come down with me to Hanmer Springs where I had a conference. We arrived a couple of days early. I offered to go biking with him. He said he wanted to ride by himself the first time. I was not so sure but let him go.

An hour later the young constable knocked on my door.

Self-blame. Rod had taken responsibility for his friend's death to the extreme. I blamed myself for Rod's death. I lost my son and ten months later my wife of twenty years left me. I prayed the Toledos would not experience the same fate that my family suffered.

•••

Day 3 of the TADSAI conference. I chaired a lively panel discussion by public and private sector representatives on initiatives for tourism development in peripheral regions. In the following session I presented my paper showing how frameworks of tourism could be integrated with recent concepts of development to improve Latin American policymaking. A prominent Chilean consultant argued that the country needed concrete, practical ideas, not airy-fairy notions from academics. I enjoy this form of intellectual skirmishing and sat down satisfied with my effort.

On the way out for coffee, Ana came up to me and said: 'Don't take any notice of Victor. He has a go at all academics, bitter that no university has offered him a job.'

'So I've heard.'

'I liked the way you structured your paper. In Chile we need fewer case studies and a more systematic—'

'Cliff, Cliff, so good to see you again.' Muñoz Muñoz glad-handed me.

'What brings you here, Hector? I didn't see your name on the programme.'

'I was tied up providing input into a new government policy. But when Felipe called and told me about that horrible accident our good friend Antoine had up in the desert, I knew I had to get away and came down late last night. Splendid idea of Vinícius to honour Lepan's memory with a festschrift.'

Good friend. Honour his memory. What a hypocrite. Muñoz Muñoz was here to shore up support for his confirmation as the new president of TADSAI.

'And how is Felipe? I hear he had to return home in a hurry. Some family emergency?'

'Ah, there's Carvalho. I need to speak to him.' With that, Muñoz Muñoz elbowed his way over to where the festschrift editor was holding court.

•••

The farewell function took place in the ballroom of one of the new international hotels in Providencia. More drinks, nibbles and circulating. Perez asked us to move back and clear the floor for a cultural spectacle. A dozen dancers in traditional dress swept in to perform the national dance, the *cueca*. Other Chileans, including Lucas and Ana, soon joined in and began waving their handkerchiefs. Members of the dance troupe split up and invited other guests to be their partners. Maria Paz, Viviana and even Pat accepted willingly. Time for me to edge to the back of the onlookers. I have no sense of rhythm and had no wish to make a fool of myself in front of my colleagues. Someone tapped me on the shoulder. I turned round, fearful that my move had not gone unnoticed. It was not one of the dancers, or Carvalho, but a smartly dressed young man.

'Professor West?'

'That's me.'

'My name's Miguel Figueroa. I wanted to thank you for autographing my book. My dad told me you would be attending the conference and I wanted to thank you in person.' He pointed to his hotel name badge. 'I'm doing my internship with the events coordinator in this hotel. It's a real honour to meet you, Professor.'

I welcomed my salvation from the dance floor and kept Miguel talking until the *cueca* finished and we were invited to take a seat at our allocated table for dinner. I handed Miguel my card, told him to email me if I could help him with anything, and asked him to pass on my regards to his father. On impulse, I asked for the sergeant's email address, *por si las moscas*, in case (of the flies), one of the Spanish sayings I find amusing but apt.

The speeches before dessert by Perez and Carvalho were routine and blessedly brief. The looks exchanged between the two suggested the third speech was not programmed. Muñoz Muñoz got to his feet and reminded us of TADSAI's annual conference in Kuala Lumpur in three months' time. He already saw himself as the next president and invited everyone to attend to learn about the exciting new directions the association would be taking. Pat muttered and shook his head.

I had avoided Carvalho all day, but he finally cornered me as I was saying my farewells to Edílson and Lucas. 'So, Cliff, I trust we will have a contribution from you for my festschrift.'

I could hardly believe hearing myself agree to his request.

•••

Viviana, Maria Paz and I shared a cab back to the Vegas. The two women made plans to do some shopping and sightseeing the following day before catching their flights to Mendoza and Madrid. We said our farewells and promised to keep in touch.

Back in my room, I shrugged off my jacket. The crumpled

serviette on which I had written Figueroa's email address fell to the floor. I picked it up. All the talk about Lepan during the conference had reminded me of something Figueroa had asked me in San Pedro, a detail which had just come back to me. And which might be important. I sent him an email:

> It was a pleasure to meet Miguel this evening. He is a fine young man and I am sure he will do well.

> You asked me the colour of the ute at the El Tatio geysers the morning of Professor Lepan's accident. I remember now that it was purple with some white on the doors. Perhaps the same colour scheme as a Mundial Mining ute.

I showered and lay on the bed thinking. Why had I agreed to contribute to the festschrift? I still doubted their value. I did not owe anything to either Lepan or Carvalho. I found Carvalho an oily character and his persistence grating. But the more I heard about Lepan the more intrigued I became with him. How had he become such a prolific scholar? Why was he such a polarising figure, admired by many and disliked by others? What led to his activism? And those glimpses of the dangers he faced. Contributing to the festschrift would help me answer some of these questions. It would also fill the void waiting for me in Wellington where I had no new projects to occupy me.

I checked my emails next morning. Nothing of interest. No response from Figueroa. I reread the email I had sent him. Mundial Mining. Who were they? I googled 'Mundial Mining'. Up popped its logo: two intertwined Ms in a white globe against a purple background. Except for one paragraph in English, Mundial Mining's home page was in Portuguese. From the little I could make out, the company's headquarters were in Belo Horizonte, the capital of Minas Gerais, the main mineral producing state in

Brazil. Mundial began mining gold there in the 1990s. Mundial appeared to be much smaller and newer than many of the other mining companies in the state. I could not find my way around a Brazilian company register to determine who the owners were.

The English commentaries of investment analysts and industry pundits depicted Mundial Mining as an ambitious upstart. The name Mundial was purely aspirational; far from having a worldwide network of mines, the company's only international operation to date was a diamond mine in Angola. Newspaper articles and internet posts by NGOs painted a picture of a mining company which cut corners, paid little heed to regulations and had little regard for the safety of its employees. Lives had been lost in an accident at its Angolan mine. Suggestions too that Mundial was pushing the Brazilian government for concessions to mine for gold in the Amazon. It was reputed to be behind several illegal mining operations in the rainforest in Pará where half a dozen members of a hitherto isolated indigenous community, including a young child, had been killed in two separate incidents. Mundial Mining's English slogan, Mining for Mankind, did not align with these reports.

There wasn't any gold or diamonds in the Atacama as far as I knew. But there was gold in the Amazon. Was this the outfit that Lepan was after there? I sent Ramón an email to see if he could remember. Was Lucas right? Had there been some funny business in the Atacama?

# CHAPTER 5

The twelve and a half hour LATAM flight back to Auckland did not leave until well past midnight. I adjusted my seat and studied my fellow passengers. That woman across the aisle, two rows up, was a dead ringer of Rosa, the Venezuelan vet whom I had met at the Sociedad Hispanica in Wellington. Her fiery temperament, exciting at first, became too hot for me to handle and our relationship soon flamed out. That was a couple of years after Wendy had divorced me. Then came Hazel, the Canadian post-doc. Another promising start which ended when she returned to Quebec and hooked up with her former partner again. I later found out that breaking up with him was the real reason Hazel had come to New Zealand, not the renown of the economics school which had offered her a scholarship. I had only been a temporary distraction. Wendy, Rosa, Hazel—three strikes and I was out, back into my work more than ever.

After dinner had been served and the cabin lights dimmed, I put on my sleeping mask. The seat next to me was empty and I was able to stretch out a little. Even so, sleep eluded me. Lepan's accident and its consequences would not leave me alone. How was young Rico? How were Alba and Pablo coping? I did not want the boy to feel any guilt and end up like our Rod. I dreaded to think that the incident at the geysers would come between Alba and Pablo.

What had I learned from our experience that might help them? Wendy and I hadn't been able to convince Rod that anything other than his suggestion that they should ride as fast as they could had caused Mark to hurtle off the trail. As much as we had assured him that it was an accident, we had nothing concrete to counter the fixation of a young teenage boy blaming himself for his friend's tragedy.

To prevent Rico going down a similar path I needed to show that something other than his scarf had led to Lepan's demise. Perhaps by doing that, by sparing Rico and his parents, I could find some redemption and ease the burden I continued to carry. That thought boosted my spirits. But what could I do? Any alternative explanation was surely to be found in the Atacama and here I was travelling further away from that desert by the minute with no future trips to Chile in the offing.

It was Figueroa's and the coroner's job to determine what had happened. I was not as convinced as Pat and Rory that Figueroa was just going through the motions, that he had already made up his mind that Lepan had had an accident, that he had simply tripped and fallen into the hot pool. Close the case as quickly as possible, don't let the word out and upset the tourists on whom San Pedro depends. True, Figueroa had said that it appeared Lepan had tripped when I asked him how his enquiries were going after I had signed Miguel's book. But some of his questions during the interview made me wonder what he was looking for. Why the interest in how professors emeriti support their activities? In how Lepan financed his activism? What he had been working on? And his hotel room being broken into? What was that all about?

And the talk at the conference about Lepan's activism. About putting himself in danger. Carvalho emphasised that. Lucas said Lepan had run into trouble years earlier in Chile with loggers and salmon farmers. What had Ramón said about using drones in the Amazon to film illegal mining? 'Without him, the project won't be going ahead.' Was that the outcome somebody wanted? To halt the project. What if Lepan's death was not an accident after all?

That got me thinking. That ute at El Tatio was the same colour as the one belonging to Mundial Mining that I had seen outside the hotel in San Pedro. What if it was a Mundial ute at the geysers and they were the ones Lepan was going after in the Amazon? What then? What were Mundial doing in San Pedro?

Slow down, Cliff. You're getting into conspiracy theory territory here. You need to be objective, structured. What are the key elements of a crime that keep cropping up in those Latin American detective stories you read to keep up your Spanish? Think… That's right, the trifecta of means, motive and opportunity.

Means? Shoving Lepan into a hot pool would no doubt kill him. It would not have been difficult; he was a small man.

Motive? Amazonian gold. Would an unscrupulous mining company threatened with exposure go so far as to eliminate an interfering activist? Lust for the precious metal has caused more than its share of murder, mayhem and misery over the centuries. Mundial did not have a clean slate.

Opportunity? The deserted geysers, early in the morning when it was barely daylight and the fumaroles were at their steamiest, would have presented an ideal opportunity to do away with Lepan unseen, as if he had tripped while viewing the hot pools alone. Lepan had a habit of keeping to himself, except when seeking publicity or needing a boost to his ego from a packed auditorium or a pliant female admirer. Doing him in at El Tatio would have reduced the risk of anyone making connections to the Amazon and to Mundial.

It was odd that we had the geysers to ourselves that morning. The usual stream of traffic had been held up by the crash involving two Australians. Were those the two I had heard in the restaurant trying to chat up the two Swedish women. From the snatches of conversation that I overheard, the Australians had been told to piss off when it appeared they had crashed deliberately and been paid to do it. By Mundial? Or by somebody else?

Yes, a case could be made that Mundial were responsible for his death if it was their ute at the geysers and they were the ones whose operations Lepan wanted Ramón to film. Possible, but just conjecture. I had no evidence. Ramón had not replied right away.

But other than the occupants of the ute, there was only our tour party at the geysers. Who else was near that hot pool where Lepan died? When I arrived, Pat Mason was stretched out trying to reach Lepan. I missed what had happened immediately before that. Later that afternoon in the bar I learnt Lepan's report had sunk Pat's chances of promotion to professor. Would that have riled Pat enough to give him an opportunistic shove in the back? He had quizzed me on what Figueroa wanted to know about him. Was Pat drinking to celebrate or to forget what he had done?

Then Rory joined us. He struck me as a dodgy character. Rory had stayed back at the hotel, supposedly indisposed, in his room across the corridor from Lepan whose room had been broken into and searched. Were Pat and Rory complicit? Were Lepan's death and the break-in connected? Rory avoided discussing that. What could he have been looking for that was so important to him or Pat?

Pat and I went back a long way. It was inconceivable that he would stoop to murder because Lepan had thwarted his academic ambitions. And if Pat was not involved, Rory could not have acted by himself since he was not at the geysers. Still, when he interviewed me, Figueroa had asked about Pat. He had also questioned the young Irishman. About Lepan's room or something else?

And the Mexicans. Where had they come from? Felipe Montoya arrived just after we pulled Lepan onto the path. He insisted the Frenchman's body not be left there. Was this to provide the deceased with some dignity? Or to remove him from the scene of a crime? Felipe left the country that evening and skipped the conference. Had the 'family matter' been attended to and had he left to be beyond the arm of Chilean law? Hector Muñoz Muñoz, Felipe's father and vice-president elect of TADSAI, had turned up unexpectedly in Santiago and set about shoring up support for his confirmation as the new president of the association now that Lepan was dead. I knew little about Felipe or Hector, but this scenario seemed as utterly fanciful as any machinations by Pat and Rory. Becoming president of TADSAI was not that big a deal despite what Edílson said.

Maybe Lepan's death was an accident. Whether he tripped on Rico's scarf or something else had caused him to fall we might never know. That would not help Rico and his parents. Or me.

The 787 struck a patch of turbulence, juddered violently and pitched into a steep dive. The cabin lights came on. The fasten your seat belt signs lit up. Oxygen masks appeared. Coats, bags, a couple of duty-free bottles of Jim Beam and other items not correctly stowed in the overhead compartments rained down on careless passengers and their neighbours. Tray tables clattered open. Young kids screamed. Flight attendants calmly emerged from the rear of the aircraft.

I've seen the statistics, how it is many times more likely you will die driving to the airport than in an air accident. I also knew that high above the Pacific—but plunging seawards—we were thousands of kilometres from the nearest airport. I have racked up thousands of air miles over the years but am still an anxious air traveller, not entirely relaxed until I am safely in the terminal building at my destination.

I was starting to fear this might be my last flight when the reassuring voice of the captain told us we would soon be out of the passing storm. In the interests of safety, we were to remain in our seats with our seatbelts securely fastened. The drama was soon over, the flight attendants gathered and stowed the fallen items, masks and tray tables were put back, mothers hushed their children, the cabin lights were dimmed again. Calm and order were restored.

I loosened my grip on the armrests. My heartbeat gradually returned to normal. The years had not flashed in front of my eyes before the plane levelled out. Nothing so dramatic. But the unnerving experience did cause me to reflect on my life.

A continuing theme quickly emerged—my work. It had dominated much of my life. I was hard-wired for hard work, brought up that way by my parents. Dad was a shearer all his life; he barely made it into his fifties before his back gave out and he went to an early grave. I began sweeping the board in woolsheds when I was at primary school. Fleece picking and wool pressing over the summer paid my way through uni. I was ambitious and found tourism research inherently interesting and rewarding, never a chore. I tried to persuade myself it was solely this interest which drove me on. But working hard meant less time for other activities.

Sure, I had a good time in France doing my doctorate—who couldn't enjoy three years in Provence? What's more, my research had taken me all over France, to resorts on the Mediterranean coast, in the Alps and in the Pyrenees. I finished my thesis and returned home to the lecturing position I had longed for. But my friends in Aix were right, I should have lifted my nose from my notes more often, made more of my stay, got a bit more *joie de vivre* as well as my degree.

Back in New Zealand, I got stuck into building my academic career. In my second year I met Wendy, a young French teacher at my old high school, when I was invited to speak at the end of year prize-giving. We married a year later. We agreed to wait until after my first research and study leave before starting a family. I wanted to complete as much fieldwork as possible, unencumbered by a young child. We spent eight months in France and Spain.

Wendy was delighted to spend a prolonged period in France. Before that she had only made a couple of ten-day visits to New Caledonia shepherding groups of high school kids. I had followed up on my resolve to learn Spanish and could now put the language of my Latin American friends to use in one of the world's leading tourist destinations. Wendy had also picked up some basic Spanish and practised that at every opportunity when we were based in Barcelona. We packed as much as we could into the trip and got a lot out of it, personally and professionally. Wendy taught for two more terms after we got back before Rod was born.

Rod was a great kid, did well at school, made friends easily, loved his sport. We were a happy trio. We had a house with a mortgage, some lawn and a garden. Wendy was a devoted mum, she did not miss teaching and got heavily involved in the Alliance Française. I settled into family life. I made sure I left my work in the office and kept my evenings and weekends free. Wendy appreciated my efforts in the kitchen. I enjoyed reading to Rod and picking out books for him at the library when he was young. I walked to primary school with him and learned about his classmates and his teachers' foibles. I cheered him on at rugby on cold Saturday mornings and at T-ball in summer. We filled our family holidays with fun and adventure.

Work did not dominate this phase of my life. Pulling back was easy when I had Wendy and Rod to share my life with. I enjoyed what self-proclaimed well-being gurus today refer to as a happy work/life balance. All that changed when we gave Rod a mountain bike for his birthday and he and I travelled down to Hanmer Springs.

Wendy blamed me for Rod's death. She would yell and scream and cry. Weeks went by when she barely said a word. We drifted apart. Wendy found a teaching job in Auckland and in due course divorced me. I buried myself in the one thing I could do, my work. I taught and researched and wrote like never before.

I volunteered for the most boring committees and accepted the most tedious administrative tasks. This behaviour became the norm, promotions followed.

Not for the first time, the irony of how I reacted to Rod's death struck me—losing myself in ever more work was my coping strategy for work-induced guilt. Was there another way forward? Was redemption to be found in coming up with an alternative explanation for Lepan's death? I was determined to find out.

I rubbed my hand over my balding pate and cratered scalp. It had been a year since the procedure. Subsequent scans had come back 'no mets'; the cancer had not spread. I tried to be positive, but the thought was always there, would it return and if it did how much time would I have left?

The Rosa lookalike got up and made her way down the aisle. That sure was a good time I had with Rosa while it lasted. Dammit, was it too late to start over, to spend my remaining years, however many they might be, with someone I cared for and who cared for me? If I could ever shake off the guilt I felt over Rod's death, or at least lessen it, I knew it would never go away completely, I might then have the courage to enter another relationship and not seek solace in my work.

Lepan, Rico, Rod, Wendy, Rosa, Hazel, Viviana—a parade of faces passed through my mind's eye as I drifted in and out of sleep as the flight continued through the night.

# CHAPTER 6

I returned to Wellington much more enthusiastic about contributing to Carvalho's festschrift. If I learnt more about Lepan's work and understood his life better, I might discover what led to his death. I might be able to offer an alternative explanation for how he ended up in a hot pool in the Atacama. Could an incident earlier in his academic career have triggered his demise? The odds were not great but researching and writing my chapter was at least a place to begin.

It was more likely an alternative explanation lay in recent events, in Lepan's activism, and that could only be found in the Atacama. If I were serious about being an amateur sleuth, I had to get back to Chile before the case grew any colder. Not that anybody else was treating Lepan's death as an unsolved murder, not an accident. I needed a *raison d'être* for being there. I couldn't just go to San Pedro and poke around by myself. My efforts would soon be noticed. If there had been foul play, I would be putting myself in danger. Let's face it, I was no Indiana Jones. I needed a cover. Some funding would also help. Nothing loomed on the horizon. I had to find or create an opportunity to return.

With the Atacama tour, the conference and the time spent at UACh beforehand, I had been away for a couple of months. I settled back into my two-bedroom townhouse in Mount Victoria. The pot plants on my deck had survived my absence. I loaded the washing machine, replenished my larder with a visit to Moore Wilson's, and sorted through my accumulated mail, mainly bills and requests for donations.

I had brought back some *alfajores* for Maisie, the neighbour who had been keeping an eye on my place, and invited her over for a coffee.

'Did you see that leaky townhouse complex in Pirie Street is all wrapped up in plastic now they've started the remediation?' she asked.

'That will be costing them a packet.'

'The same thing couldn't happen to us, could it, Cliff?'

'Don't worry, Maisie, our places were built by a more reputable developer, different architect too. We will be all right.' I hoped so. My savings and superannuation could not sustain a substantial hit like the sums mentioned for the Pirie Street townhouses. Sure, I had been on a good salary as a professor but I was now retired. My earlier assets had been halved when Wendy left me.

Figueroa had asked a good question about how professors emeriti support their travel and activities. Lepan had three wives divorce him, I only had one. I don't know how many children he left behind, no doubt several. How had Lepan funded his ex-wives and his activism? 'Follow the money.' Wasn't that the advice that Deep Throat character whispered hoarsely to those Watergate reporters, Woodward and Bernstein? That tactic worked for them; they brought down Nixon. In Lepan's case I had no idea where a money trail began.

•••

I sat at my desk in the sunny book-lined study where I do my writing and pondered how to begin my Lepan mission. I could have googled 'Antoine Lepan' and seen what that threw up. Multiple hits no doubt. Or checked him out on LinkedIn if his profile had not been deleted. I have never been a Facebook user or fan of other social media. I could have gone back to the posts on Trinet at the time of his death. However, I wanted to understand the man and his work better in my own way, not through another person's eyes.

I began by going back to some of the research I did in the late 1970s and 1980s in which I cited some of Lepan's early work. At that time my research dealt mainly with development processes. I studied how different geographical contexts gave rise to different forms of tourism and how different processes produced varying impacts. Lepan was a social anthropologist, one of the first in France to focus on tourism. Much of his early work dealt with the social structure of communities experiencing the growth of tourism, how different groups within those communities became involved in tourism and how they were affected by it. I could not remember much else.

I reached for my first book and saw I had referred to three of Lepan's papers drawn from his doctoral thesis examining inter-generational changes in occupations in resorts along the Atlantic coast of France and the attitudinal and societal shifts which had resulted. I found the few lines I had written on the changes he had reported. I had praised his work as being insightful, original and based on in-depth fieldwork. In other articles of mine I found four more references in which he had taken a similar approach to resorts along the Costa Brava and in Mallorca.

Now I was getting a better sense of what he had done and where his work intersected with mine. I had adopted a predominantly spatial perspective whereas he focused on the social. I mapped land use change from aerial photographs; he plotted occupations on family trees. I had gone through the archives of local authorities; he had accessed personal diaries. My interviews focused on those directly involved in tourism; his covered a wider range of people.

I googled 'Lepan, publications' hoping to find a CV with a complete list of his publications. No joy. His profile on the university website in Bordeaux had already been removed. I set about building up a more comprehensive list of Lepan's work using references in Scopus, Google Scholar and the Web of Science which I exported into Endnotes. There was a lot of overlap. Many of the references were in English; coverage of literature in other languages is generally much less comprehensive in these databases. I excluded references to Latin America which Viviana was dealing with and ignored the increasing number of papers addressing topics other than tourism. By the 1990s Lepan was also writing about such subjects as how the industrialisation of maize growing in Mexico had resulted in a loss of genetic diversity because the lower yielding traditional varieties cultivated by the poorer peasants in Oaxaca were no longer competitive. Many peasants were migrating to the city where they lacked a social network, became unemployed and resorted to petty crime.

To do justice to Lepan's work and to understand his contribution to the literature, I needed more than the few lines citing his work that I had written thirty or forty years earlier. The abstracts I had found in the databases were not sufficient either. I needed to reread the original papers to obtain a better appreciation of them and to read those my online search had thrown up. The day had come which I knew was inevitable—the papers that I had kept for so long because they would be useful one day had been thrown out. When I retired, I was obliged to relinquish my large professorial office in Rutherford House and downsize decades of academic accumulation. Emeritus status gave me the privilege of sharing a cramped office with another elderly colleague, Bill Broughton. More drastic culling followed when we were told we would henceforth be hot-desking and that no individual shelving or cabinets would be available.

I was able to download many of the papers I sought. Some of the journals had since ceased publication or their online issues did not go back far enough. I could not download the chapters in edited volumes published in the late 1970s. Undeterred, I reverted to submitting interloan requests, a regular exercise when I started out and the university library held few French geographical journals. I updated Maria Paz on my efforts and asked if she could check out the Universidad Autónoma de Barcelona library or see if any of her older colleagues held copies of a couple of papers relating to Lepan's early work in Spain.

I put on a Graeme Allwright CD, settled in my comfortable armchair and began reading the papers I had obtained. I enjoyed the task. I had not read much in French since retiring. Reading Lepan's early papers took me back to my early days when I first came across a few journal articles in French while still doing my master's. Moving on to the papers in Spanish also reminded me of my early skirmishes with publications in that language. Night school classes had not equipped me with the vocabulary to read scholarly papers. I needed to be able to do more than ask for a room with a double bed for two nights, please. I had to construct my own specialised vocabulary of words and phrases. Now I had no trouble, especially after my recent trip to Chile.

As I read, I began to build up a much better picture of Lepan's work. I was impressed not only by the sheer volume of his publications but also by the scope, depth and originality of his research. His early studies in France and on the Costa Brava were followed by papers elsewhere in Spain (the Balearic Islands, Galicia and Andalucía) and by an increasingly wide range of destinations: Portugal, Tunisia, Hungary, Bulgaria, Morocco, Senegal, Tanzania, Thailand and Bali. He carried out an immense amount of time-consuming ethnographic fieldwork and at the same time was able to introduce new ideas and concepts. He wrote about tourism as a form of imperialism, about cultural appropriation, about the demonstration effect whereby the arrival of Western tourists exposed people in developing countries to different mores, values and behaviours.

Lepan had made a significant contribution to the emerging stream of research on the social and cultural impacts of tourism. His work became increasingly critical of such impacts. He was one of the first to advocate for *le tourisme doux*, for soft or alternative forms of tourism development, smaller in scale and better adapted to the needs and resources of so-called host communities than the chain hotels favoured by European tour operators catering to the masses. Was it this work which subsequently led to his activism, to becoming involved with indigenous communities confronting outside developers who exploited their cultural and natural resources on an industrial scale?

Lepan stood out as a lone wolf; virtually all his papers were sole-authored. Many prolific writers boost their lists of publications by co-authoring with two, three or more colleagues or graduate students. Those with high citation indexes often deal predominantly in ideas or write overview papers instead of doing much empirical research. Lepan managed to find the time and have the skill to do both. Curiously, his reference lists rarely ran to more than a dozen articles or books, with little cross-referencing of his own research, even when he was addressing similar topics in different countries.

•••

Maria Paz emailed me a couple of the journal articles and a book chapter that she had tracked down and scanned. She saw I was online and Skyped to say she had been to a farewell function for Jordi Segarra. I knew Jordi well when I spent some time in Barcelona many years ago with Wendy.

'Pau Puig asked to be remembered to you,' she said. 'So did

Montse Domenech. Pau had a fair bit of contact with Lepan. You might be interested in what he said when I told him you were working on your festschrift chapter.'

My ears pricked up. 'And?'

'Pau didn't know much about Lepan's research as they worked in different areas, but he spoke highly of the amount of time Lepan gave to postgrad students here. In his younger days Lepan would come to Barcelona and give seminars for them. He was always approachable and happily spent hours and hours discussing their research and ideas. He didn't speak Catalan, but his Spanish was excellent.'

'That ties in with what Carvalho said about Lepan mentoring young researchers.'

'Then, as his reputation developed, Lepan used to sit on panels evaluating research applications for one of the well-known foundations in Barcelona that funds social science research.'

'Interesting. Not everyone gives up their time for those sorts of things.' Reviewing applications is time-consuming. I did my share but avoided it where possible. You don't get much out of it, except for ticking the 'service to the discipline' box on research evaluation forms or promotion applications.

'Apparently Lepan was very willing and his services as an external referee were much appreciated. Though not by the applicants. According to Pau, Lepan rejected many of the applications. The foundation didn't mind; they said it was important to maintain international standards.' I noted that down. This would help fill out my picture of the man and his impact as a scholar. You can't learn everything from what people write.

I asked Maria Paz about her own research. Her latest paper about using GPS for visitor monitoring had been accepted for *Tourism Management* subject to a few minor revisions.

'Well done. Have you heard anything more from Santiago yet?' I had started to think that if Maria Paz got invited to carry out some project with the sub-secretariat, I could join in and get back to Chile that way. Wishful thinking, no doubt; I could not see how our differing research interests might come together.

'Nothing yet, but I'm still hopeful.'

'It wouldn't hurt to send him a quick email letting him know you are still interested. Another small favour, can you send me a few of your Atacama photos, especially of the geysers and the Valle de la Luna. I'm giving a staff-student seminar in a couple of weeks—we professors emeriti must put in an appearance occasionally—and I managed to lose mine downloading them.'

She laughed. 'Same old Cliff. You need to get to grips with technology. Aren't there courses for old folk like you?'

'Well, you know the old saying about teaching old dogs new tricks.'

'How is Viviana, by the way?'

'I haven't heard much from her since Santiago.'

'I'm sure,' Maria Paz said with a chuckle and ended our call.

What had Maria Paz implied by that last remark? Viviana and I had exchanged a couple of emails after Santiago, pleasantries and views on Carvalho's guidelines for his festschrift. We agreed that it should not be a hagiography. Rather, we would write as fair and objective accounts of his research as we could.

I began thinking more about Viviana herself, about what Maria Paz hinted our relationship might be. What had the two of them been discussing that night in the restaurant in San Pedro when I had gone to the gents and waited to order another bottle of wine? At the conference, it was Viviana who had suggested we share a taxi back to the Vegas and finish the evening with a drink next door. I had always got on well with her and admired her scholarship. I assumed she regarded me in much the same way. We had known each other for a quarter of a century. As colleagues and friends. But was there anything more? Should I spend less time with my files and pay Viviana more attention? Mendoza was half a world away and even by Skyping it would be difficult to detect how she felt about me. Let alone develop a closer relationship. Still, there was nothing to be lost by maintaining contact. And if I got back to Chile, Mendoza was next door.

I waited until Tuesday morning to make it more like a business call before trying to reach Viviana on Skype. When I got hold of her, I asked how she was progressing with her festscrift chapter.

'It's taking more time and effort than I thought to track down some of his studies. He sure covered a lot of ground. He must have written a paper on every country south of the Rio Grande.'

'I heard there was a standing joke in his department: what is the difference between Antoine Lepan and God?'

'Tell me.'

'God is everywhere; Lepan is everywhere but here.'

She laughed. 'Nice one, Cliff. Lepan published a lot of his work in the region in journals based in Europe or North America, in English or French rather than in Spanish or Portuguese. I suppose that's because we only have a few good tourism journals, even anthropology journals, in Latin America.'

'No offence to you Latin Americans, but maybe he pictured himself as an international scholar and wanted to boost his profile in the more prestigious realms of academia.'

'You're right, we do have an uphill struggle gaining recognition. I also came across one of his papers in Portuguese which is set more in your territory. Deals with Borneo. That might be one of the seminal papers that Carvalho referred to in Santiago.' She fished around on her desk and held up the title page to the screen. 'I will send it to you. I know you don't read Portuguese but there's an eighty-word abstract in French.'

'Strange that it's in Portuguese. Borneo isn't my territory but I will try and see where it fits into the grand scheme of things. Did Lepan co-author much of his work in Latin America?'

'A handful of papers. Early on, only a few of us were working on tourism, especially anthropologists. Why do you ask?'

'For someone so prolific, he wrote most of his papers by himself. At least the ones I've been reading.'

'Remember, joint papers weren't so common when we were starting out, Cliff. Nowadays, a lot of papers have three or four authors, if not more. The younger ones try and boost their publications list that way.'

'That's true. What else has been keeping you busy lately?'

'I'm on the committee of a wine and food festival coming up later in the year. We're trying to encourage more artisanal producers to participate but that's not easy. I'm also organising a book club, that's a lot of fun. Not erudite books, mind you. I've introduced the good ladies in my neighbourhood to comparative readings of South American crime fiction. Last month we did a couple of Chilean writers, Díaz Eterovic and Mario Valdivia. This month we have *Una mancha más* by Alicia Plante. How about you?'

'I'm not a book club person. Listening to someone else's views on what I've been reading for pleasure doesn't do much for me. And I prefer to pick my own books. I like detective stories.' It was good to know we shared some non-work-related interests. 'Mario Valdivia is especially readable, credible characters and original plots. I met him once, in Santiago. Interesting fellow.' I reached over to the bookcase for my signed copy of *Crimen en el barrio alto* and held it up to the screen.

'You must tell me about him some time, in case we do another of his books.'

'Have you heard from Alba or Pablo lately?' I asked.

'I called Alba last week. Rico's better than he was but breaks down and cries a lot. He was always a cheerful kid before. Alba says Rico won't have a bath anymore, only a cold shower. What happened up at the geysers must still be upsetting him.'

'The thing is, Viviana, we don't know what did happen to Lepan.'

'Well, there's not much we can do except keep on supporting Alba. As always, nice talking to you, Cliff, but I've got to go meet up with one of my winegrowers. Keep in touch.'

'Keep in touch.' I would make sure that I did. But it was Viviana's other remark which played on my mind: 'there's not much we can do.' I had made a start on my festscrift chapter but not any progress on what led to Lepan's death. Still no response from Ramón confirming Mundial Mining was the company Lepan had been after in the Amazon.

But there was something I could do that might cheer Rico up. I sorted through the dust-covered boxes of books stored in my garage. I found the one I was looking for right at the bottom at the back. The box containing the French books that had given Rod so much pleasure, especially the adventures of Tintin. We must have bought him the whole series. As my fingers moved across the spines to find the one I was after, I teared up with the memories they rekindled. I quickly closed the box once I found *On a marché sur la lune*. I doubted that Rico read French, but I thought he would enjoy leafing through the book, the pictures are so imaginative and well-drawn. Some resembled the landscapes we had seen at the Valle de la Luna. We too had walked on the moon. I couriered it to Rico right away.

# CHAPTER 7

I don't receive much snail mail anymore and only check my departmental pigeonhole when I go into university for some other reason. Generally, nothing exciting awaits me these days. This time I found a large envelope from Spain, from Montse Domenech, an old acquaintance in Barcelona. Back at my hot desk I opened it. The envelope contained twenty-five photo-copied pages, a journal article and a letter that read:

Dear Cliff,

It was good to hear from Maria Paz when I met her at Jordi's farewell that you are keeping well and are as busy as ever. You should slow down now that you are retired. Being retired suits me and being a grandmother keeps me fully occupied. I am not missing lecturing or doing any research at all.

Maria Paz told me you were writing about Antonio Lepan and his research in Spain. I want to tell you something about him because it's just not right.

You probably don't remember but I did my master's thesis examining social changes brought about by the development of tourism in Calella on the Costa Brava. I spent a lot of time interviewing families in the area, some in the town itself and others involved in market gardening on the fringes. I asked them lots of questions about how they earned their livelihood, what changes had occurred with tourism and how they felt about it. It took me months but I got a very detailed picture of differences in occupations and attitudes between parents and their children. I got an excellent grade which enabled me to go on and do my doctorate at UAB. That dealt more with market gardening. I focused mainly on agricultural geography after that but I came back to tourism from time to time. Remember, that's how we met at that IGU conference in Barcelona.

Well, five years ago Jaime Valenti gave me an overview paper he had written on the history of tourism on the Costa Brava in which he referenced an article on Calella written many years earlier by Lepan for a French journal. Out of interest I asked Jaime for a copy of the original (see enclosed). My mother was from Perpignan, and I know you speak French too. I am also sending you some pages from my thesis. If you look at the long passages I have highlighted, you will see he has taken most of what he has written directly from my thesis. His introduction and conclusion are written using fancy language but the quotes from 'his' participants are word for word the same as mine. How could that be? It is outright plagiarism. Of course, it was too late then to try and prove anything. Manuel had only recently passed away and I had a lot of other things on. But if you are writing about Lepan you should be aware of this. Some people have no shame. Who knows if the 'great scholar' has not done the same thing to other students?

Please use this information as you think fit.

Warmest regards,

Montse

I shook my head in disbelief. I reread Montse's letter. I perused the pages from her thesis and the article she sent. It was one of Lepan's that I had already located. On first reading the article, I was impressed by the empirical data which followed a thoughtful introduction couched in terms of intergenerational change and the evolution of small-town attitudes. Reading it again, I saw what Montse meant. Lepan favoured technical terms, Montse used much simpler language. Nevertheless, the body of the paper was identical to hers except that it was in French. Montse called her thesis 'Changing occupations and attitudes in Calella'. Lepan chose a more generic title for his paper, 'Intergenerational changes in a Spanish coastal resort.' I double-checked his list of references, no mention of her thesis nor any other recognition of her work. Supervisors at the time often found a simple footnote sufficient acknowledgement of a student's research. In any case, Oriol had supervised Montse in Barcelona, not Lepan. Lepan's paper appeared to be a clear case of plagiarism.

I looked up from the paper when the door opened and Bill Broughton entered, struggling with a pile of books. Bill, a supply chain expert, had retired a year after me. He had cast aside the natty suit he wore when head of school in favour of his old corduroy jacket, complete with leather elbow patches. Like me, Bill preferred the printed word.

'You are looking reflective, Cliff. Found the meaning of life or are you just keeping your seat warm?'

'Grab the other chair while you can. I spotted Marsha in the distance. She will no doubt want 'her' desk once she's finished tearing strips off the AV guy. What brings you in this fine sunny day?'

'Dropping off these books and then I'm off to give my annual talk to the research methods class, about how and where to start your research.'

'And the answer is?'

'The usual. Research is about finding answers to a question. Good research starts by asking the right question.'

'And the right question is?'

'That, my friend, is a good question.' He dropped his books

where they would most annoy Marsha and set off to enlighten the troops.

I picked up Montse's letter again. What now? Her letter had dented my esteem for Lepan. I liked Montse and could sense her injustice. The pages she had sent from her thesis and Lepan's article did appear to show that he had lifted her work verbatim and used it without acknowledgement. Was there some other explanation? Had she forgotten some verbal agreement that he could have access to her material? It was a long time ago. Possible, but unlikely. Lepan was no longer around to provide his side of the story and I did not want to speak ill of the dead. Still, there was Montse's question, had he done the same thing to other students? Was hers an isolated case or symptomatic of a broader pattern of behaviour? Was his prolific output the result of wholesale plagiarism?

I was pondering all of this when Marsha stormed in. Her talk with Harold from AV had not gone well. 'Whose books are these?' she asked. She pushed them to one side and claimed the chair. 'Bill's no doubt. Doesn't he know you can read books online these days?' She glanced over the titles. 'I suppose not. They didn't have e-books in the Dark Ages.'

'Good afternoon, Marsha,' I said. I put Montse's envelope in my satchel and started to stand.

'Oh, hello Cliff. No need for you to go. It's Bill and his blasted books which get on my wick.'

I wanted to avoid another lengthy outburst about the multiple misdemeanours of my colleague, but it occurred to me Marsha might be able to help. I sat. 'Marsha, when you chaired the Ethics Committee you would have dealt with cases of plagiarism, wouldn't you?'

'We copped our share of those. Some from staff who felt their work had been ripped off by someone else. Most of the student ones involved the lazier or less capable downloading ready-made essays. We also received a few complaints from PhD students who felt their work should have been explicitly acknowledged by a supervisor. We didn't hear much from master's students. Why do you ask? Has someone been misappropriating Professor West's words of wisdom?'

'No, I was reading an article which I thought I had come across elsewhere. How did you pick up and check out plagiarism?'

'Usually, we were responding to complaints, either from a student or lecturer. We would check them out using one of those programs that are around now, generally Turnitin. A lot of journal editors nowadays use Crossref Similarity to verify if submissions are original. These programs don't catch everything, but they greatly increase the chances of picking up writing which has appeared elsewhere.'

'What about something from one of Bill's old books there?' I asked.

'Those programs only work on digital files and these books of Bill's predate the electronic age. If you don't have a digital version you would need to have a hard copy of both, the original and the one where plagiarism is suspected.'

'That would be true of theses too?'

'Right, the library only has digital copies of the more recent ones. Remember, the university changed the regulations a few years ago. Is it one of ours?'

'No, no, a paper from Spain, from way back.' I got up, not wanting to prolong the discussion. Marsha was the faculty gossip.

•••

Montse's letter and the chat with Marsha led me to take a fresh look at Lepan's publications before going any further. There were a lot of them. I needed to be systematic if I were to detect any evidence of widespread plagiarism, something which had not occurred to me previously. How would I know if Lepan was guilty of using unattributed work from students or other researchers decades ago? Without Montse's letter I would not have known about the Calella case. What's more, there would only be hardbound copies of theses from that time.

Where to start? I stared at the lengthy list of Lepan's publications that I had compiled. Running my eye up and down the list, language struck me as a central characteristic of Lepan's work. I was impressed by the fact that he published in French, Spanish, English and Portuguese. Lepan was not the only European scholar to be so multilingual, but his work shone out in the tourism literature dominated by monolingual Anglo-Americans. I was missing something, but what? I added the fields of language and the country studied to my Endnotes file and reordered the publications by language rather than date of publication. I flicked up and down the reordered list repeatedly but failed to detect any pattern.

I reordered the list by country studied. Bingo. Lepan's papers on two African countries caught my eye. His paper on the adverse effects of tourism in French-speaking Senegal appeared in an English journal; that on alternative tourism in Tanzania came out in a French periodical. This struck me as odd. A Frenchman might publish papers dealing with Tanzania in French, his native language. Or a researcher could choose to publish in a particular language because it is the language of the most highly regarded journals in a particular discipline. But Lepan was multilingual and could publish in any of four languages with relative ease. The pattern revealed a systematic bias towards publishing in a different language from that spoken in the destination in question—eleven of his thirteen papers on Spanish destinations were in French or English, both papers on Portugal appeared in English. Moreover, in the wider research community there has been a growing acceptance that researchers have a duty to give back to the participants or communities which they study. Even in the 1970s social anthropologists would have been particularly aware of such a responsibility. Publication in a foreign language would severely limit dissemination of the research findings in the places studied.

The penny dropped. Was that the very reason Lepan had adopted his publication strategy? Was he deliberately lessening the chances of his plagiarism being discovered by publishing in a different language, avoiding reference to specific places in titles and using generic terms? Many of these papers were written before online databases and search engines were available. You could not simply enter a place name or terms such as 'alpine community' AND 'social impacts' AND 'Pyrenees' and expect to identify most of what had been written worldwide on the topic in a matter of seconds as you can nowadays. Lepan's relative lack of cross-referencing his own publications also made sense now—it was a way of reducing the chances of readers making connections between them. In the absence of a CV or online profile, which I had yet to find, I was conceivably the first to compile such a comprehensive list of Lepan's tourism publications, excluding Latin America which was being covered by Viviana. No doubt Lepan needed to include his list of publications in applications for promotion or research grants. But would anyone on the relevant committees have done anything more than be impressed by his output and the international scope of his research? Apparently not. His output in any one of the languages I read, let alone all three, was so prolific and of such quality that it alone would have built a reputation which anyone would have been proud of.

Montse had only discovered by chance years afterwards what he had done with her work. I sensed that hers was not an isolated case and that Lepan may have resorted to plagiarism over many years in many places. Lepan was not a lone wolf after all. He had co-authors—silent, unwitting partners oblivious to how their work was being used. Or was I becoming cynical? Or jealous of his track record? Other than Montse's case, I only had circumstantial evidence from the patterns I had identified in my list.

Then there were Lepan's more conceptual and methodological papers which made up about a third of my list and contained no geographic references at all. This group contained such titles as: 'Concepts and criteria for appropriate forms of tourism development' and 'Culture, commodification and change: an analytical framework for anthropologists'. These papers were published in a mix of French and English journals and were amongst his most significant contributions to the literature. They were mainly theoretical in nature. Establishing the source of ideas and concepts would be much more difficult unless I could trace earlier papers from other authors and prove the links between them and Lepan's papers. Theories and conceptual models are rarely developed overnight. When the theorising has been done is less evident than with fieldwork. With fieldwork you need to indicate not only where and how the research has been done but also when the data have been collected. Dates could be falsified, of course. But if Lepan was not shy about taking results and text verbatim from another study, as in Montse's case, then maybe he was cavalier enough not to alter the periods in which the fieldwork was done.

I reread Montse's pages and Lepan's paper on Calella. *Voilà.* In both cases the fieldwork was reportedly carried out between March and June 1977. What else had Lepan been busy at around that time? I reordered the list of publications by date and country and focused on those between 1978 and 1980 (there is usually a delay of a year or two between when research is done and when it is published). I checked out if any other fieldwork had been carried out at the same time as Montse's/Lepan's was being done. According to the little table I produced, in 1977 Lepan had been doing research in Tunisia from February to April, in Senegal between April and July, and in Galicia from June to July. He had the magical ability to be in several places at once. I had no doubt that if I continued to tabulate the dates of research reported in his other papers I would find a pattern of improbable, if not impossible, overlaps in time and place. Lepan was claiming credit for other peoples' work. How he managed to access the material without detection was not yet evident, but he was without doubt plagiarising on a grand scale.

My thoughts were interrupted by a ping indicating I had mail. Viviana had sent the paper in Portuguese. I read the abstract in French and found it dealt with the role of cultural brokers in visits to longhouses in Borneo. Why would a French professor choose to publish his research in Borneo in Portuguese in a Brazilian journal, *Revista Brasileira de Estudos Etnográficos*?

I thanked Viviana and said my review of Lepan's work had taken an interesting turn. I attached the three Endnotes lists and the table with Lepan's fieldwork dates to my email and suggested she might find it revealing to do the same with his Latin American publications. Two days later Viviana got back to me with her lists. A similar pattern emerged. Most of Lepan's work in Latin America appeared in French or English journals with little in Spanish or Portuguese. Again, not surprising given that the tourism journals there, and to a lesser extent the anthropology ones, were relatively recent. None of his research in Brazil had been published in Portuguese. None of his studies dealing with Argentina had been submitted to the Spanish-language journal Viviana had edited. Two others had been. One was conceptual, the other related to Belize, the only English-speaking country in Central America. She discovered the fieldwork in Belize had been done in late 1991, the same time he had supposedly been hard at work collecting data for another study in Mexico. Nothing untoward had been noted on the two papers Lepan had submitted to her journal. The referees recommended acceptance with only minimal revision.

I checked her lists again for anything else out of the ordinary. Most of his Latin American publications, like the others I had read, were sole-authored. There were some joint articles, though. This time one of the co-authors' names caught my attention— Vinícius de Oliveira Carvalho. Carvalho had written six papers with Lepan, one on indigenous tourism in Brazil in English, an almost identical one in French, and four conceptual articles in English and French. Interesting that they were that close. Carvalho was by far Lepan's most frequent co-author. Perhaps he viewed himself as Lepan's disciple and that is why he was pushing the festschrift to honour the man.

You learn a lot from jointly writing up a research project with someone: how they write, how they think, what they see as important, whether they can be depended on to deliver on time, whether they are willing to share ideas, to split the workload and to apportion credit fairly. You might also learn if they cut corners, if they massage data to fit their hypotheses and whether they engage in other unscholarly practices. Might one also learn how to plagiarise undetected to advance one's career? Were Carvalho and Lepan working together to deceive? Was having a co-author a means of indicating that at least some of your work was being done jointly? As Bill Broughton would say, there were plenty of good questions to ask.

I had a lot to discuss with Viviana when I Skyped her the next day.

'Your Endnote tables of Lepan's publications and your table of his fieldwork dates suggest something odd is going on,' she said. 'What are you suggesting?'

I held up the tables. 'Lepan had a calculated multi-language publishing strategy designed to boost his profile internationally and minimise the risk of any large-scale plagiarism being detected.'

'I see how you could interpret the patterns in both our sets of tables that way, but it's all circumstantial as they say in those detective stories you read. What direct evidence of plagiarism do you have?'

I told her about Montse's letter and the material she had sent. Viviana's jaw dropped.

'That sounds clear-cut. Still, it's only one paper among more than a hundred and fifty we've looked at. How could we show Lepan has done this repeatedly? How would you identify any others? I've been around tourism circles in Latin America a long time and don't recall any rumours about Lepan being associated with anything like this. No red flags were raised in the papers he sent to my journal either.'

'Direct proof is an issue,' I agreed. 'Especially with the conceptual papers.' I was sure we were on to something, but we needed more evidence. I changed tack and asked about Carvalho's relationship with Lepan.

'They were closer than most of Lepan's connections in Latin America. I didn't know they had co-authored to that extent until you asked me to check it out. Maybe Carvalho collaborated with Lepan simply to publish in English and French which he doesn't speak.'

'Could be. How does what Carvalho has written with Lepan correspond with other papers he has written by himself? Is it an extension of his other work or are those papers with Lepan quite distinct?'

'No idea, but I can follow that up, Cliff.'

'Can you also check and see if Lepan collaborated at any stage with Hector Muñoz Muñoz?'

'OK, but I doubt it, given the animosity between them. Why do you ask?'

'A hunch, that's all.' There weren't any joint publications between the two on the list she had sent. But as I used to tell my students, it is generally harder to spot what is missing than what is present. If there was something, it might help explain the hostility between the two which had been mentioned over dinner in San Pedro when we had been discussing who would become the next president of TADSAI. I neglected to say that this formed part of my parallel study into Lepan's death, another potential alternative explanation being explored. Momentarily side-tracked, I nearly missed Viviana's question about what to tell Carvalho.

'What we've found out about Lepan's publications hardly makes for a chapter honouring him in a festschrift,' I said.

'Let's hit pause and think about it for a week or two. We still have some time before Carvalho's deadline.'

'Sounds a plan. I've got my seminar on tourism in Chile to prepare.'

'Keep in touch, Cliff.'

'Keep in touch'. Was that just on the work front? Lepan had at least increased my contact with Viviana. That was a positive legacy.

Discussing Montse with Viviana reminded me I needed to reply to her letter. I sent Montse an email:

I have been following up what you wrote regarding Lepan and how he plagiarised your thesis. Going through his publications, it does appear he may also have plagiarised other researchers' work. I have not been able to find any other evidence as concrete as yours. I see you refer to him as Antonio, not Antoine. Did you meet with him at any stage, or do you know how he may have come by your thesis? It is a long time ago, but do you know of anyone else who may have been working on tourism at that time and whose work he may also have taken without consent or acknowledgement. Any leads would help me uncover what he was doing and establish whether yours is an isolated case or not.

I also emailed Pau Puig to thank him for the helpful information about Lepan's activities in Barcelona, especially refereeing reports for the foundation. Was anyone still around who might have been on the foundation's assessment panels at the same time as Lepan or could he remember any successful applicants from that period?

With that, I turned to the more mundane task of preparing my seminar on tourism in Chile.

# CHAPTER 8

I got a good turnout of staff and graduate students for my seminar on tourism policy in Chile. I launched into my topic with a map of Chile and emphasised the challenges the country's geography creates for those wanting to visit—covering the long distances to visit the main attractions is expensive, time-consuming and a lot of back tracking is required. I started to illustrate this with a pictorial journey from north to south. Maria Paz's photos showed the Atacama landscape much better than mine would have done.

'Do the Chileans call those things geysers?' Bill asked. 'My little grandson Mikey could piddle higher than that and he's only three.' The students guffawed.

I pressed the key to advance to the next slide. I pressed it again. My PowerPoint had frozen. I'm helpless when technology lets me down. One of the PhD students came to my aid and fiddled with the computer and projector, checked cables and connections. I tried to keep my audience engaged by explaining it was not so much the geysers that were the attraction as the hot pools and the vast amounts of steam emanating from them. The hot pools photo would not budge. I feared I was about to overextend my knowledge of geothermal processes when Jeremy, one of the associate professors, put his hand up. My relief was short-lived.

'Isn't this the place where Antoine Lepan died? I remember reading posts about it on Trinet a few weeks ago. I'm pretty sure it was the El Tatio geysers.'

'That's right.'

The student was still bent over the computer.

'Were you there? Didn't you go on some trip to the Atacama before that conference in Santiago?'

'Yes, I did.'

'Can you tell us what happened?'

Even if I knew, I did not want my seminar to be hijacked by Lepan.

'Well...' With a flash the screen came to life, the student pressed the key to advance and a photo of the colourful houses clinging to the hillsides of Valparaíso appeared.

The rest of the seminar ran smoothly.

Afterwards, I had arranged to meet Tony Miller, one of the graduate students, to discuss his application for a scholarship to study in France. I suggested we go over to the cafe at the National Library as a hot-desking office doesn't lend itself to discussions with students. In the cafe Tony handed me a folder with his forms and research outline and asked what he could get me. His grades showed he was a bright student. Tony used to sit in the front row of my first-year class, never afraid to answer a question. He had even done a couple of French papers.

I had reached the last paragraph of his research proposal when he returned with a couple of date scones as well as the coffee. Initiative like that is always a good sign.

'So, why do you want to go to France?' I asked.

'I've never been out of New Zealand before.' His eyes lit up. 'This is the ideal opportunity to travel and do my PhD at the same time. France is the world's number one destination. Some of the French articles that I've been reading take a different slant on topics I'm interested in.'

He brimmed with the same enthusiasm that I had done four decades earlier. I remembered the encouragement and help I had received at the time from one of my lecturers. I turned to Tony's proposal, careful not to spill my mochaccino over his papers.

'This is in a pretty good shape. You need to tighten up your main research question. Be more explicit and strategic about why France is the best place to do this research. Drop in a couple of French references. Some excellent research is being done in Grenoble and Angers conceptualising destinations as clusters and networks. Show how you want to draw on that to examine the management and marketing of wine trails, if that is what you want to study.' We spent another half hour going over his application. Tony absorbed my points and asked perceptive questions. He stood a good chance of gaining a scholarship.

'Any other advice, Professor West?'

'Be prepared for a lot of differences in how things are done in France. It's more than the language. In my day a huge gap existed between staff and students. A lot of the professors didn't devote much time to supervising. They were always busy or away travelling somewhere. It was difficult to make a time to meet. Remember, we didn't have email in those days. No texting either. My supervisor lived in a little village near Arles and only showed up on campus in Aix one or two days a week when he had lectures and meetings. I used to lie in wait outside his office on those days, hoping he had some time for me.'

'No kidding?'

'It was frustrating, but I learnt to be independent and self-reliant.' That's also where I vowed that if I ever became a lecturer, I would make myself accessible to my students. The staff/student divide was probably the same in Barcelona. That's why Lepan's willingness to meet with Montse and other students to discuss their research would have gone down so well. I didn't rip off my students' work though.

'No staff-student seminars either,' I said. 'Graduate students didn't have offices or even a room to themselves like you've been used to here. All the students from first years up to PhDs made do with a handful of desks in the departmental library. Writing up, I would spend all day in my hall room, only going out for lunch and dinner at the cafeteria.'

'You must have been lonely.'

'At times, but I had a great topic and was immersed in my research.' I didn't add that I was also a bit of a loner, being by myself did not trouble me.

Tony began to look down-hearted. 'But that was forty years ago. It's different today, you will be fine, but be prepared for less attention than you've had at Vic.'

'Anything else?'

'Study hard but do make time for other things. France has a lot to offer. Take a break from your research every so often and make sure you enjoy your stay. *Bonne chance*, Tony.'

# CHAPTER 9

Dear Cliff,

I knew you were a decent man and would take my letter seriously. Now I am not so sure that I should have brought up the issue of Lepan plagiarising my thesis. I did, however, and I will answer your question even though it pains me to do so.

Lepan came to Barcelona in 1977 and gave a series of research methods seminars to a group of us post graduate students. Antonio was full of charm, he sounded so knowledgeable and showed a lot of interest in the research we were doing. After one seminar we all went out for drinks and tapas in a bar off Las Ramblas. I was infatuated with him and to my lasting regret ended up going back to his hotel and spending the night with him. Yes, I knew him in the biblical sense. At his next seminar two days later he refused to even acknowledge me. Instead, he moved on to his next target, Begoña Pi, a friend of mine. I stopped going to the seminars. I felt embarrassed and ashamed as my Manuel was already courting me at the time. I have never mentioned this to anyone before. In the seminar, and no doubt in our pillow talk, Lepan would have learned what I was working on and later he must have got hold of my thesis. It would have been in the library. He was back in Barcelona and held more seminars the following year. He used my thesis as he had used my body—for his own purposes. I do not know if the same thing happened to Begoña or any of the others. I expect it did.

Cliff, this all happened a long time ago. Lepan is dead. It would be best to let the whole matter rest. The question of plagiarism is serious, but I don't wish this personal side of it to come to light. My life now revolves around my children and grandchildren. I know I can trust you to do what is best and will leave the matter in your hands.

Warm regards,

Montse

So that was Lepan's *modus operandi*: flatter the students in seminars, charm them into bed, persuade them to share their ideas, purloin the best research, polish it up with a fancy introduction and conclusion, and submit it in a different language under his name. Poor Montse. What was I going to do? She was clearly regretting having stirred up the past, but I sensed she was still angry that Lepan had ripped off her thesis.

I moved on to Pau's reply. He had not reviewed any research grant applications for the Barcelona foundation. Francesc Vilar had done a lot of it when Lepan was around, but he had died in 2015. Jordi Segarra might have been able to help, but he was incommunicado, celebrating retirement by taking a round-the-world cruise. The foundation took confidentiality seriously and Pau thought I would not learn much from them. So, no progress on that front.

Viviana emailed to say she had started checking out Carvalho's publications.

Except for the first one, what he published with Lepan appears to be completely different to his sole-authored papers. I called him about his relationship with Lepan for my chapter on Latin America. He got quite cagey, said not to concern myself with it as he would deal with it in his introductory chapter. I told him my chapter was progressing but tracking down all Lepan had written about tourism in Latin America was taking longer than expected. 'Understandably so, he's written so much,' was his reply.

I came across a series of heated exchanges between Hector and Lepan, not in a tourism journal but in an agricultural one, Anales de la Agricultura Latina Americana. Hector favours large scale operations while Lepan supported small traditional practices. He argued they support indigenous communities better. It all centred around the industrial cultivation of maize. It was news to me that Hector was into maize but who knows, economists have a view on everything. Lepan did too. I met the editor of that journal once at a forum for journal editors, so I called him. Apparently, there was a lot of bad blood between Hector and Lepan. Well, we can leave all that if it's relevant to whoever is writing the agriculture chapter for Carvalho.

Interesting. That was the paper on Oaxaca that I had come across without appreciating its significance. What Viviana said made the bitter rivalry between Hector and Lepan to be president of TADSAI clearer; it formed part of a bigger picture. Why was Carvalho so cagey about his relationship with Lepan? Did the difference between his co-authored and sole-authored papers mean anything? If so, what? And what would we do about our chapters?

An excited Maria Paz Skyped with some welcome news.

'Armando, the guy at the sub-sec in Santiago, emailed me yesterday afternoon saying one of the other agencies, Corfo, put out a call a couple of days ago for project proposals for some new fund called Tourism, Technology and Innovation. They have some money left in their budget which they will lose if it's not allocated by the end of the month. Armando says his boss is interested in the ideas and techniques I discussed at the conference and would provide a letter of support if I can come up with a relevant project in Chile. I could apply some of my GPS techniques tracking visitors in some of the places we visited in the Atacama. Record where visitors are going, where they are stopping, are they sticking to the tracks and so on. At places like the Valle de la Luna and the geysers. And that's when I thought of you, Cliff. We could collaborate as you have a lot of experience of working in Chile. You've got expertise in visitor management and destination management plans and are a big name in that part of the world. I'm sure that wouldn't hurt.'

My pulse quickened. This was it. A chance to get back to the Atacama. To investigate what had happened to Lepan. To find the alternative explanation for Lepan's death. To follow my path to redemption. The research itself might even be interesting. But first we needed a competitive proposal. Maria Paz would not be the only one with backers somewhere in the bidding process. Some might have even more clout than Armando's boss.

'Hold on, slow down a bit, Maria Paz. Give me time to think. We need to be strategic if we are to be successful.' I jotted down some initial points. 'You're right, it's a clever idea linking visitor movements to destination management. Those agencies always want to see the practical implications of any research they fund.' That's one of my strengths and would justify my place in the team. 'We will also need to include some Chileans; they generally don't fund projects with just international experts.'

'So, I'm an international expert. That's flattering. This would be my first project outside Spain. Who would you suggest from Chile?'

'Lucas Marchena. You met him in Santiago. He's bright and easy to work with. He's an expert on collaboration, or rather the lack of cooperation, between different stakeholder groups. He did his thesis on that in Patagonia.' I could see it on my bookshelf, one of the few theses that I kept when I lost my office in Rutherford

House. 'Creating a more collaborative stakeholder network is important for implementing any visitor management strategies we might come up with. I can follow up with Lucas today.'

I glanced at my notes. 'We could also bring in Ximena, you remember, the woman who spoke to us on the way up to the lagunas. Having a local partner always scores well, transfer of knowledge and skills etcetera. In any case, we would need the backing of Ximena and her people to gain access to some sites in the first place.'

'I hadn't thought of that. I can see you have done this plenty of times and know how the system works, Cliff. What about bringing in Ramón Macedo, that Brazilian drones guy we met at the conference. OK, he's another foreigner but combining drones and GPS would bring an added dimension.'

'That isn't my field but adding drones would boost the technology side.' I might also learn more about what Lepan was up to in the Amazon from Ramón. He still hadn't answered my email. I had only spoken to him briefly at the conference and wanted to check him out first before bringing him on to the team. 'Hold back on Ramón for a couple of days and see how you go with the first draft before raising it with him. What's the deadline for the proposal?'

'Tight. The proposal is due at the end of next week, the decision is to be made by the end of the month. Some progress reports must be submitted but the project itself doesn't have be completed until the end of the year. Have you got any time over the next few months?'

'If we are talking weeks rather than months, I could fit that in,' I said, suppressing a smile. 'What's the budget?'

'Up to US$55,000. That sounds a lot.'

'Travel and accommodation would soon chew into it. We would need to hire a vehicle. Equipment, that's your field. Some local field assistants as well.' Maria Paz looked a little less confident. She hadn't worked through any of that. I used to crank out such proposals routinely. I had a lot riding on a successful outcome for this one. We needed a strong targeted proposal. Preparing an international bid would also provide Maria Paz with valuable experience. 'Why don't you draft up a proposal and have a first go at a budget,' I suggested. 'The form will seem endless. Work through it section by section. Send the draft to me and I will polish it up if I can.'

'Thanks, Cliff. I knew I could count on you.'

'Have you got much else on at present?'

'Have I? I'm moving into Jordi's old office. He hasn't cleared it out properly. He's taken home his books and personal stuff and left all his journals and papers with a note to throw away anything I don't want. I've heard stories about your old office, Cliff, but you should see some of this stuff; must have been here since he joined the department. Look at it.'

Maria Paz swivelled her laptop so I could see the chaotic sea of papers, folders and boxes. Jordi's office was reminiscent of my old one. Young colleagues today haven't experienced life in the Paper Age. She began her litany of the redundant.

'Here's a box labelled *Fieldwork: Garotxa, 1979.* Another one: *Teaching Timetables First Semester 1983, 1984, 1985.* What is this big box? *Foundation Reports 1982-1985.* I mean, really, what was the point of keeping any of this?'

'Whoa. What did you just say? Foundation reports?' Maybe Lady Luck was smiling on me today.

'That's right, *Foundation Reports...* Seems Jordi was on a panel reviewing research grant applications and he's kept everything. Aren't these reports supposed to be confidential? Shouldn't he have shredded them?'

'Jordi, bless his soul, has kept them on the same principle as I used to keep all my files.'

'That principle being?'

'That one day they may come in useful again.'

'But what possible good are they to Jordi or anyone else now?'

she said with a dismissive shake of her pretty head.

'Maybe none, but they may help me a lot. Can you have a quick look and see if you can find a summary of the results of the applications for each year? At the front or back of the files for each year.' Jordi may have been a hoarder but he was systematic.

'I will call you back.'

I crossed my fingers. Ten minutes later Maria Paz Skyped me again.

'Is this what you are looking for, Cliff?' she asked, waving a document in front of the screen.

'Hold it still… Yes, that's it. Could you see if there's another one like that, scan them and send them through to me. Don't throw that box out yet.'

Maria Paz hesitated. 'Are you sure we should be doing this?'

'Are those papers marked confidential?'

'No…still…'

'Trust me, Maria Paz, I'm not doing anything untoward. Jordi wasn't either. I think somebody else has been unethical. I want to check it out because he's no longer around.'

'If you say so.'

'One other thing, could you check the library and see if it holds two master's theses, done in 1977 or 1978? One by Montserrat Domenech, the other by Begoña Pi.'

'You mean Montse?' She wrinkled her brow. 'Montse's still around, I told you.'

'I've been in contact with her. I don't know if the online catalogue goes back that far or if you need to check the card index, providing they still have one. That would help me solve an issue which has been taking up a lot of my time. If I can clear it away with those bits of information, I can give some thought to your proposal.'

'Deal. Sounds like I caught you at the right time.'

If only she knew how timely this project was for me.

# CHAPTER 10

I made some plunger coffee and skimmed the online news until the two scanned documents from Maria Paz arrived. They did contain the information I thought I had seen. Each was a summary table of the outcomes of applications to the foundation to fund tourism research projects. One column listed the names of the projects, but not those of the applicants. Three columns recorded the recommendation of each of the reviewers. The fifth indicated whether the project was funded or not. Only the reviewers' initials appeared: JS, AL and EP. Presumably Jordi himself, Lepan and a third reviewer whose identity I could not guess, most likely from Spain. I respected Jordi's scholarship and assumed he would be a capable and fair judge. I now doubted Lepan's integrity. I had no idea about EP.

What interested me was how the three reviewers' recommendations compared. A pattern immediately emerged for both years. Where Jordi recommended acceptance, Lepan rejected. Where Jordi rejected, Lepan accepted. EP's pattern was less consistent but tended to coincide more with Jordi's. Even when both Jordi and EP shared the same view, the final decision always coincided with the recommendation of Lepan, the international reviewer. I counted more rejections than acceptances. I studied the project titles; those rejected were more conceptual in nature, the ones accepted were more empirical. Lepan appeared to be accepting applications which were of no interest to him and rejecting those with ideas and concepts that he could appropriate for his own use. Jordi only spoke Catalan and Spanish and would not have made any subsequent connection between material in the applications and that which Lepan had lifted and written up in French and English journals. The applicants, more established researchers than the thesis students, might recognise their ideas had been stolen, but how could they demonstrate that conclusively? 'Great minds think alike,' Lepan might have argued.

I had no concrete proof without going through the box which Maria Paz had stumbled across and matching up passages from the applications with passages in papers by Lepan. What would the ethics of doing that be? I had no legitimate access to those files. Was I becoming as bad as Lepan? Then there were the logistics to consider.

What else did I have? I scrolled through the titles of the proposed projects several more times. At least two of them sounded familiar: 'Cultural commodification: an anthropological approach' and 'Conceptualising appropriate forms of tourism'. Were these the source of two of the papers on my list of Lepan's publications: 'Culture, commodification and change: an analytical framework for anthropologists' and 'Concepts and criteria for appropriate forms of tourism development'? These last two papers appeared the year after the former two had been submitted to the foundation. There are limited terms relating to a particular topic so that similarities in the titles of genuinely different papers are not uncommon. By now, however, I was convinced that Lepan's willingness to review research grant applications was simply to filch ideas and models for his own conceptual and theoretical papers.

What to do? I needed more time to think things through before getting back to Viviana. I switched to Maria Paz's project. I knew I could trust Lucas who had replied enthusiastically to my email. Ramón Macedo taught at the Universidade Federal de Paraná in Curitiba, the same university as Amalina and Edílson. I emailed Edílson to see what he thought of him.

Maria Paz's email the next day confirmed my suspicions about Lepan. Montse's and Begoña's theses were in the card catalogue but with a note saying both were missing. The young librarian knew nothing about them. They may have gone missing way back. Several others from around that time were not on the shelves either. I had all the information I needed. I thanked Maria Paz and told her she could toss out the box of foundation documents.

Ping, the response from Edílson. He had not collaborated on any research with Ramón, but they taught a couple of classes together. Ramón was a good guy, reliable and straight forward to work with. I emailed Maria Paz to say we should include Ramón and his drones.

Viviana was online and I Skyped her. I told her about Montse's response, Lepan's seminars in Barcelona and the missing theses; evidence enough that he had been plagiarising students' work. I also summarised what I had discovered about the research grant applications he had reviewed and how I was convinced he had drawn on these for his conceptual articles.

'A lot of that's circumstantial, Cliff. But when we look at everything we know or suspect about Lepan, it does point to large scale plagiarism. Plagiarism isn't a capital sin and he wouldn't be the first to be guilty of it. Far from it. Remember that case of the German cabinet minister, Guttenberg if I recall right, who plagiarised a thesis and had to resign. Some Spanish politicians did the same thing. Lepan doesn't deserve a festschrift. Do we just leave it there or tell TADSAI and anyone else seeking to honour Lepan what we've found out?'

'Just withdrawing from the festschrift would be a cop out.

Think of the injustice to Montse and all the others whose work he ripped off. Plagiarists shouldn't be allowed to get away with it. But Lepan is dead. Montse, Begoña and others got their degrees. Montse may not be the only one who wouldn't appreciate us digging up the past. I don't see how we can right the wrongs done to the research grant applicants at this stage.'

'Why did he do it?' she asked. Her face clouded with a mix of puzzlement and sadness. 'He always came across to me as having a razor-sharp mind and a lot of ability. He didn't need to rely on others.'

I had wondered about that too. The first papers from his doctoral thesis were ground-breaking. His supervisor would surely have known if that research wasn't his own. But after that? 'Maybe he just fell into it, had a relationship with a student and ripped her off, either because he found that easy to do or perhaps out of spite because her work was better than his. That would have helped his early career. Would have boosted his ego too.'

'He was incredibly vain, that's for sure.'

'However it started, plagiarism soon became his *modus operandi*. What he was doing in Spain shows he was cold and calculating early on. Why spend all that time collecting and analysing primary data if you can take all the credit for someone else's hard work?' For me, fieldwork is the part I enjoy the most—visiting new places, collecting data, meeting new people. Not for Lepan apparently. 'Later, as his reputation grew and he received invitations to international conferences or as a guest lecturer overseas, he found more and more opportunities to carry on and it snowballed. We can only guess what drove him.'

'Why do you think his publications fell off after 2000?' Viviana asked. 'I mean, he continued to publish but not at the same rate. That could be age, we all slow down after a while.'

'He had already established his reputation by then. He was becoming more and more involved in his activism. That would have consumed a lot of time and energy. It enlarged his profile, standing in front of the loggers in the jungle, walking into the brothels in Bangkok to rescue poverty-stricken young girls from rural villages in the north. That got him a lot more headlines than an article in the *Annals of Tourism Research* would ever have done.'

'You're right. He was a hero amongst his left-leaning colleagues. A lot of NGOs loved him too. He always struck me as genuine in his support of those causes.' She shook her head.

His publications might also have dropped off because the risks of what he was doing would have increased considerably since online searches have become easier and more digital data bases are available nowadays. Lepan was smart enough to know this and cut back solely to what he needed to maintain his reputation using the safest sources. Staying put in Bordeaux after shifting from Aix early on in his career was also a clever move. It meant he would have been subject to less scrutiny than in applying for new positions elsewhere. I didn't have any contacts in Bordeaux who could fill me in on his behaviour there, on any rumours or doubts that all his work was not his own.

'Finding all this out has left me totally disillusioned, completely let down,' Viviana said. 'I admired his work and had no reason not to believe in him.'

'Me too. Lepan wasn't a big man, but he sure cast a long shadow. He would have lost a lot of friends and made a lot more enemies if this had come to light when he was still alive.'

Viviana looked at a mirror on her wall. If she was gazing into her own conscience, I doubted she had anything to worry about. From what I knew of her, she was fair in all her dealings. She turned back to the screen and asked me if I had ever been tempted to lift something from somebody else, fiddle my results or do anything I regretted in my research. Good questions.

I shook my head. Viviana read this as a sign of denial, whereas it was one of dismay. There's one episode that I would prefer to forget. Early on, I came across a colleague's draft analytical framework which she had forgotten to erase from the back of a rotating blackboard, one of those old ones like a roller towel in a public toilet, only bigger. Her framework dealt with a similar topic to mine but was more sophisticated. Collaborating was out of the question; our personalities clashed. By adding a couple of minor steps which she had missed, I adapted it, dusted off both sides of the blackboard and passed the framework off as my own. My proposal was much stronger as a result. I was awarded the research grant, she missed out. No one ever found out. Before I had even started, government priorities changed and the fund was cut. Justice was done but I still shudder at my opportunism. I understood more than I cared to admit how Lepan might have taken that first step down the slippery slope that characterised his career.

What I said to Viviana was, 'Anything I published from my postgrads' research I always did under joint authorship, with their name first.'

'That was a nice paper in *Annals*, the one with Lucas.'

'I consider myself a fair reviewer. The papers I rejected were plain bad or poorly written, not ones that contained any ideas I wanted to borrow. What about you? Do you think all the papers for your journal were refereed fairly?'

She picked up a copy of the latest issue of the journal lying on her desk and flicked through it. 'I've edited some where it seemed a reviewer was being exceptionally positive or overly harsh because they may have guessed who the author was and treated them as friend or foe. Overall, though, the double-blind process works well. I trust you. Over the years I've sent you some of the trickier submissions.'

'Ha, I thought that I got more than my share of those.'

'Well, you've been on the editorial board right from the first volume, since 1999. How much do you think Carvalho knew of any of this?' she asked.

'You said their joint articles were not related to any of the other research Carvalho published. It's only supposition, but he may have discovered how Lepan operated and got in on the act. He leveraged that to build his own career. Did Lepan support Carvalho when he became the regional chair of TADSAI?'

'He endorsed him strongly. Carvalho got Lepan to speak at the Santiago conference. A win-win situation: Carvalho got a big name as keynote speaker, Lepan used the invitation as a ticket back into Chile for whatever else he was up to there.'

'For whatever else he was up to there.' That, more than his unscholarly practices, was what was intriguing me. I itched to move on.

'You said Carvalho was cagey about their relationship. If all or only part of what we suspect is true, Carvalho won't want us to dig any deeper. How about we email him saying we regret that we are unable to contribute our chapters following the work we have already done on Lepan's scholarship and suggest he reconsider the idea of a festschrift and leave it at that.'

'That's a good compromise. That way, even if we are not correcting Lepan's image, his memory won't be honoured any further.'

We emailed Carvalho. The next day he contacted all the festschrift contributors:

Dear colleagues,

I regret to inform you that the publisher who was to have produced the festschrift to honour our late friend and colleague, Emeritus Professor Antoine Lepan, has reconsidered the commercial viability of this project and as a result advised me yesterday that they will no longer be able to do so. Before obtaining this publisher's initial agreement, several others whom I had approached turned down the proposal on similar grounds, a very worthy idea but one for which prospective sales would never recover their costs. I know many of you have already put in a lot of time and effort but now, with a heavy heart, I have no other option but to cancel the project.

Thank you all for your understanding.

Yours most sincerely,
Vinicius de Oliveira Carvalho

Carvalho's festschrift project, like the person it was to honour, was dead in the water. In researching his tourism output, Viviana and I had discovered a lot about Lepan's life. He had wronged numerous people throughout his career but nothing we had read shed any new light on his death. With the festschrift aborted, I could concentrate on finding an alternative explanation in the Atacama for how Lepan had died at El Tatio. For that, I needed Maria Paz's project proposal to be accepted.

# CHAPTER 11

We called our project 'Improved visitor management through technological innovation: using GPS and drones to monitor visitor movements in the Atacama.' Its relevance to the Tourism, Technology and Innovation fund was immediately apparent. Strategically, that was a good beginning. The aim was to develop a better understanding of visitor movements at the four sites we visited on our tour: Chaxa Laguna, Valle de la Luna, the El Tatio geysers and the Miscanti and Miñiques lagunas. Using GPS and the drones would give us a detailed picture of visitor movements. That would enable us to identify how visitors moved around, where and when congestion occurred, and what trails or areas were under-used. With that information, Lucas and I could develop more effective management strategies, such as measures to schedule demand and redirect flows to relieve pressure on hot spots. Implementing such measures requires the creation of collaborative stakeholder networks. Lucas's expertise would be invaluable for that part of the project.

Maria Paz called for feedback on her draft.

'It needs tweaking in places, but we're not far away,' I said. 'You're right about bringing Ramón in. The drones and GPS will be complementary.'

'We will convert you to a believer in technology yet.'

'I'm no Luddite, I just can't operate all these new gadgets.' I consulted my notes. 'What error margin do you have with your GPS?'

'See, a technical question. Five to ten metres. Is that accurate enough?'

'It would be for movements along the tracks but not for relatively minor movements off them. You could calibrate the GPS data with images from the drones.'

'The drones wouldn't work at the geysers because of all that steam, would they? We can just use GPS there.'

'You may need special permission to fly drones in the flamingo reserve,' I said. 'They might disturb and endanger the birds. Add a sentence or two about the work you've already done tracking visitor movements on the Ebro delta where there are also flamingos. That would reinforce your expertise.'

'Good idea. We will also have to check out the ethics of using drones to video tourists. What about the visitor management side of the proposal?'

'We should focus on analysing how visitors disperse along the trails and whether they stick to the trails or stray off them into areas which might affect any wildlife and the vegetation. And keep an eye out for any implications for visitor safety without mentioning Lepan's accident explicitly. The distinct types of environment and variety of trails will add to the comparative side of things.'

I added that Lucas was enthusiastic and that I had asked him to develop the section on implementing recommendations through network collaboration. I was looking forward to working with him in the field.

'Ximena is keen to be on the team and will write a letter of support and provide some contacts,' Maria Paz said. 'She says we will have to work around her other engagements; she's spending a lot of time protesting some new mining exploration.'

'Ask her if she knows of a house to rent in San Pedro; that could work out cheaper for us. And contact Marisela and see if we could distribute the GPS loggers to her tour groups. Most of the visitors come by bus.'

'Good idea. I haven't got on to those practicalities yet. I'm learning what a big job this is.'

I knew what she meant. They don't teach you about logistical practicalities and collaboration in research methods courses. That comes with experience, generally after making mistakes.

'And we would also want some field assistants to hand out the loggers and collect them back in, record arrival and departure times of the buses and so on.' I had Miguel Figueroa in mind. Not only because he was bright and hailed from San Pedro; having him on the team might be a way of maintaining contact with his father in my quest to determine what had happened to Lepan.

'No room in the project to bring in the expertise of Professor Arévalo?' Maria Paz asked deadpan.

'Not without upsetting the already delicate international/Chilean mix in the team,' I said. I had pondered over how we might include Viviana but couldn't justify it, other than wanting to see her again. Viviana's strengths were in wine tourism and distribution channels for tourism, neither of which meshed with our Atacama project.

'Does August suit you? I don't have classes over the summer,' she said.

'No domestic commitments either?' I asked with a straight face.

'Both my parents are in good health, thank you.'

'August works for me. It's not peak season, so we won't get as much of an idea about crowding as over their summer, but it would be more manageable for us. That gives us time to finish the analysis and write up by the end of the year.'

We were making good progress.

Miguel replied to my email the next day, excited by the

prospect of being a research assistant in an international team in his hometown. His internship finished at the end of July.

Almost lost in all the project emails was one that gladdened my heart. From Rico.

Dear Professor Cliff,

Thank you so much for the Tintin book. I really like it. I can't read the French but the pictures are super. I can follow the story from them. Some of the pictures are like what we saw at the Valle de la Luna. In that photo you took of me I look just like Tintin. All it needs is a rocket in the background. I will show the book to my cousins in Armstrong next time we visit them.

Yours sincerely,
Rico Toledo

Alba also sent her thanks. She said Rico looked at the book every night in bed and then got up, pulled back the curtains and gazed up at the moon. I almost choked on the lump in my throat—Rod used to do the same night after night until diplodocus, triceratops and pterodactyls replaced the moon, Mars and Jupiter. I knew what a bright kid I had when Rod explained to me the link between his passions, that meteorites had wiped out the dinosaurs.

•••

Emails and Skype sessions intensified between Maria Paz and me until we were satisfied with the proposal. She submitted it a day before the deadline. It was her first time as lead on a multimember project, and an international one at that. The team had a good mix of skills and experience. We should get on well together. Nothing holds back a group project more than personality clashes, dissent in the ranks, people not doing their share or holding back with their ideas. We had a strong proposal and my chances of getting back to the Atacama were promising.

Moreover, I now had a lead to follow. Maria Paz's contact with Ramón must have jolted his memory. He emailed to apologise for the delay in answering my question about Lepan. He had spent several anxious weeks in Bahia with his mother who had gone down with yellow fever right after he had returned to Brazil. Ramón was not one hundred per cent certain but thought the company mining for gold in the Amazon that Lepan wanted him to film was called Mundial something. Perhaps Mundial Mining. I had no doubts, the ute I had seen at the geysers the morning Lepan died belonged to Mundial Mining. But what were they doing at El Tatio? No gold there that I had read about.

•••

Ximena kept reminding us of the need for flexibility because of her protest activities. Why was mining in the Atacama such a big issue? I realised I knew little about the Atacama other than what I had seen at the few places we had visited on our tour. On our trip up to the lagunas, Ximena had mentioned that Lepan would have raised the issue of mining had the workshop in San Pedro been held. Something about lithium mining reducing the water table due to the popularity of smart phones. I had forgotten how that all fitted together. I searched online and soon discovered the problem.

Rechargeable lithium batteries powered not only my iPhone and Acer, and everybody else's, but also the world's electric cars and some power grids. Smart phone and laptop batteries contain only a few grams of lithium. Batteries for each electric car require 20 kg. The demand for lithium had soared and would continue to expand exponentially because of the strategic role electric cars have in reducing our global dependence on fossil fuels. So much for buying a Tesla and saving the planet.

To my surprise, the Atacama salar produced forty percent of the world's lithium. All the lithium is mined by two massive corporations: Albemarle, an American firm, and the largely Chilean owned SQM which had been privatised during Pinochet's regime. The general's son-in-law had been a major player in SQM. Chinese interests were now after a large stake in the company.

I had assumed mining lithium involved digging it out of the ground in a massive pit, such as the one at Chuquicamata, the world's largest open pit copper mine near Calama. But no. In the Atacama, lithium is found in a saline solution or brine in the aquifers below the salar. The lithium occurs in such minute traces that enormous amounts of brine are pumped out into huge ponds and left for years to evaporate in the hot Atacama sun. When it is concentrated sufficiently, the brine is transported to Antofagasta to be processed further and then exported. We had not come across the ponds on our tour because they are located at the southern end of the salar, away from San Pedro. Had we been over that way, we could not have missed them due to the sheer scale of the operations—the ponds cover approximately eighty square kilometres. Unfathomable amounts of water are needed. Most of the brine used in the extraction process is evaporated. Extraction of the lithium also required freshwater to be pumped in from nearby mountains.

Water, already a scarce resource in the fragile environment of the Atacama, became hotly contested as the effects of the lithium extraction became evident. The mining operations led to severe depletion of the aquifers. Environmentalists became concerned about the impacts that shrinking bodies of water on the salar were having on the flamingos and on the microorganisms that play a critical role in the whole salar ecosystem. The mining companies, of course, contested the nature and extent of these impacts. Local communities began to experience a loss of drinking water, their irrigation canals dried up and their pastoral activities declined. Because of the Atacameños' spiritual connections with water, the impacts were not only physical but also cultural. They filed lawsuits against one of the mining companies for unauthorised withdrawal of water and for not respecting indigenous peoples' rights. In 2016 a state environmental agency started sanctions for extracting more brine than the company's quota allowed.

What exactly was Ximena protesting? She had not mentioned anything specific about her mining protest. I searched the Chilean papers. Nothing in *La Tercera* or *El Mercurio*. I scrolled through the most recent issues of the Calama newspaper. I just about missed it; a five-centimetre column about a group from San Pedro protesting the application for a lithium mining licence by a multinational company new to the Atacama salar, Mundial Mining.

The expansion of lithium mining, that's what concerned Ximena.

Lithium mining, that's why Mundial Mining were in San Pedro. That was why the company had utes there, like the one I had seen up at the geysers and outside our hotel. Was the threat Lepan posed to the company related to their lithium mining bid in the Atacama salar, not his opposition to gold mining in the Amazon as I had earlier assumed? I had missed their lithium mining activities in all the Portuguese text when I had checked them out online.

I could see Lepan fitting right in and lending his experience to drawing the world's attention to the Atacameños' cause. Was that why he had been so upset when Rico had scared away the flamingos—he had wanted some photos of the adorable birds to illustrate their endangered habitat. I knew from my earlier research that Mundial Mining were unscrupulous. Would they go so far as to silence him to eliminate the threat he presented to their interests in the Atacama?

And was Ximena putting herself at risk by leading the protest against Mundial Mining? Had she told me everything about her connection to Lepan?

Lithium mining was not the only cause of demonstrations in the region. A couple of references mentioned protests at the El Tatio geysers. The first wells to explore the potential for a geothermal power plant had been drilled in the early 1960s but nothing eventuated. Nevertheless, interest in geothermal electricity remained as Chile sought to diversify its energy sources. More exploratory drilling was carried out in 2009 when one of the older wells exploded, belching toxic ground water fluids into the atmosphere and depositing arsenic rich salts. Such blow-outs created not only health risks but could also upset the geothermal balance of the basin. Local communities protested strongly and further exploration was discontinued. Some private sector developers argued this stymied economic growth, ignoring the impact on tourism if a blow-out caused the geysers to dry up. The anthropologist/tourism researcher/activist Antoine Lepan would have been right at home protesting energy exploration.

What had Lepan been doing in the Atacama? Had he come into the area under the guise of an academic on a pre-conference tour with some other objective in mind? Was all his running around with a long-lensed camera just for show? Or was he taking photos to gain evidence of some new operation? What was he going to reveal at the workshop? Was it related to the new application for mining lithium which Ximena was concerned about? Or was it connected to the geysers where he had met his death? Was it related to his involvement in something we knew nothing about? If so, what? Who would have reason to see him dead? Did the local police suspect anything? Did Sergeant Figueroa know more than he had let on? Was Lepan's death related to his hotel room being ransacked? And his missing camera bag? Was there a single alternative explanation or several? I had a lot to think about.

Time for a long walk along Oriental Parade to Point Jerningham and back. I leant into the strong northerly whipping up whitecaps in the harbour and buffeting the smaller planes taking off into the greying sky. I did not envy the businessmen flying back to Timaru or New Plymouth or wherever else they were heading after an exhausting day meeting bureaucrats or lobbying politicians. Would I be taking off in a few weeks' time and heading back to Chile? I hoped so. The Atacama held the answer to what had happened to Lepan. If foul play was involved, and I was now certain it was, being able to show that would absolve Rico of any responsibility.

# CHAPTER 12

Recent weeks had been busier than usual since I had retired. My digital files and folders were as cluttered as their Paper Age forebears had often been. It was time to tidy up and take stock.

I tackled the Lepan articles first. I say Lepan articles, though I now knew he was not the real author of many of them. I had ordered and re-ordered the articles and tabulated and cross-tabulated the references so many times that I was pleased to be filing them away. I created another folder for the material I had downloaded on the Atacama.

Tidy folders also act as silos. They compartmentalise papers and prevent connections, serendipitous or systematic, between topics. This thought generated another. Had Lepan written anything on the Atacama? I checked; nothing in the Lepan folder on the Atacama, nothing in the Atacama folder by Lepan. He must have written something given what I had read about mining/water use issues and the possible links between Mundial Mining and Lepan's activism. I looked at the Atacama folder again; all the articles were in English.

I attacked the search engines again, in French for Lepan+Atacama+*eau* and in Spanish for Lepan+Atacama+*agua*. I got two hits, one from 1996, the other from 1998. They were variations on the same theme, an ethnographic study of water rituals by the Atacameños and the growing threat lithium mining posed to traditional lifestyles in villages on the margins of the salar. I also came across half a dozen Chilean newspaper articles and a French NGO blog referring to his involvement in the 2009 protests at El Tatio. Lepan appeared in one grainy photo up at the geysers flanked by a dozen banner waving supporters. In another shot he was being led away by the San Pedro carabineros to be charged with public disorder. The accompanying text said the charge was subsequently dismissed providing he left the country.

Lepan was much more familiar with the region than he had let on. When Marisela had asked at the start of our tour if anyone had been to the Atacama before, everyone had said no. I understood now why Figueroa was familiar with Lepan's activism. I could not make out from the photo if Figueroa had been one of the officers who had arrested him in 2009. But why had Lepan returned to San Pedro on our tour and acted as if he was one of the party on his first visit? The Frenchman continued to intrigue me.

I moved on to ordering the various sets of photos I had used in preparing my seminar. I corralled them all in a Chile folder and ran through my presentation to make sure I had not missed any. I stopped on the one of the geysers which had been on the screen when my PowerPoint froze. I could see why Maria Paz had selected it. A striking steamy shot which captured the ethereal nature of El Tatio perfectly; a metre high geyser was erupting in the foreground sending ripples across the hot pool, two fumaroles further back emitted clouds of steam broken by weak shafts of the early morning sun, the stones that edged the path framed the lower right. Perfect for a postcard, scenic calendar or travel brochure. I clicked through the rest of the presentation to check I had filed everything but was drawn back to this photo. What was it about the scene aside from Maria Paz's superb photography? When it had frozen on the screen I had been playing for time as the PhD student sorted out the problem. Then Jeremy had asked me about Lepan's death. I kept staring at the photo but could not see what it was telling me. It might come to me if I recreated that moment in the seminar room. The monitor there was much larger than the screen of my laptop.

The dean had asked to see me the next day so I took the bus to Rutherford House early in the hope the seminar room would be free at lunch time. It was. I inserted my memory stick and brought up the slide I was after. I stepped back and studied it on the monitor. Bill Broughton broke my concentration when he stuck his head through the door, looked around the empty room and said, 'You've lost your audience, Cliff. No wonder, if all you show them is that one slide.'

'Feel free to join in, Bill.'

'Sorry, must grab my hot seat before Marsha does.'

I closed the door after him and studied the monitor from a different angle. This time the slide gave up its secret; right at the top of the photo in one of the shafts of dawn sunlight I made out a faint green spot. I peered at it. Green. The colour of Lepan's jacket. Could it be that Maria Paz had caught Lepan in the background in what must have been the last few minutes of his life?

I needed a bigger image to confirm it was Lepan and not some piece of vegetation. Harold, the AV guy, could help. I was in luck; he was finishing his rounds.

'What's the problem, Cliff?' I explained what I was trying to do.

'You don't need a bigger screen. What you want is to be able to enhance that part of the photo you are interested in. Right, let's see what you've got.' He played around with the photo until he had enlarged and enhanced the green spot. 'Is this what you're after? It's still not that clear, but it looks like somebody standing there.'

I peered at the image and could just make out the top half of someone dressed in green. It had to be Lepan. As far as I could recall nobody else in our party that morning was wearing a green jacket. We were all blues, blacks and greys, except for Maria Paz who had been wearing a dressy white number.

'You're a real wizard, Harold. Can you print that off please and save it on my memory stick?'

'Done,' he said and with a couple of more clicks of the mouse he handed back the memory stick and reached over to retrieve the printout. 'Who is the mystery man in the mist?'

'One of the members of our tour party on my last trip to Chile. Thanks, Harold, must rush off to see the dean.'

I was not sure what, if anything, Lepan's appearance in Maria Paz's photo signified. At least I had been right in sensing some connection between what had been on the screen at the time and Jeremy's question about Lepan's death.

I took the lift to the twelfth floor, territory I never frequented these days, wondering what the dean wanted. I had been keeping my end up as an emeritus professor and my office entitlement could not be downsized much further.

'Cliff, they tell me you are keeping active around the place. Don't overdo it. You are officially retired,' the dean said.

I trotted out my old line of being in reactive mode, responding to any interesting propositions if they fitted in with anything else I had on the go.

'Good, good. That's what I was hoping to hear,' he said with a smile. 'The thing is, Cliff, I've got a clash of commitments and you might be able to help me out. I was due to go to South America at the end of August with a delegation from Education New Zealand and some representatives from other New Zealand universities to strengthen academic exchanges, drum up international enrolments etcetera, etcetera. Two days ago we learnt that visit has been brought forward to the end of July when I'm scheduled to be in Los Angeles for a business schools' accreditation meeting. Maintaining accreditation and being recognised internationally is critical. I need to go LA.' The dean waved his hand at the framed accreditation certificates lining one wall. 'To be honest, Julie, my eldest, is being awarded her PhD from UCLA around the same time and I promised her mother we would be there. And one shouldn't disappoint the good lady, as you know.' He hurried on, remembering that I had no good lady to disappoint. 'So, I thought you might be able to step in and take my place for the Chilean leg, I can fly down to São Paulo after that. You are highly regarded in that part of the world. And you speak Spanish. That's important, shows we are truly international in outlook and practice.'

'I will need to check my diary but I should be free around that time,' I said, trying to keep a straight face. 'You would need to brief me fully beforehand.'

'Of course. And naturally you would be flying business class; those long flights are exhausting. And I'm sure the delegation will be staying in good hotels. You need to be well looked after; those meetings can take it out of you. Much appreciated, Cliff.'

'Only too pleased to fly the flag, Malcolm.'

# CHAPTER 13

I needed a break. Bill Broughton had told me several times that I was welcome to use his bach over in the Wairarapa whenever I needed to escape the city. I phoned him to see if the cottage would be available over the next few days.

'It was about time you asked, Cliff. Mary and I are going over late Friday afternoon for the weekend but it's vacant until then. Why don't you stay on over the weekend with us? Mary is a non-drinking driver so she can take us around some of the vineyards on Saturday. It's much more fun tasting a few wines if you have a friend to compare notes with.'

'That would suit me fine, Bill. I'm not sure my notes would be very insightful. I enjoy my wine without waxing lyrical. Are you sure I wouldn't be imposing?'

'Not at all, not at all. It would make my weekend. It's not a mansion but it's got a couple of bedrooms. Would you be going by yourself or taking a friend?'

'Just me, Bill.'

'That's a pity.'

'How about I make dinner on Friday?' I asked, giving Bill no time to go down that path. 'Give your driver a break. Say seven pm.'

'Sounds good. I'll flick you through a map.'

I needed no further urging. I packed a few supplies from Moore Wilson's into the car, tossed some clothes in a bag along with a couple of Spanish crime novels and hesitated for ten seconds before deciding to leave my laptop behind. This was to be a few days' break. I headed out along the motorway and up the winding Remutaka Hill road. I always find that part of the trip to the Wairarapa never ending. It's beyond me how some people manage the commute daily. Once over the hill I started to relax, with the city behind and the small towns of rural New Zealand ahead of me. I stopped in Featherston to buy some goat's cheese and scout the offerings in a second-hand book shop. I picked up a copy of Owen Marshall's *Pearly Gates* in good condition. I bought a couple of bottles of wine at one of the newer vineyards on the outskirts of Martinborough and a gourmet pie at the bakery. I studied Bill's map and carried on into the gently rolling sheep country on the back road to Gladstone and down a long gravel farm road until I reached the bach.

The bach must once have been a shepherd's cottage or home for the farm's married couple. It sat on a slight rise, back from the road, flanked by cabbage trees. Paint was peeling from the pitched corrugated iron roof and the weather board exterior could have done with a fresh coat. Bill obviously came to relax, not to paint. I was determined to follow his example.

I settled into an old armchair on the deck to eat my pie and have a leisurely read of *The Dominion Post*. The rain set in mid-afternoon. It did not dampen my spirits; the sound of the raindrops tap dancing on the iron roof only increased the distance from the aridity of the Atacama. The next two days sped by. I lost myself in reading and drank the local pinot noir. When the rain reduced to a drizzle I enjoyed Bill's—or was it Mary's? —selection of CDs. I discovered a Joan Baez CD in Spanish. It included a few songs I had heard her sing in Aix at a concert I had attended with Esperanza many summers ago: *Gracias a la vida, Llego con tres heridas, Guantanamera*. I doubt if that was Bill's choice.

I knew Bill to be a carnivore; he invariably opted for lamb shanks, pork belly or steak and chips when I had meals out with him. I had only met Mary a couple of times but got the impression she was more adventurous than her husband. With her in mind, and to shake up Bill's taste buds, I prepared a quinoa risotto with braised endive for dinner on Friday evening.

'Cliff, that smells heavenly,' Mary said.

'Evening chef, what's under the grill?' Bill asked.

I handed Mary a juice and poured Bill a wine.

'What's this you're serving, Cliff?' he asked, reaching over to read the wine label. 'Carmenere! Some Chilean plonk. Coals to Newcastle! They do make some decent wine in the Wairarapa, you know.'

'And I'm sure we will sample some tomorrow. Tonight we have a wine and food match.' I set the risotto on the table. 'Mary, go ahead, serve yourself.'

'And fancy foreign tucker to go with it,' Bill said. His lip drooped as he could find no discernible trace of meat on his plate.

'Manners, Bill, manners,' Mary said. She savoured her first mouthful. 'Cliff, this is delicious. It's quinoa, right?'

'Quinoa, miracle food of the Incas.'

'Bill tells me you've spent a bit of time in South America. What's Patagonia like?'

'Take the Southern Alps, the Mackenzie Country and the West Coast and scale them up several times. Then think of condors rather than keas, Emperor penguins rather than our little blue ones.'

An hour later Mary excused herself, saying she was bushed after a hectic week dealing with ongoing glitches in some new software at Inland Revenue where she was a senior manager. And to leave the dishes for the morning. Bill pronounced the carmenere drinkable but would need another glass or two to be sure. Did I happen to have another bottle that we might open? I did. Bill cleared away while I uncorked the second bottle. We moved over to the armchairs to continue our judgement of the carmenere.

We talked some more about Chile before Bill came out with the question he had been dying to ask, confident my tongue would have been loosened after the first bottle. Bill does not miss much. 'So, what's the story with that slide of the hot pools you were peering at the other day?'

I thought I had left that behind for a couple of days but there was no escaping the direct question from my host. I recounted the whole Lepan saga and explained how everything I had learnt had left me disillusioned with somebody whose work I had once respected. I omitted the bit about Rico and his parents in case that led on to Rod's death and Wendy leaving me. Bill probably knew some of that history. But not how it was driving me to find out what had happened to Lepan in the hope that doing so would provide me some redemption.

'Sounds a proper bastard to me. How you realise your academic ambitions surely has limits. I've seen the effort you have put in over the years to earn your chair, Cliff. That's been hard yakker. You have to put in the mahi as the saying goes. I'm not sure what's been driving you,' he said with a quizzical look, 'but I'm sure it's not greedy ambition. More like you've retreated into your research as a means of escape.' He was right about that. 'The world is better off without buggers like Lepan, careerists scrambling to the top on the backs of others. Once they make it, they assume a sense of entitlement, that rules and morals are for others and don't apply to them. A bit like Boris Johnson in that respect.' He drank some more carmenere and waited for me to continue.

'It's not as though Lepan didn't have a sharp mind. I've seen him cut leading scholars to shreds at conferences with a spontaneous incisiveness that was all his own. Not pretty, but intellectually impressive. Must have had a double persona. All his activism seems to have been genuine enough. He would have ticked that engagement box the senior leadership team has brought into our promotions criteria.'

'But what was he engaged in? Does anyone know? His activism could be as dubious and self-serving as his scholarship.'

'Fair point. I don't know much other than he was involved with lots of issues in different parts of the world. He got kicked out of Chile a while back, protesting logging on Mapuche land and salmon farming in Patagonia.'

'Coming back to that slide of the hot pool, what do you think happened? Did he fall or was he pushed?'

'The age-old murder mystery question. The most probable explanation is he tripped while taking a photo. That's the conclusion the carabineros had come to when we left, although the inquest hadn't been completed.'

'But you're not convinced?' Bill persisted, looking me in the eye.

'Well, Lepan was not short of enemies, or at least of people who would not mourn his passing. Would anyone go as far as to kill him? I suppose it's possible, but I doubt it. Besides, only our group and a ute were at the geysers that morning.'

'Wasn't it Churchill who said "You have enemies? Good, that means you have stood up for something, sometime in your life." You could rule out a bunch of academics, though. Our colleagues may piss us off from time to time, but doing them in because they nicked your ideas, wrote a damning promotion report or rejected your paper would be going too far.' Bill shook his head as if to dismiss the malevolence of fellow academics and changed tack. 'Tell me about this ute. If this place, El Tater or whatever you call it, was such an attraction as you made out in your seminar, it's odd that there were so few visitors the morning the Frenchman met his maker.'

'It may sound far-fetched, but whoever was in that ute might have been involved.' I outlined the conversation between the Australians and the Swedes, the hold-up after us on the road to the geysers, the ute I had seen outside our hotel in Mundial

Mining colours, what I had read up about the company's shady record, Lepan's research on lithium mining and water, and his protests at El Tatio in 2009. They could all be connected.

'I didn't take you for a conspiracy theorist, Cliff. Yes, all those incidents could be connected. Could be. But think about it. How could Mundial Mining be sure their plan would work? Yes, the ute could have left early enough to ensure they would be at the geysers first and lie in wait for Lepan. But how could they be sure your bus would be next in the convoy, that a couple of Australian larrikins would carry out their part, that is, be right behind your bus and crash their cars in the ford in such a way that the road would be blocked for an hour or more? How could the Mundial malefactors be sure they could isolate Lepan and do away with him without anyone seeing? Admittedly, that part would have been easier if the roadblock worked and yours was the only group at the geysers. It all seems tenuous if you ask me.'

'Put like that, it does sound rather conspiratorial.' Was it all conjecture and wishful thinking on my part that Mundial Mining was the villain of the piece?

'Lepan was from France, right? What's that saying they have?' Bill scratched his head. 'Got it, *cherchez la femme*. How about a jealous woman, a *femme fatale*, in there somewhere?'

I laughed. 'He certainly had a reputation as a womaniser. From what I've heard, his three wives divorced him for having affairs and casually sleeping with students. Well, maybe not casually, generally with purpose. However, none of those were on our tour and none of the women in our party seemed unduly saddened or over-joyed when they learnt what had happened. I doubt if there was a woman in that Mundial ute.'

'A heart attack, then. We professors emeriti aren't getting any younger.'

'Speaking of which, we should turn in if we are to do those local wines justice tomorrow.'

'Not so fast, Cliff. Are you going to leave it there?' He looked over his glass at me.

I sipped my wine before replying. 'I'm now certain the answer lies in the Atacama. A Spanish colleague has put in for a project that would take me back to San Pedro for a few weeks next month if we're successful. That will give me an opportunity to poke around. I don't have any concrete leads to follow. All that I've come up with so far is circumstantial.'

'And didn't I hear you've got the dean's junket to Santiago?' He put down his empty glass. 'I was hoping that might have come my way.'

'Not a chance, Bill. A demonstrated liking for Chilean wine and food was a prerequisite. See, I'm trying to educate you in case a similar opportunity arises in the future.'

We looked at the half full bottle, shook our heads and left Bill's oenological education for another day. We took Mary at her word, left the dishes in the sink and retired for the night.

Despite the wine, or perhaps because of it, I could not sleep but tossed fitfully in my bunk. Bill's comments about academic ambition swirled around in my head. Was it just Lepan's ambition I should be considering? Who else on our tour had ambitions that might have been thwarted by Lepan? Earlier, I had considered Pat Mason and Hector Muñoz Muñoz whose son Felipe Montoya was in our party, but I had dismissed those ideas as too fanciful. Bill had pooh-poohed the idea of anyone's academic ambitions having fatal consequences. At least not intentionally, I thought, with an ache in my heart.

Thinking of what Bill said reminded me of what he had told the graduate students, that good research starts by asking the right question. Had I been asking the right question about the relationship between Pat and Lepan? Was the real question, why had Lepan been so negative in his report? What had the Frenchman stood to gain? Was he the one who had been vindictive for some earlier slight, not Pat? Where had their paths crossed in the past? Other than the issue of the promotions report, Pat had not hinted at any shared history. I could not recall any ideological debates between the two like the rift between Lepan and Muñoz Muñoz. Rory had joined us in the bar before I had the chance to ask Pat what the Frenchman held against him. Was it pure arrogance on Lepan's part? Or something else?

Carvalho came to mind. Not as a suspect—he wasn't at the geysers and stood to gain more with Lepan alive—but how he had structured his tribute to his co-plagiarist at the conference in Santiago. The Brazilian spoke of Lepan's outstanding publications record, his mentoring of young researchers and his activism. We now knew that the first two facets of his career were connected—his publications output was based in part on the large-scale plagiarism of those he had so freely mentored. But other than Montse, we hadn't identified anyone who had discovered their work had been ripped off by Lepan. And even if one of his mentees had been so aggrieved as to want to take his life—a doubtful proposition, Montse wanted to forget the whole episode—no one who had been on our tour had known Lepan in his early days or had been mentored by him. As far as I knew. Only Pat, Viviana and I would have been old enough for that. Neither of them had ever mentioned knowing Lepan in their younger days. Viviana had been shocked when I first told her about Montse.

That left Lepan's activism. Lepan had been effective in many of the causes he had championed around the world. I did not know why he had come on the tour to the Atacama or what he intended to say at the workshop. Opposing Mundial Mining's lithium mining licence application would have brought him up against a well-resourced and unscrupulous foe who would not brook any opposition to their ambitious expansion plans. I had no proof of any wrongdoing, but the presence of their ute at the geysers pointed the finger at them. I was determined to find out what had happened to Lepan.

The rain had stopped by the time we got up, lingered over a late breakfast and set off to taste the wines of the Wairarapa. Many of the vineyards around Martinborough are small and close together, you can walk or cycle from one to another. However, having Mary driving suited two elderly gents who had spent the previous evening drinking and talking until late. We sampled pinot noir at Atarangi, appreciated the Coney rieslings and stopped for lunch at the Margrain vineyard. Mary and I enjoyed the Spanish gypsy stew and Bill got his pork belly. Re-energised, we carried on. Mary deviated from Bill's itinerary so we could stroll through one of the nearby olive groves before we sampled some more pinot noir and chardonnay at the Palliser Estate and headed back to the bach with some pizza for tea. We again talked late but avoided Chile and Lepan.

Bill and Mary needed some time by themselves and next morning I made my excuses, expressed my thanks with the Palliser wines and two bottles of olive oil, and headed back to Wellington. It had been the break I needed. Bill's questions and comments and the ideas they had triggered stayed with me, however. Turning them over in my mind, the journey back over the Remutaka Hill seemed shorter than usual.

The only email of interest that had come in while I was away in the Wairarapa was from the secretary of TADSAI advising that Hector Muñoz Muñoz had been confirmed as the association's new president at the annual conference in Kuala Lumpur. The Mexican now held the position he had long coveted but had been denied by the election of Lepan earlier in the year. Pat Mason had been voted vice-president, nominated by Jose Ortiz, one of his Colombian collaborators. Knowing how admin adverse Pat was, I was surprised he had accepted. He was sure to be a thorn in the side of the new president. Perhaps that was what appealed to his ornery nature.

I selected a few shots of our lunch at the Margrain vineyard and a couple of our wine tastings and sent them off to Viviana suggesting she extend her already extensive wine knowledge by some *catas* of New Zealand wines, *in situ* of course. Viviana replied right away. She thanked me for the photos but made no comment about coming and tasting the wines. Rather, she was concerned for Alba, Pablo and Rico. The boy was still very unsettled after his experience at the geysers, relations between Alba and Pablo had reached breaking point, Alba had taken leave from the university, she and Rico were living with her parents in Mendoza. Alba was at her wit's end and was coming round to see Viviana every other day. All Viviana could do was listen. Did I have any suggestions? What could I say? I needed to get back to San Pedro to pursue the alternative explanation. That depended on Maria Paz's proposal being accepted.

# CHAPTER 14

Maria Paz's emerald eyes sparkled when she Skyped me.

'We did it, Cliff. Our proposal's been accepted. We got it. The funding's been cut back by $8,000—no new toys for Ramón this time—but otherwise no changes to what we submitted. Thank you so much. We wouldn't have got there without all your experience, using the right terminology, knowing what to say in each part of the form, bringing in Lucas, Ximena and Miguel.'

I imagine my eyes were starting to sparkle too. This was my way back. Atacama here I come.

'If you hadn't impressed the guy from the sub-sec with your paper at the conference we wouldn't have known to put in a proposal. You're the one with the technological expertise.'

'This is a major step up for me. I've never led a team before. And on an international project. My head of department will be impressed,' she said. 'You're still right for early August I hope?'

'Timing's perfect. My dean has asked me to go to some meetings in Santiago in the last week of July. They are covering the air fare.'

We carried on discussing all the practicalities now we were in business.

I was pleased for Maria Paz; the project would be a significant boost for her career. It would also help Lucas and Ramón broaden their research experience. I was not sure how many more of these projects I had in me. Although interesting and generally enjoyable, field work is physically demanding and I knew I was slowing down. We would be making multiple trips to each of the four sites we were studying: travelling to and from the geysers would be especially exhausting. Working in a different language and culture adds spice to a project; it also can have an edge that is mentally draining. None of that mattered. What counted was going back to Chile and finding out what had happened to Lepan at the geysers.

•••

Annie Ortega, the cultural attaché at the New Zealand embassy, briefed the delegation the evening we arrived in Santiago. She emphasised the need for a New Zealand Inc approach in all our meetings. This would be interesting, international recruitment and research collaborations are extremely competitive. Each member of the delegation would be vying for as much attention as possible for their own institution.

The meeting next morning began with the representatives from Conicyt, the government agency that manages postgraduate scholarships, outlining their policies regarding scholarships for promising Chilean students to study abroad at the leading universities in their field. These had been relatively generous but fewer scholarships were now being awarded following the fall in world copper prices and the drop in government revenue from royalties. Rapid fire PowerPoint presentations from members of our delegation followed Annie's overview of the New Zealand tertiary sector. Or not so rapid in some cases. When my turn eventually came, I was squeezed for time. The Conicyt officials looked at their watches and I feared the meeting would end before Victoria had got much of a hearing. Annie came to my rescue by inviting me to share my experiences at UACh which had been funded through Conicyt's visiting professor scheme. The Conicyt representatives sat back in their seats to hear what they had got for their money. Their questions and comments showed they were well pleased. The rest of our delegation were not.

After lunch we met with the deans of eight business schools to discuss ways in which we might collaborate on projects of mutual research interest. Annie managed to rein in two of the more prolix members of our delegation and maintained some sense of direction in the discussions so that several potential projects were identified. This was as good an outcome as we might have hoped for, especially after one of our party had referred to the University of Contraception, much to the indignation of the dean from Concepción and the amusement of his colleagues.

At a forum for the postgraduate students the following day, Annie brought Lucas in to share his experiences as a PhD student in Wellington. His enthusiastic presentation generated numerous questions about studying at Victoria, much to the displeasure of the other members of our delegation. The afternoon consisted of a speed dating procession of educational agents who assured each of us that they possessed endless pipelines into the brightest kids, or at least the richest parents, and that they could boost enrolments if only we were able to relax our strict position on English language scores and other entry requirements.

After the rest of the delegation left to catch their flight to São Paulo, Annie invited me for dinner. Her husband was looking forward to meeting me.

He picked me up at my hotel on his way home. In his early forties, he wore a charcoal grey suit, a fawn shirt but no tie. He introduced himself with a confident smile and a firm handshake, 'Arturo Eterovic.'

'No relation to Ramón Díaz Eterovic, by any chance?' I asked, thinking of the Chilean crime writer whose books I enjoy.

'No, but I get asked that a lot.'

'How come?'

'I'm with the PDI, narcotics. People often think I'm the source for all those detective stories he writes.'

'Well, if you had that gumshoe Heredia for a colleague, Chile wouldn't have a narcotics problem for long.'

'For sure. I don't know how he does it. Must be all that talking to his cat.' Arturo laughed.

Annie and Arturo lived in a compact but modern apartment in the Barrio Italia. She had prepared a simple Chilean salad of onions and tomatoes, followed by baked corvina and a *torta tres leches* for dessert. The bottle of Cloudy Bay sauvignon blanc that I had picked up duty-free at Auckland airport matched the fish perfectly. Annie suggested Arturo and I adjourn to the lounge while she cleared the table and prepared coffee. He made full use of the time she had given him.

'Annie tells me you knew Antoine Lepan.'

'That's right.' Strange, I could not recall discussing Lepan with Annie.

'And you were writing about him for some book.'

'That's right. But that project was cancelled a few weeks back, not commercially viable.'

'I heard there were other issues, the suitability of Lepan being honoured with a festschrift.'

'That too.' Where had he found out about the festschrift? 'Why the interest, Arturo?'

'Let's say that we had him on our radar.'

'Your radar. You mean the Chilean narcotics squad were interested in Lepan?' I stared at Arturo.

'Liaising with Interpol is part of my role. They had been following Lepan's movements for the past three years. His life as a gypsy academic, jetting from one conference to another, being a visiting professor here, an activist there, gave him a perfect cover for coordinating drug trafficking operations all over the world:

Afghanistan, Morocco, Thailand, Mexico, Colombia… You name it, he had been to where they grow, where they sell and all points in between. Hiding in plain sight. Giving public addresses, agitating for the betterment of the poor and downtrodden, but also, Interpol believe, making contacts, doing deals behind the scenes. He may have been altruistic, but where do you think he got the funding from to support all those good causes as well as his three ex-wives?'

I thought I knew Lepan's character and background by now, but Arturo's revelation shocked me more than Montse's letter.

'San Pedro is a gateway for drugs being brought into Chile, both by organised rings and by amateurs, backpackers coming down from Bolivia wanting to finance their tripping around South America. He was in Colombia the week before he entered Chile. Supposedly at some tourism colloquium. We don't know why he went on your tour to the Atacama. We hope to uncover who he was working with in Chile through his movements and activities.'

'Surely your colleagues up north will have already filled you in on what happened on the tour. We were all interviewed by that sergeant, Figueroa. He gave me the impression Lepan had tripped taking a photo. Has that theory changed?'

'No. That's the official finding of the coroner. I'm looking at the bigger picture. You might be able to help me understand the academic angle better. What can you tell me about that?'

What did I know about Lepan that Interpol and the Chilean PDI didn't? I repeated what I had told others, that I had not known him well and that his academic career turned out to have been built on the work of others. 'But surely you knew most of that, Arturo?'

'Much of it, though not the extent of his plagiarism. See, an academic's perspective adds background.' His expression implied we were a race apart. Perhaps we were. How learning more about Lepan's plagiarism would help Arturo uncover a drug smuggling network was beyond me.

'You mean, it takes a thief to catch a thief?' I said. That made some sense. Viviana and I had uncovered aspects of Lepan's past that had escaped Figueroa and Arturo because we knew how to check out his research. On the other hand, I had made little progress in finding out how Lepan had met his death. I was tackling that as an amateur.

Arturo smiled wryly. 'I would not put it quite like that, but you get the idea. Would you say Lepan was a shady character?'

'No doubt about it in terms of his research. But there's a huge gulf between being a plagiarist and a kingpin in an international drug smuggling ring. Interpol would surely have arrested him if they had any concrete evidence, wouldn't they?'

'True. Their evidence is largely circumstantial.'

Largely circumstantial, like how I had built up my picture of Lepan's plagiarism.

'Would you say Lepan had many enemies in academia?' he asked.

I looked at him with growing interest. Did Arturo have doubts that Lepan's death was an accident?

'It would be fair to say he was not everyone's favourite anthropologist.' I repeated the point that Bill and I had discussed, that professional enmity would hardly have led to anyone killing him.

'What do you know about his trip to Bogotá?'

'Nothing at all. It was only after I had been asked to contribute to the festschrift that I took more interest in him.'

'There were a couple of Colombians at the conference here, Ortiz and Sanchez. How close were they to Lepan?'

Jose and Jorge, Pat's collaborators. 'I've only met them once, very briefly. Our research interests don't overlap.'

'But they work with Patrick Mason and Rory O'Connor.'

Arturo had done his homework. 'That's correct. The four of them presented a joint paper at the conference.'

'Would you say Mason and O'Connor were close to Lepan?'

'Pat wasn't a big fan of his. O'Connor, I can't say.'

'Were you aware Mason and O'Connor were at the same colloquium as Lepan in Bogotá?'

'No.' Where was this going?

'Would Mason engage in any extra-curricular activities?'

'You mean drug smuggling? No, I've known Pat a long time. Never a hint or rumour that he's anything other than a university professor.' Where was Annie with the coffee?

'Associate professor,' he corrected. Arturo knew the nuances of the academic hierarchy; Annie's job must have rubbed off on him. Surely he wasn't aware of Lepan's role in Pat's unsuccessful promotion application. I said nothing.

'Was Lepan close to anyone at the Santiago conference?'

'I don't know, he never made it here. I suppose the Brazilian, de Oliveira Carvalho, must have held him in high regard; he was the one who invited him as keynote speaker. I gather he was also going to meet with a young Brazilian lecturer about using drones to film illegal gold mining in the Amazon.'

'Who was that?'

'Ramón Macedo'

'Interesting. Anti gold mining, you say.' Arturo seemed to make a mental note then moved on.

'Who did Lepan mix with on the tour in the Atacama?'

'No one. On the first day he was busy taking a lot of photos and he sat by himself on the bus. The second day, well, you know what happened.'

'Had he gone out the night before?'

'No idea.' What was Arturo driving at? I was dying to know but Annie entered with the coffee.

'I see you two have found plenty to chat about,' she said with a quick glance at her husband. 'We should not keep Cliff too late, dear. He's flying down to Valdivia tomorrow for another round of meetings; no one from UACh was able to come up here. That should all go smoothly, Cliff, they're only too eager to firm up an exchange agreement with Victoria.'

I had hoped to discuss Lepan further with Arturo on the way back to the hotel. But having drunk a few glasses of the Cloudy Bay, he called a taxi for me. I thanked them both for their hospitality and gave Annie a look which I hoped she interpreted as 'You might have told me beforehand.'

Arturo had given me a lot to think about and hope that I might find an alternative explanation after all. Could Lepan possibly have been involved in drug smuggling? Gypsy academic, how apt. Drug smuggler, hard to believe. Presumably Interpol and the Chilean PDI would not be wasting their time on the matter if there was nothing behind it. Carvalho? I could not see him as a drug smuggler; he was weak and lacked substance. It seemed even less likely that Pat or Rory were involved. Jorge and Jose? Who knows what goes on in Colombia?

# CHAPTER 15

I flew to Valdivia on Thursday and spent the afternoon with a mix of academic and administrative staff at the Universidad Austral going through the process of establishing the equivalence of courses in our respective undergraduate curricula and dealing with the issues raised by the different dates of our trimesters. My colleagues in tourism management invited me out that evening; a round of pisco sours, then carmenere from the Maule with the large steaks which followed. They were all for including a staff exchange in the agreement. More meetings Friday morning to explore the opportunities for postgraduate exchanges. Lunch with the dean to discuss the Memorandum of Understanding which he had drafted. The arrangements looked good to me. I had no authority to sign and sent the draft MOU on to Malcolm in São Paulo for his approval and signature. I also updated him on the meetings in Santiago, including some interest at the Universidad de Chile in a research project with Bill. All told, I had earned my business class ticket.

Tony Miller emailed me to say that he had been awarded a scholarship to Angers, starting at the *rentrée* in October. I sent my congratulations and wished him well.

Malcolm's reply arrived with the signed MOU. I printed it off and delivered it to the dean who celebrated the new partnership by opening a bottle of wine. And another when my tourism management colleagues learned of the news and the inclusion of the provision for staff exchanges. And another. I was a popular fellow.

Saturday morning, Esperanza's husband Max picked me up at the hotel. They had invited me for the weekend before I flew back up to Santiago. I had known Esperanza for over forty years. We met in 1975, during my last summer in Aix-en-Provence where we were students. We only overlapped for six months but became good friends. She was the only one from that time I've kept in touch with. Our continuing friendship was one way of keeping alive the fond memories we each had of our time in Aix. I had missed her earlier in the year when she and Max were on an extended visit to Europe.

'Cliff, Cliff, so good to see you again,' Esperanza said. '*Trois bisous*, like in the old days,' she said as our cheeks touched for the third time. 'You're looking well.'

And so was she. Esperanza was tall and blonde, of German stock from southern Chile. Age had been kind to her. I could still see her as that attractive newcomer in the kitchen of the Arc de Meyran who had asked if she could borrow my saucepan.

We had a long catch up over coffee before she brought out her laptop, itching to show me all the latest photos she had taken of Aix and other parts of Provence. She also had an old Hanimex slide projector on the living room table loaded and ready to go. 'I thought it would be fun to go through some of my old slides,' she said. 'Max has been digitising a lot of them so I can have them printed off for a photobook.' Her husband left us to it; he needed to tune the Mustang he was restoring and take it for a drive. 'Max doesn't know most of my old friends but I'm sure you would enjoy seeing them.'

'*Bien sûr*' I said. I figured it would be enjoyable to take a trip down memory lane with Esperanza. We had reverted to French to enhance our nostalgia.

I had mainly photographed places not people. Most of my old slides were of the resorts I was studying or landscapes of France, taken in the hope that they would be useful one day when I realised my ambition of becoming a geography lecturer.

Esperanza's slides, on the other hand, were full of student friends and acquaintances. Many were of bright-eyed twenty-somethings sitting around cafes on the Cours Mirabeau, sun-dappled by the light filtering through the plane trees that lined the avenue. I did not feature in any of them. 'You weren't much of a café goer were you, Cliff? Carmen and I used to go into town most days. *Les Deux Garçons* is still going strong.'

Other slides were taken on outings organised for international students: ski weekends in the Alpes de Haute Provence; day trips to Arles and Avignon, the pont du Gard and the picturesque villages of Gordes and Roussillon. I rarely missed those trips because they gave me a chance to see more of Provence and the opportunity to meet people. I recognised quite a few of the faces, though I could not put a name to many. More often it was a case of 'Wasn't she from Peru?' or 'Isn't that the know-all American who was always spouting Mistral?'

'*Voilà*, one with you in it, Cliff.' I recognised it right away; half a dozen people dancing on Avignon's truncated bridge, two figures to one side looking on. I was one of them.

'*Sur le pont d'Avignon, on y danse tous en rond.*' Esperanza sang the refrain which made the bridge famous. 'You weren't much of a dancer either.'

'No sense of rhythm, that's my trouble. A total disconnect between ear and feet.'

'Who's that standing beside you?'

'Zu.'

'Who?'

'Zu, from Malaysia.'

'Oh, I remember her now. I knew her as Zubaida. She was on our floor at Cuques. I didn't know her very well, just to say '*bonjour*, what's that you're making?' That sort of thing. She used to make these curries you could smell right down the hallway.'

'That's Zu. Her curries were out of this world.'

'Hang on, I think I've got another one of her somewhere.' Esperanza hunted through half a dozen boxes of slides before she found it. 'This is at a Bastille Day party in 1976. After your time.'

'You're right, that's Zu at the back, beside Carmen. Whose party was it?'

'A young French lecturer who used to throw a lot of parties, mainly for international students. They were fun. Tasty nibbles and plenty of wine. Not plastic buckets of sangria like at some of those other parties. That's Tony there, raising his glass of champagne. He was a party animal. Used to make a pass at all us girls. He didn't have any luck with me but lots of the others fell for his French charm.' Esperanza laughed at the recollection.

'Looks a bit familiar.' I couldn't place him, though. 'Do you know what became of Zu?'

'No. She was usually bright and cheerful but one day I heard her sobbing in her room. I didn't see her again. Carmen told me she had to go back home to Malaysia as she had lost all her fieldwork notes and had nothing to write up for her thesis. She was on a scholarship, wasn't granted an extension and didn't have any money to start over again.'

'Poor old Zu. She would have already put in a lot of effort to get that far. She was working on tourism but I'm not sure what. That also explains why I didn't hear from her again. Not being able to complete her degree would have meant a huge loss of face back home.'

We stopped for lunch.

'Come on through to the kitchen and make yourself a pastis while I finish off the ratatouille.'

Max was late so we started without him. Esperanza's ratatouille brought back more memories, a true Provençal dish which she had mastered. The phone rang. Max was having problems with the car and would not be back until much later in the afternoon. Esperanza clenched her fist. 'Damned thing is always breaking down and costs a fortune to keep on the road.' She had planned for us to go out to Niebla. What were we going to do now?

I had a thought. Right before Malcolm had emailed me the MOU and the dean had opened the first of several bottles, I had been reading Tony Miller's email. He had signed off with 'or should that be Antoine from now on?' Tony is the diminutive of Anthony; the French equivalent of Anthony is Antoine. That charming young lecturer named Tony in that party photo of Esperanza's. Could it be?

'Esperanza, could I see that party photo again, the one with Zu in it?'

Esperanza blinked, got up and turned the projector on.

'The guy with the glass of champagne, you said his name was Tony, if I remember correctly.'

'That's Tony, all right.'

I stepped closer to the screen. Tony, a short slightly built figure. Unfortunately, the raised glass concealed part of his face and I could not make out the distinguishing feature I was looking for. 'Do you have any others of this party.'

'Let me check.' She hunted through one of the boxes.

The next slide was almost identical. But in the one after that Tony had lowered his glass revealing a bluish birthmark the size of a bantam's egg below his right eye. I was looking at a much younger but no less arrogant version of the recently deceased Antoine Lepan. My pulse quickened.

'Do you remember Tony's last name?'

'No, I only knew him as Tony, the guy who threw parties. Why the interest, Cliff?'

'I'm pretty sure that's Antoine Lepan. He became a famous professor. He was on that Atacama tour in April. He tripped and fell in a hot pool at the geysers. I helped pull his body out. Died instantly, nothing we could do.'

Esperanza gasped and raised her hand to her mouth. 'That's awful. I didn't know him well. Just went to a couple of his parties. Still, what a horrible way to go. I've been to the geysers; you do have to watch your step.'

'Who else do you know in that slide, other than Carmen and Zubaida?'

'I can't remember any of their names. I didn't know them beforehand. They were mainly students of Tony's. One of them was a good friend of Carmen; that's how we got invited.'

My mind swirled, making connections. Esperanza's party slide confirmed Tony was Antoine Lepan, the same Antoine Lepan who showed up as Antonio in Montse's account of the parties he had invited her and other postgrad students to in Barcelona. Zu also appeared in Esperanza's slide—Lepan had known Zu. Shortly afterwards she had to return home to Malaysia without completing her thesis because her fieldwork notes had disappeared. Antonio Lepan had lifted and published Montse's material. Was it too much of a leap to think it was Tony Lepan who had purloined Zu's notes and wrote an article based on them?

Think, Cliff, think. Malaysia? Malaysia? No, not Malaysia as such, parts of it. The states of Sarawak and Sabah are located on the island of Borneo, not peninsular Malaysia. Was the famous article in Portuguese on longhouses in Borneo not just the seminal article on culture brokers in tourism, as Carvalho had glowingly described it in Santiago, but also one of the first in a long line of Lepan's plagiarised papers? It had to be. Lepan had developed his *modus operandi* with students and parties in Aix and gone international with Montse and others.

'What is it Cliff, is something the matter?'

'Sorry, that slide with Tony and Zubaida triggered a lot of thoughts. How's your Portuguese these days?'

'My spoken Portuguese is rusty. I can still read it quite well. Why?'

'Can you take a quick look at an article in Portuguese for me? Written by Lepan, by Tony.'

'Sure, if it will help. Where is it?'

'Let me get my computer,' I said. I retrieved my Acer from Esperanza's guest room and quickly located the paper from my now well-organised files. 'I don't need all the details; a general idea will do.'

'Oof,' she said after quarter of an hour, having reached for her large dictionary several times. 'This is heavy going, Cliff. I'm not familiar with all this theoretical stuff and these long technical words. I'm just getting into the methodology section. He refers to ethnographic research; is there such a thing?'

'That's what anthropologists do, they spend weeks or months in communities, observing their culture, making notes on how they live. Don't worry too much about that, concentrate on the findings. They should be in the next section.'

'Right, I've got it,' Esperanza said an hour and a half later. 'Quite interesting, actually. Is that what you tourism researchers write about? I sometimes wondered.' *Just give me the gist without the editorial comment.* 'Basically, it deals with tourism in longhouses in Borneo. Longhouses are where a community in the rainforest live together under one long roof, spending much of their time in communal living spaces. Apparently, these people, the Iban, used to be head-hunters and used blowpipes. Oh, I think I saw a documentary on them once on TV. Or was that in the Amazon? They had blowpipes. I can't remember seeing any longhouses though. Max would know.' *Please Esperanza, just get on with it.* 'Anyway, back then they were becoming a tourist attraction and tours were being organised so visitors could take a trip up the river, the Skrang it says, and spend a night in a longhouse and experience how the head-hunters lived. That would be exciting. I don't suppose they still do that, head hunt, I mean.' *Pleeease, Esperanza.* 'Well, these tours were organised by operators based in the city, that's Kuching. I've never heard of that before. Have you? All of the tour operators were Chinese except one run by a Malay. The tours were led by a guide who would act as a go-between, the link between the tourists and the head-hunters, explaining the Iban culture and making sure the tourists knew how to behave properly in the longhouse. The guides, as well as the tour operators, are what the author, that's Tony, right, calls culture brokers. The author spent a lot of time living in the longhouse that the Malay operator organised tours to, observing the behaviour of the head-hunters and the tourists and how life in the longhouse was changing because of all these tourists coming in.'

'Are there any acknowledgements? Look for a footnote at the bottom of the first page or at the end of the article.'

'No, nothing I can see,' she said as she scrolled through the paper again. 'Why are you so interested in this article, Cliff? Aren't Europe and South America your thing?'

'They are. I'm pretty sure this paper is based on Zubaida's fieldwork, on her notes that went missing.'

'You mean Tony stole Zubaida's notes?' Esperanza looked up with widened eyes. 'I can't imagine him doing that. He was such a friendly guy.'

'Sorry to disillusion you, Esperanza, Antoine Lepan was not all that he seemed. He spent his career ripping off other people's work.'

She frowned, puzzled. 'How can you be sure that paper is based on Zubaida's fieldwork?'

'I can't be one hundred per cent certain, but it fits a pattern.' I recapped what I knew of Lepan, what he had done to Montse and others. 'What I don't know is what happened to Zu after I left

Aix. She was from somewhere on the peninsula, somewhere in the north. I thought she was doing her research there, not in Sarawak. And you didn't know her well either. Who was close to her?'

'Carmen might know. Hey, why don't we Skype her?'

Our luck was in, we got through to Carmen, who lived in Montevideo, on our first attempt.

'Carmen, I've got a visitor with me.'

'Good afternoon, Carmen. It's been a long time.' I leant towards the screen; Esperanza pulled back.

'Good afternoon… Who's that with you, Esperanza?'

'You don't remember me?' I said. 'Aix-en-Provence…'

'It can't be… Cliff!'

'In person. How are you, Carmen?' Identity established; we caught up with what we had been doing since we had lost touch before I got down to the purpose of my call. 'Carmen, do you remember Zubaida, a girl from Malaysia who used to be along the corridor from you in Cuques.'

'Zubaida… Zubaida.' Carmen knitted her brow, trying to remember.

'She used to make those strong-smelling curries,' Esperanza said. Food is often a good prompt. It is for me anyway. Worked for Carmen too.

'Right, Zubaida, I remember her now. From Malaysia?'

'That's the one. Did you hear anything from her when she was back in Malaysia doing her fieldwork? That would be early 1976. I'm trying to find out where she went.'

'That's a long time ago, Cliff. Let me think… She might have sent me a postcard now you mention it. I may even be able to dig it out, I've got all my cards from that time in an album. Honey, Esperanza and a friend of ours from Aix, Cliff, are on Skype. Come and say hello while I look in my albums.'

Her husband's face filled the screen. We chitchatted for ten minutes before Carmen reappeared waving an album.

'It will be in here somewhere. Let me see. That one is from Switzerland, that's from Brazil…this is more like it.' She held up a postcard of a large river running through a jungle and an orang-utan hanging from a tree. 'Yes, this is it. "Dear Carmen, I'm having a fabulous time in Sarawak. My research is going well thanks to my uncle. He's a tour operator and has lots of contacts I've just spent a week in a longhouse up the Skrang. What an experience! Looking forward to spending more time there. Regards to everyone at Cuques, Zubaida." Is that what you were looking for?'

'Exactly. Is there a date on it?' I held my breath.

'The postmark is "Kuching 18 March 1976".'

Bingo! My adrenaline surged. 'That fits perfectly. Many thanks, Carmen.'

Esperanza poked her head over my shoulder and said: 'Carmen, Cliff was also asking about Tony, you remember, that young French lecturer who threw those parties we went to a couple of times. Can you remember his last name?'

'Tony, Tony… Le Pain. No, that means bread.' She chuckled. 'Le Pain, Le Pain. Got it, Lepan. Tony Lepan. Did you know him, Cliff?'

'Not when I was in Aix, only much later. He died a few months back, an accident here in Chile.'

'That's too bad. I liked him. He threw terrific parties. Zubaida went to some of them as well. She hadn't been long back from Malaysia when we were at Tony's Bastille Day party. Was there anything else you wanted to know? My grandkids are due any minute.'

'No, that's all. Good talking to you Carmen. You've been very helpful.' More helpful than she would ever realise.

I pumped my fist in the air. I no longer had any doubts. Lepan had got hold of Zu's notes and written an article based on them. The same as he had done with Montse, Begoña Pi and many others. No, not quite the same. Zu was even more of a victim; she had to go back to Malaysia without graduating. Lepan was an utter bastard.

However, I was no closer to finding out what had happened to him. It seemed inconceivable that he had been pushed to his death in some drug deal that had gone wrong as Arturo's questions had implied. Or was it? I couldn't wait to get up to San Pedro.

'Esperanza, if Max has already digitised the slide of us on the Pont d'Avignon, could you send me a copy?'

'Sure, he's done that one already. Any of the others?'

'That one of you, me and Carmen at Gordes. And that last party shot.'

'That was in one of the boxes Max hasn't got onto yet. But I'll make sure he does it soon. It's the least he could do after messing up the afternoon.'

The misfiring Mustang had made my afternoon, not messed it up. I had fitted another couple of pieces in the puzzle that was Antoine Lepan.

# CHAPTER 16

I flew up to Santiago on the Sunday afternoon and caught up with Maria Paz that evening. She had flown in from Madrid the previous day, looked fully recovered from the flight and was rearing to go. Oh, the energy and enthusiasm of the young. We caught up over a drink and meal at the café beside the Vegas.

'Cliff, who would have thought when we were here in April that we would be back again so soon and working together on a project in the Atacama?'

'Here's to a successful project,' I said, raising my glass. Or rather to two projects. I kept the second to myself.

Lucas joined us the following morning for the meeting with Corfo, the funding agency. We were able to handle all their questions about the project. Maria Paz had much more technical expertise than the funders. Lucas dealt effectively with stakeholder matters. I sat back and admired the next generation of researchers at work, answering only the occasional query relating to how the monitoring data would be used in visitor management.

Ramón Macedo had arrived that morning and was waiting for us in the domestic departure lounge. He was excited to be part of the team and to see what his drones could do in a completely different type of environment. He jealously guarded the two bags which contained his drones.

After arriving in Calama, we took a shuttle to San Pedro where Ximena met us at her cousin's house. It was an old, single storeyed place with whitewashed walls, not far from the centre of town. The four bedrooms were small and sparsely furnished. Ramón got the one with the largest bed. Showers would be at a premium as the house had only one bathroom. A kitchen cum dining room with an assortment of chairs and a family sized wooden table would also serve as our office. Three mismatched armchairs against the back wall constituted the lounge.

Our new quarters were not spacious by any means. We would have to watch we did not get on each other's nerves. Fortunately, we would be out in the field much of the time. Ximena looked relieved that international academics would put up with such conditions. I doubted Lepan would have.

Ximena had also arranged for us to hire a red double-cab Toyota ute from another cousin who had a garage. The wash he had given it could not hide the fact that the ute had seen thousands of kilometres over rough desert roads. Just the ride for Barry and Scotty. Lucas took the ute for a drive and pronounced it serviceable enough for us.

Maria Paz suggested going out for dinner so we could get to know each other better. If Ximena was apprehensive about working with a bunch of academics, three foreigners at that, she did not show it. Relations between the two local members of our team were cooler. Ximena probably knew Miguel's dad was a sergeant with the carabineros and thought they might end up confronting each other in any mining protests she organised. Maria Paz's cheerfulness soon dispelled any initial awkwardness. We had a thoroughly enjoyable evening. I hoped this boded well for the project.

Next morning, we gathered around the table and got down

to business. Maria Paz recapped the meeting in Santiago before asking each of us to outline the key points of our respective roles. An air of enthusiasm and anticipation filled the room. Maria Paz and Ramón were impatient to test their technology in the field and compare their results. Miguel leant forward, soaking it all in, eager to do his part. He kept fiddling with the data logger Maria Paz had given him. As this was his first time in the Atacama, Lucas looked forward to visiting all four sites so that he had a clearer idea of which stakeholders he needed to talk to and what their concerns and interests were. I needed to visit each of the sites so I could see them from a visitor management perspective. I was particularly interested in returning to the geysers, though not for that reason. Ximena's role was to facilitate our work; she would accompany us on our first site visits and assist Lucas with arranging the stakeholder meetings. Her local knowledge and contacts were essential. Ximena admired the way Maria Paz had guided the discussion firmly and made sure everyone had their say. So that's how you manage a diverse group of males. Once everyone had spoken, Maria Paz ended the meeting, saying the boys no doubt wanted to check out Ramón's drones.

We stood around the empty weed infested plot behind the house and admired the skill with which Ramón manoeuvred his drones. He had them buzzing up and down and around the back yard, circling a couple of the neighbour's trees to show his expertise. How far can they go? How high can they go? Will a drone that size really produce good video? Ramón answered all our questions patiently without looking down his nose at us like many technical experts do. Miguel and Lucas pleaded to have a go at the controls. 'Maybe later' was all Ramón would commit to. Whether he wanted to maintain his technologically dominant position in the team or protect the hardware from enthusiastic but inexpert hands I could not say. It would be easy to send the drones plummeting to the ground. Maria Paz's data loggers had less of an immediate impact. I looked on, amazed at the advances taking place in tourism research. Ximena, too, was getting caught up in the general excitement.

Marisela was pleased to catch up with Maria Paz and me at lunch. She already knew Miguel because he had done one of his university assignments on her company. Over lunch we explained what we wanted to do. How it would be best if Marisela or whoever was the guide on a particular tour could outline our research project and explain how the visitors could help. All they had to do was wear the data loggers like a sports watch, forget all about them and act naturally while they visited the attraction. Miguel's job was to hand out the data loggers and make sure he got them all back when the visitors reboarded the bus. The information would be confidential. None of it could be traced to any individual. We only had twenty data loggers and would be doing one tour at a time. We discussed a possible programme of tours to make sure we got a representative selection of sites. Marisela was intrigued by it all and looked forward to seeing the results.

The six of us could not fit into our ute for the afternoon trip out to the lagunas, so I rode with Ximena in her little Suzuki SUV. It was the first chance I had to probe her for more information about Lepan.

'So, what did you think of Ramón's drones?' I asked.

'Amazing the way he can manoeuvre them. I'm not sure what they will give us. I suppose he's used them on similar projects in Brazil.'

'He's had a lot of experience, but this is his first visitor management project. Ramón was going to help Professor Lepan in the Amazon before... well, until the professor's accident.'

'Really! What was that about?' she asked, looking at me rather than at the winding road.

I held onto the strap above the door. 'Something to do with collecting evidence on illegal mining and the harm being done to some of the isolated rainforest communities. You will need to ask Ramón for the details. Lepan was after a company called Mundial Mining.'

'Mundial Mining!' This time we nearly swerved off the road. 'Mundial Mining are the ones giving us all the trouble here. They're the ones we're protesting against.'

'Are they? What are they doing?'

'They're planning to apply for a licence to mine lithium, at a site much closer to San Pedro and the Chaxa Laguna than the operations of SQM and Albemarle. Mundial Mining have a terrible reputation. If they get the licence, it would be an ecological disaster. We must stop them. That's what's been keeping me busy and why I can't give much time to your project.'

So, the proposed mining site was much closer to the Chaxa Laguna. That could explain why Lepan had bombarded Marisela with questions about ecological issues on the salar the morning Rico had upset him when he was taking photos of the flamingos.

'Was Lepan going to help you to take on Mundial?'

'I'm pretty sure he was but he died before he could tell us anything.' She fell silent and concentrated on her driving. I couldn't tell whether Lepan had not said anything or whether she was not letting on if he had. A few curves later she turned and faced me directly. 'You don't think Mundial had anything to do with the professor's so-called 'accident'?' she asked, putting 'accident' in quotation marks with her fingers. 'I mean, what he was doing in Brazil. Their plans to apply for a lithium mining licence here hadn't been made public when you were in San Pedro before. But he might have had inside information. He had a lot of good sources. It makes you wonder. What do you think?'

'I don't know much about what he was doing in the Amazon. Wasn't his death accidental? He tripped and fell in the hot pool. Isn't that what the coroner ruled?' I asked. 'Death by misadventure.'

'That's how it was reported. I always thought there was more to it. Lepan wasn't a spring chicken but he had been all around the world. He wouldn't have been that careless. What you've said about Mundial makes me wonder even more.'

I waited until we were on a straight stretch of road before telling Ximena about the ute I had seen in the car park at the geysers which I later identified as belonging to Mundial Mining.

'There you are.' She slammed both hands on the steering wheel. 'That confirms it. They must have had something to do with the professor falling into the pool.'

'But we didn't see anyone nearby.'

'Well, you could easily miss someone in all that steam. It would still have been quite dark.'

'True. I suppose they could have gone the other way along the path and we would have missed them. Even so, the ute being there doesn't prove whoever was in it had anything to do with Lepan's death.'

'I'm sure they did. They're a pack of villains. We need to make the authorities see that. We need to make sure that Mundial don't get a licence, that they don't do any more harm, that they pack up and go back to Brazil. We'll need to protest even louder.'

'When are you holding the demonstration?'

'We are already using social media a lot and have the support of some international NGOs. We've a protest march next week in San Pedro. We'll show them.'

'Have you been involved in earlier protests?'

'Ha! Have I?' A light burned in her eyes at the recollection. 'My first one was in 2009, after that bore blew out at El Tatio. I was protesting alongside my uncle and cousins. I was only thirteen at the time. Since then I've marched against the other mining companies, lobbied for more infrastructure from regional and central government, protested against a multi-national hotel project. That one we won. The mining companies are different; they have a lot more money and we don't have the resources to take them on in court. I'm just about a full-time protester these days. We have to fight to get justice for our people, but we need more money.'

No mention of Lepan's involvement in the 2009 protest. Why had she left that out? I did not push my luck and instead asked her what she did when she was not protesting.

'I help run an early childhood learning centre. As well as all the usual activities, we try to immerse our kids in their language and culture.' That topic exhausted, we fell silent until we reached the lagunas.

The others were already out of the ute and organising the equipment. Before our trial run Ximena introduced us to the people managing the reserve. Maria Paz issued Ximena, Lucas, Miguel and me with a data logger each and instructed us to leave the car park at intervals and wander around looking at the lagunas as though we were tourists. That was no trouble for Lucas. The beauty and tranquillity of the lagunas was a marked contrast to the hillside sprawl of Valparaíso. Meanwhile, Ramón had his drone up and started videoing our movements and those of the tour party who were there when we arrived. After a couple of hours Ramón and Maria Paz were confident everything was working properly.

Ximena asked if I would mind swapping places with Ramón for the return trip because she wanted to learn more about drones from him. She had more than technology on her mind.

Marisela had a tour with a dozen people to see the flamingos the following morning. This provided Maria Paz with her first opportunity to try out her system on visitors, a group of young Europeans curious about our research and willing to be guinea pigs. Miguel distributed the data loggers and off they went. I spent the time examining the layout of the site and observing the visitors rather than the flamingos. It was straightforward; visitors paid their entrance fee at a small visitor centre, then followed a well-formed path alongside the laguna out and back to view the flamingos and other birds. Some visitors spent more time out with the flamingos, others looked at the display in the centre or hung around the bus waiting for the keen ones to return. No readily apparent visitor management issues here. No little Ricos running up and down this morning. The main problem with the monitoring was recovering all the data loggers.

We tested the data loggers again on the afternoon trip to the Valle de la Luna where Ramón was also able to do a trial run with the drones. Lucas stared in amazement and wondered how come he had waited so long to visit the Atacama. The multi-hued lunar landscape had lost none of its magic for me. I stood transfixed until Maria Paz broke the spell: 'C'mon, Cliff, we can't test the data loggers unless you move around.'

The GPS side of the monitoring proved promising. We were confident it would give us a good idea of how the visitors from different groups dispersed along the trail. Some of them charged ahead, others were challenged by the sandy slopes and lagged, like me in April. As a result, visitors from different groups merged and some congestion occurred, depending on where the visitors stopped to take photos or where the guides waited for the laggards to catch up. I could see how this might result in some track widening, lessen the visitor experience, or even create some safety issues when those in a hurry skirted around others or clustered together to listen to a guide.

Ramón had problems with his drones. The technical issues escaped me. Something to do with how he wanted to retain an overall view of the trails but to operate a drone he also needed to keep sight of it all the time. He found he could not do that at the Valle de la Luna because of the jagged terrain and the sinuous nature of the trails visitors followed. Or maybe it was something to do with the thin air at that altitude and the type of drones he had. 'Now you can see why I wanted to buy better equipment,' he lamented.

Back in San Pedro, Lucas and Maria Paz bought pizza from a place Miguel had recommended. I chatted with Ramón while we waited at the house, hoping to get some more information about who Lepan was after in the Amazon.

'So, what do think so far, Ramón?' I asked.

'I'm glad Maria Paz invited me to join this project. Back in Curitiba they think all I do is play around with my drones. My head of department doesn't understand how challenging working with new technology is, that you need to master the drones first before you can do any research with them. He keeps telling me I need to publish more, show this technical expertise of mine is useful, that it can provide some meaningful answers to real world problems. I'm hoping to get a couple of papers from this project to prove that.'

'Quite a contrast to the one you were going to be working on with Antoine Lepan in the Amazon,' I said.

'Sure is. There are no trees to get in the way here, but as you saw, I've got other issues to sort out at the Valle de la Luna.'

'Remember I asked if there was anything more you could tell me about who Lepan was after in the Amazon.'

'Yeah, nothing really. Just they were illegally mining for gold and making an environmental mess. We mainly discussed the technical side of things, what I could do with my drones in the rainforest. But I'm sure it was Mundial Mining. Ximena tells me they're the bad buggers she's up against here.'

'Apparently.'

'I don't know if Mundial were involved with lithium mining in Brazil. But now they're in the Atacama as well. Strange that Lepan was in both places too.'

'That is odd.'

'Why are you so interested, Cliff?'

'Curious, that's all. I was one of the ones asked to contribute to that festschrift. That got me more interested in him. Some of our early research interests overlapped.'

'What's happening with the festscrift?'
'It got canned. Carvalho's publisher let him down.'
'Pity, Lepan struck me as a good man.'
If you only knew.

# CHAPTER 17

Leaving for the geysers at 4am next day was no less demanding than it had been on our April visit. We were jolted around even more this time. Whether that was because of Lucas's driving or the condition of the shock absorbers of our ute was debatable. It did not seem quite as dark and steamy on our arrival at El Tatio as I remembered. This time we did not have the place to ourselves. The car park was two thirds full of buses, utes and SUVs. Tourists swarmed everywhere, chatting loudly as they expressed their wonder and recorded the experience on their selfies.

Lucas was less impressed than the tourists. 'Hey, Cliff, your geysers are much bigger than ours, but all this steam is pretty amazing,' he remarked as we wandered along the path. 'I can see why Ramón can't video here.' Further along he asked, 'Was it around here that Lepan fell in? I see how he might have tripped on these stones marking the edge of the path.'

'It must have been nearby, I'm not sure where exactly. After we pulled him out, I was too shocked to be thinking about that.' I had in fact been looking closely, trying to figure it out, but it was difficult now with so many people around. 'Can you remember, Maria Paz?'

'No. Once I reached Rico, Ana and I were busy trying to calm him down and get him back to his parents.'

'Well, we can try to work it out and tie it in with the visitor movements in case there's some particular issue about the spot that we need to consider from a safety point of view,' I said.

'Maybe one of the steamier places along the path,' Lucas said.

'Mmm, maybe.' I wanted to locate the pool where Lepan had died without seeming preoccupied with it.

'Let's head back and see how Miguel is faring collecting my data loggers,' Maria Paz said.

Miguel was doing a good job and the tourists had already handed them all in. We thanked Marisela and headed back. This time we did stop in Machuca. We bought some llama empanadas at a stall. They tasted a bit gamier than the usual *piño* ones.

Ramón had stayed back at the house trying to decide the best way to overcome the problem with the drones at the Valle de la Luna. The best solution, he decided, would be to have two operators at different points along the main trail. This would mean one of us would have to learn how to fly the second drone. Lucas's and Miguel's hands shot up. Ramón explained the basics of piloting drones and organised trials in the back yard. Lucas sent us scattering as he narrowly missed flying a drone into the back wall. Miguel proved a quick learner and was far more adept. He was stoked to be named associate drone pilot. As a result, I would have the task of distributing and collecting the data loggers much of the time.

After an early dinner of pizza, we reviewed the first results from the GPS tracking. Maria Paz had downloaded the GPS data onto detailed maps of the lagunas and the flamingo reserve. At the lagunas she was able to show the movements of the four of us from the car park to the Miscanti Laguna and then Miñiques.

'That's you, Miguel, you set off first,' she explained. 'It's obvious you already knew the place well and haven't moved very far off the paths. And that line there is you, Lucas. See how you've wandered around a lot more trying for better pictures, seeing as it was your first time.'

'Which one is me?' Ximena asked, peering at the map.

'There, and that last one is Cliff. See how you've all come together at the end.'

'That's amazing how you can keep track of us,' Ximena said.

'But remember, we're interested in the overall patterns, not the movements of any individual tourist. You can see how at the flamingos the tourists initially stay close together and then start to disperse. Some are more interested in the birds than others.'

'I've got the video from our trial run at the lagunas on my computer,' Ramón said, not to be out done. 'I'll freeze it here where we have got a good overhead shot. Lucas, if you look carefully, you can make yourself out on the bottom right because of that blue hat you're wearing. It's more difficult to identify the rest of you because of the other visitors. But again, we're interested in the overall picture, not what Lucas is doing.'

'Will you two be able to combine your results, map the movement patterns onto a still taken from the video?' I asked.

'We are still working on that but it's looking promising,' Maria Paz said.

'Now I have a much better idea of what you are trying to do. Impressive,' Ximena said.

'As Cliff would say, a triumph of technology,' Maria Paz added.

'But the real work lies in the interpretation, how we use these patterns to identify and solve any visitor management issues.'

'That's right, Cliff,' Lucas said. 'Then we must persuade all the stakeholders to respond to our recommendations, that's the challenging part.'

Truth was, although each of us had our role to play, we were all entranced by the video and maps and continued to pore over them long into the evening, our early start forgotten.

•••

Wednesday evening. Esperanza sent through the copies of the slides I had asked her for. The digitised photos turned out well despite the age of the slides. The Pont d'Avignon one was exceptionally clear. I cropped the photo to just Zu and me and looked at it for a long while. Those were the days. They might have been even better had I got my head out of my notes more often. I had come home with my degree, though. Zu hadn't. The photo reinforced my resolve to find out what had happened to Lepan.

No news from Viviana. Leave her be or act? I rubbed my hand over my head, accustomed now to the feel of the craters left by the surgery. Time might not be on my side. Act. I emailed her saying I had discovered that the paper on longhouses in Borneo had been based on the unacknowledged research of an old friend of mine. I attached the party shot with Zu and Lepan. I also told her I had bought a copy of Mario Valdivia's latest book when I was in Santiago—any excuse to remind her I was back in Chile.

Bill Broughton emailed to say he was not sure what magic I had worked in Santiago, but he had received an enthusiastic invitation from the dean at the Universidad de Chile to participate in a joint project on supply chain vulnerability in the Pacific. Bottles of pinot noir would be waiting the next time I wanted to use the bach.

•••

We soon settled into a routine and started making good progress with our research. The two-drone approach solved the problems at the Valle de la Luna and cemented Miguel as a valuable member of the team. Maria Paz's side of the project was also going well, with good cooperation from Marisela and only the occasional technical hiccup. Lucas was moving ahead with identifying and interviewing key stakeholders thanks to the contacts and introductions provided by Ximena and Marisela. Every couple of days we would gather round Maria Paz's maps and Ramón's videos and study the emerging patterns.

In between distributing and collecting the data loggers I spent my time noting the arrivals and departures of the groups of visitors and observing their movements at each site. Good old-fashioned participant observation still has its place. Following the visitors, noting what they said and did when they stopped and moved on again, provided some insights not captured by GPS. I was developing a good understanding of the visitor dynamics at each site which would help with interpreting the video and GPS data.

I was particularly interested in the pattern of activity at the geysers and put up with the early starts and the exhausting travelling involved. Most mornings the place teemed with visitors. It would be much more difficult to push somebody into a hot pool unnoticed than on the morning Lepan died. I kept trying to identify from the photo Harold had enlarged for me the spot where we had found Lepan's body, but without success.

I also got to know the drivers of Marisela's buses. I would often have a coffee with them while waiting for all the visitors to return. I did not come across Jorge who had driven us to the geysers in April. His sudden departure from the company right after Lepan's death had me wondering if the two events might be connected. How? I had no idea. I asked Carlos about him one morning.

'Which Jorge do you mean? There are two or three drivers called Jorge.'

'The one who was driving for Marisela before you took us up to the lagunas on our tour in April.'

'Oh, you mean Jorge Soto.' Carlos put down his coffee mug. 'He left the company back in April, moved down to Santiago so I heard. I don't know why. I doubt if he would enjoy it in the capital, too many people, everyone rushing around, too much noise, a crazy place to drive. He had spent all his life in San Pedro or in that little settlement out near the geysers.'

'He's Atacameño?' I had assumed his bronzed complexion came from having spent so much time in the Atacama sun.

'No, but he married one, lived like one.'

'Have you seen him lately?'

'Not since he left the company. It's worked out well for me,' Carlos said with a grin. 'I got his job. I had only been driving coaches part time before that.'

•••

Sergeant Figueroa called round to pick up Miguel one afternoon. He and Ramón were not yet back from the Valle de la Luna, so I invited the carabinero in for a cup of coffee while he waited.

'Professor West, thank you for inviting Miguel to be part of your project. I've never seen him so enthusiastic. He says you treat him like one of the team, as an equal, not merely an assistant. He's learning a lot and can't stop talking when he comes home each day. I don't always understand what he's been doing or know exactly what your project is all about.'

'Well, have a look at this,' I said. I opened my laptop and brought up some of our maps. 'What we are trying to do is get a better idea of visitor movements so your attractions can be managed better. If we understand what is going on, we can protect the resources more effectively and give visitors a better experience. See, here at the Valle de la Luna we have different pulses of visitors moving up the trail as people in one group spread out and other groups arrive.' Figueroa moved in for a closer view. 'See here, and here, it's congested. That could be avoided if the tour buses could be scheduled so they don't all arrive at the same time. That's the part we are working on next. Now on this map we have visitors to the flamingo reserve. Fewer problems there as the path is flat and wide. Everyone can see the birds easily. Miguel has been helping us monitor the visitors using GPS and with videoing them from the drones. He's a real asset to the team.'

'Interesting. And at El Tatio?'

'The problem at the geysers, as you know, is that the place is at its best for only a couple hours each morning before the steam has dissipated. So, on the busiest days a lot of crowding occurs. Our maps, as you can see on this next one, show a lot of toing and froing along the main path. More circular movement would ease the pressure. We are still working on that.'

I was about to drop in Lepan's name to see if there was anything new when the door opened and Miguel and Ramón entered.

'Hey, Dad, sorry we are late. Another tour group arrived as we were about to leave. I see you've met Cliff again. This is Ramón, he's the drone wizard I've been telling you about.'

'Pleased to meet you, er… Sergeant Figueroa,' Ramón said after recognising the carabinero's rank from his uniform. 'Miguel's doing a great job. Miguel, why don't you take your father out back and show him what you can do?'

'Well, quickly then. It's Miguel's sister's birthday today. I won't hear the last of it if we are late. Nice to have seen you again, Professor West. Thank you for the explanations. And to have met you, Ramón.' The latter, in a more formal tone.

'I didn't know Miguel's dad was a cop,' Ramón said. His expression suggested he was wary of close contact with law enforcement. 'Explanations? What was that all about?'

'I was showing him a few of our maps so he had a better idea of what Miguel is helping us with. Best to keep on the right side of the law.'

# CHAPTER 18

Tuesday of our second week. We were on our way back from the Valle de la Luna in the ute. Maria Paz was driving, only the second time she had been at the wheel. Usually we were with a tour bus and Lucas or Ramón drove the ute, but this afternoon Lucas was in San Pedro and Ramón was over at the lagunas with Ximena.

'I'm amazed at how well the project is going,' Maria Paz said. 'Ramón and I are collecting some fantastic data. How's progress on the visitor management front and with the operators?'

'We can already see some pressure points in the patterns we've got so far. We may have to recommend limiting visits during peak periods, especially as it's not summer yet. Or persuade the operators to organise their schedules to spread visits more evenly across the four sites and throughout the day.'

'How easy would that be?'

'Could be tricky, especially at the geysers. Lucas says that some of the companies aren't cooperating. He's having trouble arranging interviews with them. That's what he was trying to do this morning, nail down the ones who aren't responding to emails or phone calls. He's only missing a few but we need as complete a coverage as possible.'

'I'm sure he'll sort it out. You were right, Lucas is good, knows what ... That guy behind us is sitting right on my tail. And in a hurry.'

I looked over my shoulder. A battered minibus loomed large in our rear window. Maria Paz slowed and moved as far as possible to the right on the narrow and winding stretch of unsealed road to let it pass. The driver blasted his horn, the minibus sideswiped our ute with a tremendous thump, cut in in front and barrelled down the road in a cloud of dust and gravel. Maria Paz had no time to take the corner. She pumped the brakes. I hung on. The ute smashed through a roadside sign and ground to a halt.

We dared not move or say a word. The ute tilted. I looked out the side window. The front wheel on my side hung over a yawning gully. Not the time for a dangling conversation. I reached over and turned off the ignition.

'Ease yourself out gently,' I said.

'What about you?'

Another slight tilt.

'Get out. Now. But gently.'

Maria Paz opened her door and delicately edged her way back onto the roadside. The ute rocked. I yanked my door open and leapt back. The ute rocked again. I hastily rolled a large boulder in front of the back wheel. Maria Paz grabbed a post from the broken road sign and did the same on the other side. The ute steadied. Tilted some more.

'My laptop and loggers are in the back seat,' Maria Paz said and moved to retrieve them.

'Don't worry about them now. It could go over any minute.'

'We can't afford to lose them.'

Priorities, priorities.

The back door on my side swung open as the ute tilted again. I picked up a metal strip from the sign and gingerly hooked it over the strap of the bag with the loggers and pulled it out. Another two attempts and I managed to pull the laptop clear without sending the ute over the edge.

We stood back. Maria Paz had turned pale. She was shaking and bleeding from a graze on her forehead.

'That was close,' I said. I pressed my handkerchief to the graze. I only had a couple of scratches. My heart was pounding. I had gone pale too, no doubt. 'We're OK now.'

'He did that on purpose,' Maria Paz said. 'He deliberately forced us off the road. Mad devil very nearly got us killed.'

'Didn't stop either. You did well to stay in control. Did you see who it was?'

'No, I was too busy trying to stay on the road. Did you?'

'Only the colour, red and yellow. You're right, looked like he did it on purpose. Or he was just a reckless driver.'

'Why would anyone want to force us off the road?'

'I don't know. You weren't going that slow. Just some random act of road rage.'

'You've had a lucky escape,' said a voice behind us. We had not heard the truck pull up.

'You can say that again,' I said.

We explained what had occurred.

'Happens a lot around here,' the truck driver said. 'Those tourist bus drivers are always in a hurry. Show those foreigners as much as possible as quickly as they can to make sure they're getting their money's worth. Doesn't pay to be in a hurry in the Atacama.' He sized us up. 'And you folks would be strangers around these parts. Our roads aren't the easiest to drive on.' Maria Paz's pale cheeks flushed red.

'Let's see what we can do.' The driver, a wiry man wearing dusty overalls, hitched his vehicle to ours and hauled it back from the edge. He got out of his truck, unhooked the tow rope and scrambled under the ute. 'Nothing looks broken to me,' he said. He got in, reversed the ute, drove it down the road a little way and parked on the side. We picked up the loggers and laptop and joined him.

'You should be right to drive back into town, just take it easy,' he said. He handed the keys over to me. Maria Paz did not object. I drove cautiously back to San Pedro with a wary eye on the rear vision mirror for speeding minibuses. Maria Paz called Ximena and told her what had happened.

We got back without incident and parked out front. I opened the door to find we had had visitors while we were out. Unwelcome visitors. The dining room table was upended, our printer lay smashed on the floor, project papers were scattered across the room.

I checked my bedroom. The wardrobe doors hung open wide. My clothes were tossed all over the floor. I was relieved to see that my laptop was still in its basic hiding place behind the window curtain. My paperbacks lay in a pile beside the bed; the intruder was a perpetrator, not a reader of crime novels.

'Anything missing?' I asked Maria Paz.

'Not that I can see.'

Lucas's and Ramón's rooms had also been ransacked but we could not tell if anything had been stolen.

Maria Paz looked around the dining room, arms spread wide in disbelief. 'What were they after?'

'No idea. Can't have known we were academics. My laptop was the only thing of value, Ramón and Lucas had theirs with them.'

'That printer was expensive. Why would they trash it rather than take it? We'll have to replace it. I know you prefer working with hard copy when you're interpreting my maps.'

We righted the table and gathered up the printouts.

'Some of the latest maps are missing,' Maria Paz said. 'They were on the top of the pile; I printed them off last night.' She leafed through the pile again.

'Which ones?'

'The ones from El Tatio.'

'That's funny, who would want those?'

Ximena pulled up outside and dashed in with Ramón and Lucas whom they had picked up in town.

'Are you two all right?' she asked.

'A few scratches and grazes, that's all,' Maria Paz said. 'But we've had a break-in.'

'What?'

Maria Paz pointed to the broken printer. 'And the latest printouts of El Tatio are missing.'

Lucas and Ramón checked their rooms.

'Somebody's gone through everything but nothing's missing,' Lucas said when he reappeared.

'Same with me. Lucky I had my two little beauties with me,' Ramón said. He bent over and patted his drones.

'Some coincidence,' Lucas said, 'you two being run off the road and coming back to find a break-in.'

The same thought had crossed my mind.

'Ignacio, that's my cousin, is on his way with another ute while he goes over this one tomorrow to make sure nothing's been damaged. Your programme won't be affected at all,' Ximena said.

'Should we report this to the police?' Maria Paz asked her. 'And that driver too.'

'I wouldn't bother if your insurance covers the printer and the only things missing are some maps. You can print those out again once you get another one. The San Pedro police are always busy. You're not international tourists who have lost expensive cameras or had a lot of money and your passports stolen. It would be difficult to identify the minibus and hard to prove anything if you did. But I will ask around.'

'Yeah, not worth it,' Ramón said.

Did he and Ximena have little faith in the carabineros? Or did they want to steer clear of having anything to do with them?

'What if it happens again? We're often all away during the day. This place isn't secure at all,' Maria Paz said.

'Don't worry, leave it to me,' Ximena said. 'I must make tracks. I've got a demonstration to organise.'

We sat around discussing the two incidents, thankful that neither of us had been hurt and that we had lost nothing of value except the printer. The others thought it strange but just a coincidence. I was not so sure. They had to be linked. But how? The last break-in I knew of was the one at Lepan's hotel room the day he died. That wasn't a coincidence, though I had yet to work out what the link to his death was. There had been a crash that day too, the one staged by the Australians on the way to the geysers. And now we had stopped inches short of plunging down a gully and our house had been broken into. Coincidence? How could anyone in the minibus have broken into the house? Unless we had been run off the road to provide them the time to do so?

Were the crash and the break-in related to the events in April? Ramón usually drove the ute. If we were forced off the road, not by a random act of road rage but deliberately, had the driver of the minibus been trying to scare Ramón, or worse, injure or kill him? But why? He had not been with us in April, and he had not lost anything in the break-in. The missing documents were maps of the GPS tracking at the geysers, not photos or video taken from the drones. Ramón did have that incipient connection to Lepan, and the Frenchman had died at the geysers, but that was over four months ago.

Or was I the target? An icy finger ran down my spine. A common *modus operandi*. I remembered Lucas saying a logging truck had almost forced Lepan into a ravine years earlier. Unlike Ramón, I had been here in April. Maria Paz as well, for that matter. Had someone found out I was following up on Lepan's death? Or trying to? Impossible. I had been discreet in looking around at the geysers and had no real evidence yet of any foul play. How could anyone have known I would have been in the ute this afternoon? Anyway, we had been driven off the road by a minibus, not by a logging truck or even a Mundial vehicle. And why take the geyser maps? Nothing in them was related to Lepan. Only to visitor management. That was a harmless topic.

'Do you think anyone will do that again?' Maria Paz asked.

'I doubt it,' I said to reassure her, though not fully convinced.

'I've got the ute for the next few days so don't worry, Maria Paz. Anyone tries running me off the road, let them see how far they get,' Ramón said.

'OK, but be careful.'

'You've got copies of those maps backed up, haven't you?' I asked Maria Paz.

'Always.'

'Let's have a look.'

She brought the maps up on the screen. They showed the movements of the visitors at the geysers in a series of overlapping dotted lines. It would not have been easy for anyone else to interpret them because Maria Paz had not yet added the key.

'I can't see why anybody else would want these,' she said.

'Maybe someone wants to see what we are working on,' I said.

'Or to scare us off,' Lucas said, pulling on his beard. 'Some locals don't like foreigners sticking their noses in. Or mistrust foreigners, full stop.' He looked at the three of us: a Spaniard, a Brazilian and a New Zealander. 'You're the ones out in the field every day. You would have been noticed by the regular guides and drivers by now.'

'You think that's it? But we've also got three Chileans on the team. Cliff insisted we needed a balance,' Maria Paz said.

Lucas looked at me as if to ask if that was the only reason he was part of the project. I shook my head. He should know me better, know that I value his expertise.

'You're the one interviewing the operators, Lucas,' Maria Paz continued. 'Cliff tells me you've been having trouble with a few of them, that some aren't cooperating.'

'And Miguel, he's doing a great job but he's a cop's son,' Ramón said. 'I respect Ximena for what she is doing but she's not everybody's cup of tea around town.'

I could see this speculation rapidly degenerating into a foreigner versus Chilean argument. That could split the team. I tried to depersonalise the issue. 'It's most likely some general anti-tourism sentiment. Some locals will resent the way tourism here has been expanding so rapidly. That's common at this stage of the growth curve. You've seen how backpackers and other tourists take over streets. Prices will have risen on every-day goods. The council is struggling to keep up with infrastructure. I've seen researchers and consultants cop it in other places. I've been abused in the street, shouted down at public meetings, ignored by barmen.'

'Still, a break-in is a bit extreme for what we're doing,' Lucas said. 'We're the good guys, our research will improve destination management, not encourage an unsustainable boom.'

'Good guys don't always win,' Ramón said, crouched over his laptop. 'I was hoping I could identify that minibus from some of the shots I've taken. But I've been filming visitors on the tracks and don't have anything much on the car parks.'

'All right, whoever it was and whatever the reason, we need to keep our eyes and ears open from now on,' Maria Paz said. 'Ramón, or whoever is driving, be extra alert. And let's see what Ximena has in mind for improving our security.'

Ximena's cousin Ignacio turned up the following afternoon with our ute and our security solution. He slapped the bonnet of the Toyota and said 'She's all good to go. I've checked it thoroughly, nothing damaged, just a few scrapes underneath. You were very lucky.' He passed the keys to Ramón. 'Now, if you'll give me a hand, I've something else Ximena said you needed.'

It was an old oak chest, about two metres long. 'She said you could put any valuables in this whenever you're out.' We took a corner each and with a lot of cursing and effort lugged it inside. If the lock was strong, we had a basic safe. No intruders would be walking off with that in a hurry.

•••

Carlos might have had an idea about the red and yellow minibus. I did not see him until Thursday morning when he drove Marisela's bus to the flamingos. He had been away on a full day trip on Wednesday and another driver had taken us to the geysers and the lagunas. I had checked out the car parks in both those places but found no sign of the minibus. Carlos was the one who raised the subject over coffee.

'I hear you had a bit of excitement on Tuesday.'

'Word spreads quickly in San Pedro.'

'My neighbour mentioned it, he works for Ignacio and was the one who checked out your ute.'

'Do you know who has a battered red and yellow minibus, probably a ten- or twelve-seater?'

'Sounds like P2P.'

'P2P?'

'Peru to Patagonia, better known as Peril to Peril,' Carlos said.

'Why's that?'

'Their motto is 'low cost, high adventure.' More like 'low cost, high risk' if you ask me. I wouldn't be seen dead on any of their tours. Or rather I might be if I ever took one.' He laughed. I must have looked blank. 'They've had more than their share of crashes. P2P is run by a couple of mad Brits. They cater to the ultra-low end of the market, try to go as far as they can as fast as they can. Often drive all through the night.'

'Are they local?'

'No, based in Lima. They operate on this side of the Andes.

They're linked with another cowboy company, A2B, Argentina to Brazil, on the other side. So, you can go one way with P2P and the other with A2B, or vice versa. That's if you survive.'

'Why would they try and run us off the road?'

'You must have been holding them up. They will be halfway to La Paz by now. Right, time for us to pack up and be on our way.'

What Carlos said matched the truck driver's comments. Ximena was right; there would have been little point in going to the police if P2P was not a local company and they were well gone. I could not see what interest they would have had in breaking into our house. That meant someone else had.

# CHAPTER 19

Ximena's demonstration took place on Friday afternoon. We were all due for a break and out of solidarity went along for a look. Maria Paz warned us to stay in the background and not become involved. Ximena had rallied a hundred or so demonstrators of all ages in the square where the protest began. From what I could tell, most were Atacameños, some with toddlers and young children. There was also a noticeable group of urban ecologists and, according to Miguel, some local teachers. Their placards were all hand painted, not mass produced: DOWN WITH MUNDIAL, LIVES NOT LITHIUM, SAVE OUR WATER and my favourite, LLAMAS NOT LITHIUM. In full voice, Ximena emphasised the problems lithium mining had already created in the Salar de Atacama, decried Mundial Mining's plans to seek a licence and urged the authorities to reject their application. Her supporters applauded raucously. Many of the onlookers booed.

Ximena had also managed to have some TV cameras along to film the event. Once the cameramen had sufficient coverage of her speech, the protesters began their march towards Mundial's offices, shouting 'Say no, Mundial must go.' Ramón made to join them. I placed a restraining hand on his shoulder and with the other pointed out the four carabineros shadowing the march. He shrugged my hand off in disgust and looked hard at Miguel. We had all recognised Sergeant Figueroa amongst the carabineros. And he had seen us. Tall and Black, Ramón would stand out in any Chilean crowd.

'Come on, let's all go and have a drink,' Maria Paz said. 'On the project. We've had a busy week and there's nothing we can do here.'

Ramón muttered to Lucas and the two of them headed off. Miguel made some excuse about doing errands for his mother. That left Maria Paz and me to have a drink and a catch up.

She looked at her watch. 'We had better make that a coffee for now.'

We found a cafe that served more than Nescafe.

'So, what's the big issue with lithium that has got Ximena all steamed up?' Maria Paz asked. 'I've never understood it.'

I had forgotten that she had not done all the background reading that I had on the subject. I gave her a rundown on the link between lithium mining and the effects the drawdown of the water table was having on the Atacameños' way of life. I also summarised what I had found out about Mundial Mining. 'And that's the link to our project.'

'What do you mean?' Maria Paz asked, eyebrows raised.

'Mundial was the company that Lepan was investigating in the Amazon, the one he approached Ramón about videoing their operations in the rainforest with his drones. The one Carvalho mentioned at the conference.'

'Ah, now I see why Ramón wanted to join the march. I think he's been around at Ximena's just about every night this week. He doesn't have to get up before dawn for the geyser tours. We must keep an eye on him and make sure he doesn't get carried away. And Ximena too. We can't afford to have her protest linked to our project in any way.' She paused while the waiter served our coffee. 'It always comes back to Lepan, doesn't it? We can't escape the man.'

'He cast a long shadow, that's for sure.'

'Changing the subject, any news from Viviana lately?'

I felt like saying, 'That's a broken record.' Instead, I said, 'Well, that's not changing the subject much either.'

Maria Paz wrinkled her brow.

'Viviana's become preoccupied with Alba and Rico. They're now in Mendoza staying with Alba's mother.'

'We need to clear up once and for all what happened to Lepan, for their sake,' Maria Paz said. 'I know you're still trying to show it wasn't Rico's fault and that you've been spending time figuring out where it was exactly that he fell in.'

'You noticed that did you?'

'What's your theory, Cliff?' Maria Paz sat back in her chair, cradling her mug in both hands.

'Let's start with Mundial Mining. You may not remember, but there was a ute in the car park that morning. It had gone when we got back to the bus.' I outlined the conversation between the Australians and the Swedes in the bar, how I thought the crash which had delayed the rest of the convoy to the geysers had been deliberately caused at the behest of Mundial. 'So, one possibility is Mundial were trying to eliminate Lepan because he was obstructing what they were doing in the Amazon and the geysers were a convenient place to make it seem like an accident.'

Maria Paz's eyes grew wider and wider as she listened. 'That's incredible. I can't believe it.'

'Just a theory. I can't prove anything.'

'So, what happened on Tuesday might be related to Lepan after all. Whoever ran us off the road thought Ramón and Ximena were in the ute, not us, and they wanted to stop the protest by putting them out of action.'

'I doubt it.' I explained what Carlos had said about P2P. 'But who the intruders were and what they were after at the house, I'm none the wiser.'

'Nobody's been back, thank goodness. Any other theories about Lepan?'

'An even more unlikely one, someone else's.' I recapped what Arturo had told me about Interpol's belief that Lepan was involved in international drug smuggling and how a deal gone wrong may have led to his death.

'Drug smuggling! That's even more incredible.' She leaned forward. 'Do theories come in threes?'

'Well, not so much a theory as a mystery.' I mentioned Lepan's articles on lithium mining in the Atacama, his involvement in the protest at the geysers in 2009 and Ximena's youthful participation. 'Where all that fits in, I don't know. Was his death at the geysers coincidence or was it related to the earlier protest? Mundial weren't involved in the geothermal project and don't have any energy interests.'

'Any more theories?'

'It could be that he just had a heart attack and fell in. I'm not sure how we could convince Rico of that. Or of any of the other theories for that matter. He would probably believe drug smugglers pushed him in. That's the sort of story that might appeal to a ten-year-old. We would also have to convince Alba and Pablo that it wasn't Rico's fault. That would require concrete evidence, something we still don't have. Time for that wine.'

•••

We were relieved to find Ramón and Lucas at breakfast next day. The protest had gone off peacefully and neither Ximena nor any of her fellow protestors had been arrested. We had a busy day, a tour to the flamingos in the morning and to the Valle de la Luna in the afternoon. Marisela joined us for dinner that evening. She was good company and regaled us with tales of some of the more eccentric tourists and drivers she had dealt with over the years. Her presence lessened any tension that might otherwise have existed within the team. I asked her about Jorge Soto but all she said was that he had quit and gone to live in Santiago.

As we were about to bid each other good night, Marisela checked that we would be finishing our data collection over the coming week.

'We should be all done by Wednesday or Thursday,' Maria Paz said. 'Is that a problem?'

'No, no problem. My boss, Señor Alvarez, knows your research will be very useful, that we need more information if tourism in the Atacama is to be managed properly. It's not sustainable the way we're going at present. But he's getting a bit of pushback from some of the other operators. Rumours are going around because of all the questions you've been asking and what you are doing with the drones. People are saying that the authorities will be tightening up, that tours will be restricted. If that's true, some operators won't be very happy. Others have got it into their heads our company must be benefitting somehow because you've been working with us. They think that means working for us. Señor Alvarez must be careful. San Pedro is a small town; he has to keep onside with the other operators. I'm sure you understand.'

'We do. We know how competitive tourism is here. Please reassure Señor Alvarez we will be finished in a few days and tell him how much we have appreciated his and your assistance.'

'That's good to hear. Well, good night and thank you for an enjoyable evening.'

Maria Paz and I looked at each other as she walked away.

'Well, that might explain our break-in,' I said. 'Our intruder was trying to scare us off, not rob us. That would explain the smashed printer.'

'But the maps they stole?'

'To prove that they had done the job they were sent to do by whoever is behind it all.'

'But we're still here, we've got another printer and will be out in the field again on Monday,' Maria Paz said with a determined glint in her eye.

But we still didn't know who was behind the break-in.

•••

We took Sunday off. Although it was late when I got up none of the others were around or had eaten breakfast. I ate a banana and a couple of kiwifruit. While the coffee brewed, I started playing around with my Lepan files. Maria Paz was right; we needed to clear up what had happened to Lepan if we were to move on with the rest of our lives. Ximena's demonstration on Friday prompted me to go back to the 2009 El Tatio protest and the newspaper photo of Lepan being arrested. I saw no sign of Ximena in the photo nor mention of her name in the accompanying text. One name in the caption did jump out at me now—Jorge Soto. I had not recognised him in the photo earlier. Even now it was difficult to tell it was him as the photo was grainy. The caption left no doubt; our bus driver had been arrested along with Lepan for disturbing the peace at El Tatio. They had known each other years before our tour yet Lepan had given no indication of this. He scarcely exchanged a word with the driver even though he had been sitting up front. However, Jorge had seemed unsettled and kept looking over at Lepan's empty seat on our way back from the geysers. This made more sense now; a common cause had previously brought them together. Lepan's behaviour failed to explain why he had ignored Jorge so blatantly on our tour. Was it just his general aloofness, or a calculated display of a lack of familiarity between the two?

'You can't let it go, can you?' Maria Paz said, looking over my shoulder. 'Anything I can do to help?'

'Grab a coffee and then I want to take another look at some of your photos from our tour, the ones up at the geysers, if you have them on your laptop.'

When Maria Paz came back, I laid out the photo of the hot pool with the green spot in the background which Harold's enlargement had shown to be Lepan. 'I've been trying to locate exactly where Lepan died from these two fumaroles and the geyser. There's so many of them. Trying to identify these ones with all that steam around is proving impossible, even later in the morning. Pat mentioned coming from where the path forked but that hasn't helped either.'

'And you say that's Lepan,' Maria Paz said, putting her finger on the green spot.

'Must be. He was the only one with a bright green jacket.'

'You're right, he did stand out from the rest of the group.'

'Made a point it. We all had darkish jackets, except you in your white one'. Which wouldn't be easy to see in the steam. Don't go there, Cliff, you can't suspect everyone. Besides, Maria Paz had been with you until we heard Rico cry out.

'We don't know about the guys in the ute, though. We didn't see them at all.'

'It had to be one of Mundial's. It was gone by the time we got back.'

'They were the only ones there other than our group...No...' Maria Paz had joined the dots. 'If it wasn't an accident then it must have been someone in our group. It can't be, Cliff, can it?'

I hastened to say that I had some initial doubts about Pat and the two Mexicans but had soon dismissed them. And it was inconceivable that Amalina and Edílson, Pablo, Alba, or Viviana were involved.

Reassured, Maria Paz turned back to her photos.

'That's the one I sent for your seminar, right? I'm rather proud of that one, captured the atmosphere at the geysers perfectly.'

'Picture postcard material. Impressed them all at the seminar. It's not helping me now, though.'

'I only sent you the best ones. I've loads more.'

'Let's concentrate on those you took just before or after that one.'

Maria Paz flipped back and forth but none of the photos gave us anything more than the one Harold had enlarged. Until she pointed to the top of the screen and exclaimed: 'What's that there? Something red.'

I studied the photo closely. I could not see why she was becoming excited.

'There. There's a red dot behind that green spot that you say is Lepan. Let me see what I can do.' With that, Maria Paz zoomed in and out, cropping and enlarging the corner of the photo in which the two colours appeared. As she did, the image pixelated and we could not make out what we were seeing.

'Hey guys, what's so fascinating on this bright Sunday morning?' asked a bleary-eyed Ramón as he came into the room, his pyjama shorts sagging dangerously.

'We're trying to make out what's in this corner of one of my photos,' Maria Paz said, aware from my look not to elaborate.

'Here, let me have a go.' His fingers danced over the touchpad. The image became a little clearer. 'We can do better than that. Maria Paz, send me that photo and make me a strong coffee and I'll see what I can do on my computer. I've got some programs that I use to edit my videos and make stills which are a lot more sophisticated than what you've got.'

'Deal, Ramón, but get dressed first.'

'OK, ma'am, I wouldn't want to distract you.'

Ten minutes later, dressed in jeans and a Neymar tee-shirt, Ramón began enhancing the photo. 'Let's see what a professional can do.' His initial confidence turned to frustration. 'Sorry folks, that's the best I can manage. You need a better camera, Maria Paz.' She looked offended. Ramón carried on: 'You can tell from the shape that the green spot is a person, but it's not clear enough to make out who. That red dot behind is more blurred. It also looks to be a person, or part of somebody, but no telling who.'

Maria Paz and I looked at each other with sudden realisation.

'Whaaat?' Ramón asked. 'Oh, now I get it. It's what you've been obsessing about, isn't it, Cliff? The one in the green must be Lepan and the little red dot must be that little Argentine kid, the one whose scarf the professor tripped on. Yeah, Lucas mentioned it.'

He was right. What Maria Paz had captured on film was Rico about to bump into Lepan while he was running up and down the path. It was not the scarf but the little kid himself who had caused Lepan's death. That explained why he had been so upset at the time. Why he remained so traumatised.

# CHAPTER 20

'So, that's it, no more drug smuggling, multinational mining baddies or protests to worry about,' Maria Paz said as we wandered around town looking for somewhere for lunch. There was no point in searching through more of her photos and we needed a break away from the house. Ramón and Lucas had a rendezvous with Miguel to have a drink and meet some of his female friends.

'It looks that way. We still don't know what Lepan was up to, not that it matters anymore. Your photo with Rico in it pretty much shows he was responsible for what happened to Lepan. It's made things worse not better.' I kicked out at a stone and stubbed my toe. 'Dammit.'

'Cliff, you're a good man. You were right to be concerned for Rico and his parents. However, there's nothing more you can do. You need to put Lepan behind you. We've just got one week to go. The project is what we came for and that's been going well. I'm so pleased with how the team has gelled. We should get three or four papers at least out of the data we're collecting.'

'Be careful you don't slice the chorizo too thinly,' I said, adapting the saying to Maria Paz's culinary tradition.

'We deserve something more than chorizo for lunch.'

'A metaphor.' I laughed. 'Make sure you don't spread your

material thinly across more papers to boost your list of publications. We would be much better off writing a couple of strong papers integrating ideas, methods, results and management implications rather than spinning out a series of weaker ones dealing with a single aspect of the project. Quality not quantity.'

'Oh, I see, I think. But wouldn't producing more papers boost our chances for getting other grants and projects. Your track record astounds me, the one you submitted with our proposal.'

'Enough about work for now. And no more Lepan from me if you order the finest dish the Atacama has to offer,' I said. I had spotted the restaurant where we had dinner during the tour.

We had a leisurely lunch, beginning with a pisco sour, before moving on to a carmenere to accompany the *pataska*. Maria Paz conceded it was not such a bad dish after all. A change from pizza and empanadas anyway. The restaurant was relatively quiet. The flute player whose music had tormented us on our first visit either did not do afternoons or the grumpy barman/bouncer had got the message across that he was not welcome. When we were mellowed by the wine, Maria Paz brought up the subject of Wendy and Rod.

'Cliff, when we were here the first time, I could see you were uncomfortable when Amalina asked if you had children. Viviana told me about your wife and son.'

'Maria Paz, I don't—'

'You can't go on torturing yourself over what happened, how you feel responsible for your son's death because he blamed himself for his friend's accident while you were busy correcting your proofs. And then you let him go out alone when he started mountain biking again. Nobody could have foreseen what he was going to do.'

'Maria Paz—' I could not stem her well-intentioned flow of advice.

'I know you see parallels between what happened with Rod, what Rico is convinced he has done, and what you fear he might do if he continues to dwell on it. How that could become a wedge between Alba and Pablo in the same way that Rod's reaction to the other boy's accident split you and Wendy apart. Cliff, you must let go and move on. You have become obsessed with Lepan. We both know now that it appears Rico accidentally bumped into Lepan. Lepan was a well-travelled man, not a young boy on a bike. He should have been able to take care of himself. It was an accident. It wasn't Rico's fault. There's nothing more you can do. You won't find redemption by trying to prove someone other than Rico was responsible for Lepan's death. Let Lepan go. Go with the person who is waiting for you.'

'Waiting for me?'

'In Mendoza. Viviana. It's five years since her husband died. She's extremely fond of you, admires you. Don't hold back.'

'Maria Paz—'

'And don't think it would be unfair on her knowing your cancer may return one day. We both know, you can't hide that scalp of yours under a hat all the time. Viviana knows what it's like—'

My chilly look froze the conversation. We finished our coffees and walked back to the house separated by our silence.

What Maria Paz had said about Viviana sent my heart racing. But why hadn't Viviana answered my previous email if she was that fond of me? The news that a friend of mine had done the research on which Lepan's Borneo paper was based surely warranted a reply. Telling her I had bought a copy of Mario Valdivia's latest book signalled I was back in Chile. Had the intensity of our exchanges while we were working on our festschrift chapters simply run its course? A shared interest in Latin American crime fiction was just that, I conceded, not the foundation for a stronger relationship. What was I thinking?

Forget Lepan, focus on Viviana, my young colleague had urged me. But the two were intertwined. I felt gutted that my path to redemption had been taken from me now that I knew Rico had bumped into him. Without it, I wasn't sure I was able to move on, that I was ready for a relationship with Viviana, whatever her feelings towards me.

Dammit. Despite that photo there had to be another explanation out there. We only had a week left in San Pedro and I was going to find it. After that I would see about visiting Mendoza.

# CHAPTER 21

We attacked our last week with gusto. On the Monday morning Ramón, Miguel and Lucas headed off to the Valle de la Luna, taking half of the data loggers with them. Maria Paz and I had the early morning shift at the geysers and travelled out on the bus with Marisela's tour group which consisted of only ten tourists that day. I kept my word to Maria Paz and refrained from continuing my search for the site where Lepan died.

After handing out the data loggers to the group, Maria Paz and I spent some time observing the behaviour of visitors who had driven out to El Tatio by themselves. There weren't many, but we still needed to take account of them in any overall visitor management strategy. I was particularly interested in how the independent visitors interacted with those who had come on the buses.

'This is real fieldwork,' I said. We were retreating into our academic shells, both conscious that she had crossed into delicate personal territory over lunch the day before.

While we waited to collect the last of the data loggers, Maria Paz chatted with a couple of the independent tourists who she discovered were from Alicante. I had a coffee with Carlos.

'I didn't see you at the protest on Friday afternoon,' I said.

'Friday afternoon is when we check over our buses for the weekend, do any maintenance, give them a thorough clean. Weekends are generally a busy time for us. Protesting is not my thing, anyway.'

'What do you make of lithium mining?' I bit into the ham and cheese roll which he offered me.

'Well, I started out truck driving for SQM. They created a lot of jobs, there weren't many other opportunities in San Pedro before tourism boomed. Me, I love driving tourists better than hauling that brine to Antofagasta. That's why I was glad to be taken on full time. I don't get tired of flamingos or the geysers.'

'Ximena had all her supporters fired up.'

'She gets that from her uncle, Jorge Soto, the guy you were asking about the other day. He's a real stirrer. Always has been.'

'So, Jorge is Ximena's uncle?' I should not have been surprised; she had mentioned being at the 2009 protest with an uncle.

'Yeah, he married her mother's sister. He didn't turn up at Friday's protest, did he?'

'Didn't see him. You haven't been getting any stick from any of the other drivers for having a coffee with us, have you?' I looked around at the other buses parked nearby.

'What do you mean?' He followed my gaze.

'I hear we're not popular in all quarters with the research we're doing?'

'Oh, that. Yeah, one or two drivers have been pumping me for information about what you're up to. I just say I don't understand what you're doing, that it's all mumbo-jumbo to me, that I'm just a driver and do what Marisela says.'

'You heard we had a break-in on Tuesday?'

'Yeah, I got that from the neighbour as well.'

'Do you think the break-in might be related to our unpopularity?'

'Could be. Ah, here come my tourists. Group photo time. You should see this Mr Tourism Professor.' He marshalled his group into different poses, some sat on the bumper bar, others on the bonnet, a couple leaned out of the door, one climbed up on the roof. Once he had positioned them all, Carlos took photos for everyone, including me. His staging produced a much more engaging shot than the one of our group at the Tropic of Capricorn.

'What was that all about, Carlos?'

'I'm doing an online tourism marketing course. What do you see here, Professor?' He pointed to the photo.

'A happy group of tourists sitting on a bus.'

'Aha, but not just any bus. An Adventures Atacama bus.' He pointed to the company's name emblazoned across the front of the bus at the top of the photo. 'They will be posting their photos on Facebook and Instagram, Whatsapping and emailing copies to all their friends and family saying what a fantastic time they had. Everyone will see they took an Adventures Atacama tour. Who will their friends or family choose to travel with if they come to San Pedro? Adventures Atacama. Free international advertising, the power of social media, you can't beat it.'

'You've missed your calling, Carlos. You should ask Marisela for a raise.' Carlos was smart, more than just a driver. He knew what was going on, but I doubted I would draw any more information out of him about the break-in. Tour bus drivers were a clan of their own, a clan from which the owner/drivers of P2P were excluded.

•••

Back in San Pedro, Sergeant Figueroa phoned as I was stepping off the bus and asked me to call by the commissariat. 'I wonder what he wants,' I said to Maria Paz.

'I hope nothing has happened to Miguel. I will pick up some empanadas for lunch and meet you back at the house.'

At the commissariat I was shown into a room with a bare table, a couple of chairs and no window. I had to wait twenty minutes before Figueroa appeared. Was the wait and the grimness of the room designed to make me nervous—that's what happened in those Chilean detective stories I read—or was he just busy?

'Good morning, Professor West, sorry to keep you waiting. I thought you might have been out in the field, as my boy refers to it.'

'I'm just back from the geysers. Miguel is at the Valle de la Luna this morning. A couple of more runs with the drones and they should be done.'

He sat. 'Well, I haven't asked you in to discuss your research, however interesting that is.'

'Then how can I help you, Sergeant?'

'I will come to that in a moment. But first, I heard you were involved in a couple of incidents last Tuesday. You should have reported those. We are here to assist anyone who has been harassed in anyway.'

'We didn't want to trouble you. We know how busy you are and no real harm was done.'

'The printer?' he asked, eyebrows raised.

How much did he know? 'Insured.'

'Another time, make sure you report it. We want to crack down on petty criminals in San Pedro.'

Were we dealing with petty criminals, or some larger opposition to our project? 'Understood. We will be finished by the end of the week.'

'Now, you will recall that a few days after you left San Pedro in April, you emailed me saying that the ute you had seen on the morning Professor Lepan died was the same colour, purple and white, as Mundial Mining's vehicles.'

'That's right.'

'Could there be a connection between Professor Lepan's death and Mundial Mining?'

'Maybe.' I summarised what I had heard between the Australians and the Swedes and how that indicated the vehicles behind our bus had been deliberately held up. 'I found out afterwards that Lepan had been following Mundial's illegal mining operations in the Amazon. He's got a reputation for drawing attention to these sorts of activities, in some cases shutting them down, so it's possible there has been some foul play. The connection is tenuous, but the ones in the Mundial ute were the only other people at the geysers that morning. At that stage I hadn't heard Mundial were after a lithium mining licence in the Salar de Atacama.'

Figueroa wrote in his notebook.

'Sergeant Figueroa, why are you asking me about this now? We've been in town for a couple of weeks. Has something new come up?'

'We're seeing heightened interest in Mundial Mining's activities in the district, more than interest from some quarters, opposition, as you saw on Friday. We are following up all leads to make sure nothing gets out of hand. Your break-in may be connected to the protest leader being part of your team. Another reason you should have reported it.'

And your son is also working with us. 'So, Mundial Mining might have been behind our break-in?'

'I didn't say that.'

My turn to pump him. 'You told me at the time that Lepan tripped and fell into the hot pool. Did the coroner confirm that?'

'Please, Professor West, I am the one asking the questions. However, since you have been helpful, I can tell you the coroner's findings were not one hundred per cent conclusive. He may have had a heart attack. The state of his body made it too difficult to ascertain exactly why he fell, tripping on that boy's scarf or on the stones or a heart attack.'

That did not help me much.

'Now, one of our colleagues from Santiago also wants to talk to you.' Figueroa got up and left.

Ten minutes later Arturo Eterovic entered the room.

'Figueroa told me that you were still around. So, a good opportunity to update you on what we were discussing in Santiago. Another informal chat between acquaintances, nothing more. That is, if you have the time, Cliff.'

'Of course. My empanadas can be reheated.' My stomach rumbled.

'Good. You will recall from our last little chat that Interpol had been following the travels of the late Professor Lepan, including his visit to Bogotá before coming to Chile.'

'I remember.'

'Last week my Colombian counterparts arrested Dr Ortiz on suspicion of drug trafficking. We know that Ortiz attended the same colloquium that Lepan spoke at. He also met with the professor privately on several occasions.'

Arturo waited for me to react. Ortiz's arrest surprised me—he struck me as a number-crunching nerd. I could not see any link between his statistical expertise and drug smuggling. I waited for Arturo to continue.

'This confirms our belief that Lepan was involved in bringing drugs into Chile. We saw signs of increased trafficking in San Pedro around the time of your tour.'

'Lepan wouldn't be so naïve as to carry drugs with him, particularly if he knew he was being watched?'

'Of course not, Cliff. He would have been arranging a shipment from Colombia. Either overland through Bolivia to San Pedro with the aid of local accomplices, or… he was working with other international travellers who were acting as couriers or were going to acquire drugs while they were here.' He tapped his pen on the desk. 'Which brings us again to your tour group. Anything new about Mason and O'Connor, your two Irish colleagues who were also in Colombia.'

'Mason was recently elected vice-president of TADSAI, our international tourism and development association. Ortiz nominated him.'

Arturo made a note. 'A payoff?'

'Hardly; the position is not that big a deal.' I stirred a little to see if I could learn anything from the detective. 'Lepan was president-elect but died before he could take up the role.'

'Was he now? Who became president?'

'Hector Muñoz Muñoz.'

Arturo consulted a file, could not find what he was looking for and asked who Hector was.

'Felipe Montoya's father.' Chew on that, Arturo.

He looked up at me, down again at his file and nodded. 'Montoya left for Mexico unexpectedly the next day. Do you know why?'

'A family matter, I believe.'

The detective scribbled in the margin and carried on. 'Now, Cliff, can you tell me if we've got all of the members of that tour group on this list right?'

I scanned it. 'It looks right to me, though I'm not sure of the surnames of the Chileans. I didn't have much contact with them during the tour.'

'Anything to add about the two Brazilians?'

'Forget Amalina and Edílson; they didn't know Lepan beforehand. They're a young couple expecting their first child.'

He moved down his list, skipping Felipe and his colleague. 'The Argentines?'

'Would drug smugglers bring along their ten-year-old son? And Professor Arévalo I've known for a long time. No way.'

'Which leaves us with you and Dr Casals.' He smiled. 'What can you tell me about the young lady.'

'No way would she have been involved with drugs or Lepan. Maria Paz was with me most of the time we were in San Pedro.'

'Quite so. At night, too?' His smile evolved into a smirk.

My hackles rose. 'Look, Arturo, enough informal chatting. Don't beat around the bush. Come straight out with it. Go on record if necessary.'

'Now, now, Cliff, no need to take offence. I would point out that you and Dr Casals are the only two members of the tour group who are back in San Pedro.' An overly dramatic pause. 'At a time when reports are coming in of increased deliveries of cocaine passing through the town. And you have a Brazilian in your team.'

'And three Chileans. Inspector Eterovic, why don't you take off your Interpol liaison hat and concentrate on the Chileans in that tour group? All seven of them. Or are your compatriots above suspicion?' I asked, raising my voice.

'All seven? There were only five names on that list.' He peered at it.

'You're forgetting our guide, Marisela, and the driver, Jorge Soto. Soto resigned in a hurry and left for Santiago the day after Lepan died. Coincidence?'

'My, my, you are well informed, Cliff.'

'Our professions aren't that different; you're an investigator, I'm a researcher. Ask the right questions, analyse the data, interpret your findings, draw your conclusions.'

'Indeed. Then I will allow you one question and won't detain you from your empanadas any longer. They're never the same reheated. Annie would not forgive me if our little chat created a spat in Kiwi-Chilean relations.'

'Did Lepan visit Colombia immediately before coming to San Pedro or go somewhere else in between times?'

'After he arrived in Santiago from Bogotá he spent a couple of days on Easter Island, some conference on cultural tourism, and a few days in the capital.' He frowned. 'Why do you ask?'

No reason, I just wanted to imply he should have been more thorough. 'You've already had your last question, Arturo,' I said with some satisfaction. 'Please pass on my regards to Annie.'

At the door I stopped and offered him a crumb to show that I too had the interests of Kiwi-Chilean relations at heart. A possible link between Ortiz, stats and smuggling had occurred to me as the inspector had continued with his questions. After I retired, I acted occasionally as a language buddy on the short intensive English courses the university used to run for various groups of government officials from Asia and Latin America, classes in the morning, more informal activities in the afternoon. As language buddies, our role was to chat about anything and everything to improve the officials' conversational English. Chatting with Cecilia was hard going at times. She was more a numbers than a words person. She worked in the Bolivian Customs Department, running statistical probability tests on where and how drugs were being intercepted so that the department could deploy its under-resourced staff more effectively. Could the converse apply? Was Ortiz using his stats expertise to identify which routes and channels had the least chance of being intercepted? Possibly. Drug smuggling is a sophisticated business nowadays.

'You might keep an eye out for any of Lepan's Chilean associates who are experts in probability statistics,' I suggested. Puzzlement creased the inspector's face. 'And check with Sergeant Figueroa to see if your interests are related to his in any way. Silo thinking can be a problem in large organisations.'

# CHAPTER 22

I got back to the house at two o'clock, hungry and drained after the morning at the geysers and then matching wits with Arturo. I flopped down at the table.

'You were a while, Cliff. I had to take the empanadas out of the oven so that they didn't burn. What did Figueroa want?'

'Just following up some points about Lepan. Sorry, you did ask. I think he got me to call by more on behalf of his PDI colleague from Santiago, Arturo, you know, the narcotics squad inspector. The one with the drug smuggling theory. He took me through the list of people on our tour again. I said I wasn't sure about you.'

'Cliff, that's not funny. You always need to watch what you say to the police.'

'Sorry, just joking. Arturo was getting under my skin, so I suggested he concentrate on the Chileans rather than pick on us foreigners. The seven of them.'

'Seven? There were only five on the tour.'

'You are another one overlooking the invisible people, the ones taken for granted because they're workers. We also had a guide and driver with us,' I reminded her.

'You're not suggesting Marisela is involved with drugs?'

'Not at all. I'm not so sure about Jorge Soto. Anyway, that's

Arturo's job, not ours. Lepan visited Easter Island before our tour, keynote speaker at a conference on cultural tourism. Do you know anything about that conference?' I wanted to fill the gap in what I knew about the Frenchman's time in Chile.

'I saw the call for papers; they were trying to tie it in with the TADSAI conference in Santiago to attract more participants. Cultural tourism is not my thing but I considered going. A good excuse to visit Easter Island. Sounds a fascinating place, all those statues. The dates didn't fit and my travel budget was already stretched. I've still got the information somewhere. Why the interest? Didn't we agree to put Lepan behind us. You promised.'

'Blame Arturo, he brought Lepan's name up again. And I won't look into it on company time. Now, how about those empanadas?'

'Did someone say empanadas?' Lucas came into the kitchen. I hadn't heard the ute pull up.

Maria Paz sighed. 'A project leader's work is never done. I will put some more in to reheat. Where are Ramón and Miguel?'

'They lost one of the drones and were still hunting for it so I caught a ride with the tour bus back into town.' He pulled up a chair. 'What have you been up to, Cliff?'

'Cliff's been interrogated by the cops,' Maria Paz said deadpan.

'Seriously?'

'No, just a friendly chat with Miguel's dad,' I said. 'He's keeping his ear to the ground about Mundial Mining. Ximena's protest is getting them worried. Then a talk with a narcotics cop who thinks Lepan was involved with drug trafficking and one of our tour party was an accomplice.'

'Far out. Who?'

'Pure speculation, no names, no evidence at all. I told him to stop picking on us foreigners and concentrate on his compatriots.'

'Careful, Cliff, they would be my compatriots as well. Whose names did he have?

'Hang on, I've still got all that tour stuff on my laptop. Grab an empanada and I will get it.'

'Here you are Lucas. *Piño* is all that's left.' Maria Paz set down two empanadas in front of him.

'Super, they're my favourites.' He munched into one. 'Meaty.' Took another bite. 'Could do with more olives.'

'Right, here's the list: Castro, Jaime; Hernandez, Maria Eugenia; Morales Espinoza, Luis; Rojas, Ana; Sepulveda, Antonio. But also, as I pointed out to the good inspector, Marisela is Chilean, so too was the driver, Jorge Soto. That makes seven Chileans who might have had some connection to Lepan.'

'Technically seven, but one of them was originally a foreigner like you, Cliff. Ana Rojas is from somewhere in Asia—Indonesia, Malaysia or the Philippines, I can't remember. She met and married Fernando when they were studying tourism at James Cook Uni in Australia. She must have been living here for the best part of twenty years and is a Chilean citizen. She takes Fernando's name, Rojas; never includes her Asian name, whatever that is. I guess that's to fit in more easily.'

A little bell tinkled at the back of my mind. I didn't recognise right away what it was telling me. 'Where did you meet her?'

'I got to know them when I was doing my research in Patagonia. Ana teaches at the Coyhaique campus of UACh. Fernando is a researcher with CIEP, that Patagonian research place. He's from down that way originally. They're good guys; your cop friend can count them out. I don't know the other four.'

'I remember Ana, she's nice,' Maria Paz said. 'She was the one who came across Rico first. She was consoling him when I got there. You could tell she was good around kids, the way she calmed him down.'

'My money's on Jorge Soto as the cocaine accomplice,' I said. 'If Lepan was involved with drugs, I reckon Soto was too. He's hiding, running scared.'

'Cliff, that's a substantial if,' Lucas protested, coming to the defence of a compatriot he had never met.

'That's it, you guys.' Maria Paz handed us a coffee. 'We are back on company time. No more drugs, no more Lepan. What have you got lined up for this afternoon, Lucas?'

'Cliff and I have some meetings in town to tie up some visitor management issues with three of the tour operators.'

'OK. I've got more GPS data to process, so I will see you later.'

•••

Lucas did most of the talking with the operators. He encouraged them to stagger their arrival times to reduce congestion and enhance the visitors' experience. Were there any other attractions, so-called 'honey pots', that could be developed to divert some of the demand elsewhere? It was tough going. Competition, not cooperation, was where they fitted on the coopetition spectrum.

When we got back, I retired to my room and immediately opened my laptop to follow up Arturo's mention of Lepan's visit to Easter Island. I got a couple of hits for the cultural tourism conference, including the full programme. Sure enough, it listed Lepan as the keynote speaker. His topic: 'Culture brokers or culture breakers: a longitudinal perspective.' A forced title. I read the abstract. An overview of how intermediaries—the culture brokers—in indigenous tourism destinations had progressively shaped the portrayal of native peoples to such an extent that it no longer depicted their reality, if indeed it ever had. The way they were portrayed corresponded to what the visitors had been conditioned to see—primitive people in picturesque surroundings. Drawing on a selection of cases he had studied throughout his long career, including a very early one from Borneo, he would demonstrate that the intermediaries were in effect culture breakers perpetuating myths. I had no doubt that he was referring to his/ Zu's paper on longhouses.

I ran my eye down the other papers and presenters. Four or five dealing with the host destination, a sprinkling of papers from throughout the Pacific, a couple examining Māori tourism businesses in Rotorua and on the East Coast, a session on cultural tourism in the Amazon, and another larger session devoted to more examples of cultural tourism in Chile. I almost missed her name in this last group: 'Acculturation of Mapuche traditions: asset or abuse,' Ana Rojas (UACh, Coyhaique).

My mind raced. What did I have? Ana, a Malaysian, had been at a conference on Easter Island where Lepan had delivered a keynote address featuring Zu's longhouse research. Ana, a Malaysian, had been on our tour and the first on the scene to console Rico near where Lepan had died. Ana, a Malaysian, who had been overlooked throughout as one of the invisible group of Chileans. I had pegged her as a comforter of small boys, nothing more. All my attention, and seemingly Figueroa's and Arturo's, had been on the international members of the tour group. I double-checked the list of presenters giving papers on Easter Island; Ana was the only person other than Lepan who had been to that conference and taken our tour.

I started looking through my photos for the group shot that Carlos had taken at the Tropic of Capricorn, the only one I had with Ana in it.

Maria Paz knocked on my door and came in carrying her open laptop. 'Cliff, we need to talk,' she said. She perched on the bed.

'What's up?' Our bedrooms were private spaces, not places for discussing project business.

'Look at this.' She pointed to a map with a dotted line plotted on it. It was not one of the detailed maps of our four study sites that I was familiar with. This one one covered a much larger area of the Salar de Atacama. The map showed a line from San Pedro

to the Valle de la Luna, out on to the salar and back towards San
Pedro.

'What's this?'

'A plot of where our ute went today, where Ramón and Miguel
have been.'

'Where did that come from?' I said, intrigued.

'You've probably gathered that Ramón's been seeing a bit of
Ximena lately, mainly in the evenings. I thought it was personal
and didn't say anything. Seeing how he reacted to the protest on
Friday, I was worried he might be getting involved in something
more. So, this morning I dropped a tracking device in the ute,
not one of the loggers we've been using for the project, but a bug
with a larger range which I brought along *por si las moscas*.'

'You did what?'

'Tracked the ute. I was worried that whatever Ramón was up
to would impact the project. He had Miguel with him too and
we don't need any trouble with his dad. Then Lucas comes back
at lunch time with this story that they were delayed because they
were hunting for a lost drone. So, while you two were out this
afternoon I've been keeping an eye on them and this is the result,'
she said, pointing to the map. At that moment the unmistakeable
rumble of the ute signalled Ramón's return. 'I'm not sure how to
handle this, Cliff.'

'Leave it to me.'

As we left the bedroom Lucas was coming out of the bathroom.
'Had a good rest, Cliff?' He gave me a wink that I ignored.

Ramón entered with his two drones.

'Hi, Ramón. I see you found it,' I said.

'What?'

'Your drone. Lucas said you lost one.'

'Oh, that. Yeah. Miguel was operating up at the top of the
ridge this morning, got the controls wrong and managed to send
my best drone over the back, way off the track, down amongst

199

all those rocks. I shouldn't have let him have a go, the controls are slightly different to the one he's been using but he persisted, and I relented. We hunted high and low all afternoon before we found it. I've dropped him home. I'm pretty sure the drone is OK.' Ramón held up the one in his right hand. 'I want to check it and make sure we haven't lost any video before I grab a quick shower. Ximena's coming by to pick me up at seven, so I won't be eating out with you tonight.' With that, he disappeared into his room. He normally worked at the dining room table.

Maria Paz looked at me as if to say, now what? We did not want to retreat into my room in front of Lucas nor bring him into the discussion about what Ramón and Miguel might have been up to during the afternoon. He solved that problem for us.

'I won't be joining you either. Ramón's not the only one with a lady friend in town.' He grinned and opened the front door. 'Don't wait up for me.'

'What's going on, Cliff? Ramón has just lied to us. We know he was out on the salar this afternoon, not searching for his missing drone.'

'Let's wait and see. Do you have another one of those trackers?'

'I do. Why?' I told her what I had in mind.

While we waited, we had a coffee and studied the maps of tourist movements she had been working on. We had collected a wealth of detailed information about how tourists behave at natural attractions.

When Ximena turned up in her SUV shortly after seven, I stepped out to speak to her. Ramón arranged his long frame in the passenger seat and carefully placed his laptop between his legs. The pair were in a hurry to be off.

'Evening, Ximena. I've been wondering what we might do to thank all those who have been so helpful with our project, you know, CONAF, Sernatur, your community groups, some of the tour operators. What do you suggest?'

'Evening, Cliff. I'm not sure that's necessary,' she said in a cool tone.

'We should show our appreciation in some way, give some feedback. It would be a good thing to do after all they have done for us. They've gone out of their way to be helpful.'

'Let me think about it.'

'Have a good time, you two,' Maria Paz said and rapped on the door.

'Thanks, Maria Paz, we will,' Ximena said. She put the Suzuki into gear and sped off into the night.

'No problems?' I asked.

'No, provided the magnet holds on these bumpy roads we will be able to keep tabs on where they go all night.'

# CHAPTER 23

Back inside, Maria Paz tapped on her touchpad a couple of times and said, 'Look, it's working OK. That's them.' She pointed to a moving dot on the screen. 'I wonder where they are going.'

'Can you bring up that trace again of where Ramón and Miguel went?'

'I spent quite a bit of time trying to figure it out this afternoon but no luck so far. Looks as though they followed the B-241 down the western side of the salar, turned off the road and drove in towards the salar. But there's nothing there that I can see. Even on the satellite image there's nothing but barren salt flat. Here, you have a go.'

I peered at the map and image but could not make out anything either. Why were Ramón and Miguel so interested in this desolate piece of salar? And why had they lied about it? I zoomed in and out on the satellite image trying for a better perspective but soon lost track of whereabouts I was on the salar. It all looked the same, no distinguishing features anywhere.

'What's that there?' Maria Paz pointed to some large white and bluish rectangles. 'They must be man-made.'

'That's the evaporation ponds where they get the lithium from. They're right at the other end of the salar though, not where

Ramón stopped. Damn, I've lost where Ramón and Miguel were. Here, you take over, I've never got the hang of using a touchpad. I need a mouse.'

Maria Paz circled round the evaporation ponds, amazed at their extent. 'So, this is what Ximena is against. They must take up huge amounts of water. I can see now why she doesn't want any more and why she's anti Mundial.'

'That's it.'

'What?' She looked up at me.

'That's where Ramón and Miguel went. To the site where Mundial hope to get a lithium mining licence. I bet they were using the drones to collect some evidence. Ximena said the site Mundial were after was closer to San Pedro. That's what they were doing this afternoon.'

'But they would be seen out there, it's all flat, nowhere to hide and watch from.'

'Maybe nobody from Mundial was there this afternoon. Or they could use the drones from such a distance that they had enough time to get away when they were spotted. I'm sure that's what they were up to. Mundial shouldn't be doing anything before being granted an exploration permit. If Ximena can show they were already doing some exploratory work on the salar that would be damning evidence if she took Mundial to court. She's used Ramón and Miguel to film that evidence from the drones.'

'Let's check where Ximena and Ramón are heading now.' Another few taps on the touchpad and up came the map with the little flashing light. 'That's funny, it looks like they're heading for the geysers. What would they be doing up at El Tatio at this time of day?'

'No, they're turning off.' We followed the light until it appeared to leave the road and stop in the middle of nowhere.

'What could they be doing out in the desert? Funny place for a date,' Maria Paz said.

'And you don't usually take your laptop with you.'

'If you're right about Ramón videoing whatever Mundial were doing, they must have gone to show it to someone. Must be important to rush away tonight. But who would live way out there?'

'Atacameños… some other protestors…' I drummed my fingers on the table.

'But that's nowhere near the salar.'

'Or a protestor married to an Atacameña, someone who's lying low. Jorge Soto. Has to be.'

'Jorge who?'

'Jorge Soto, our bus driver, the invisible Chilean I mentioned earlier. He's Ximena's uncle. He was involved in that demonstration at El Tatio in 2009. According to Carlos, he's a stirrer, protests a lot. Remember, he left Marisela's company the day after Lepan died and supposedly moved to Santiago. Hasn't been seen around San Pedro since.'

'What would they want with him now?'

'To show him the video Ramón shot today.'

'Ramón and Miguel, actually. Why would Ramón have taken Miguel with him? That would be a bit of a risk.'

'Or insurance,' I said. 'Having Miguel with him might have been useful if they had run up against the carabineros at some stage. He or Ximena must have converted him to their cause.'

'What do we do now? Confront Ramón? How could he lie to us like that?' Maria Paz stamped her foot in a rare display of anger. 'If he must do something, he could have at least waited a few more days and we would have finished all our fieldwork. Now he could mess everything up.'

'Well, he hasn't done anything illegal… yet. I don't know what he and Ximena are up to with Jorge—if that is who they have gone to see—but Ramón isn't on company time this evening. Ximena did warn us she would be busy protesting. To be fair, she's opened a lot of doors for us on the project.'

'Still, I feel let down. I trusted Ramón, he lied about this afternoon. And if Miguel's dad finds out, there's sure to be trouble.'

We sat back, each trying to work through what might be going on between Ramón, Ximena and her uncle. Ramón and Ximena might have been taking something to Jorge. Conversely, they might have been going to get something from him. They would not need a laptop for that. Unless what was on the laptop would persuade Jorge to give them what they were after. What Ximena needed to fight Mundial was evidence—which she maybe had now—and money. She needed money to take Mundial to court. Would Jorge have that sort of money? Unlikely; he had just been a tour coach driver and had not even been doing that for the past four months.

Maria Paz made the connection before I did, though not in the way she intended.

'You don't suppose there's a link between Mundial and drugs do you? From what you say, Mundial is a shady outfit. Maybe Ximena is so anti Mundial because she has proof they're running drugs as well as proposing to mine lithium.'

'No, but you're on to something. Ximena needs money to fight Mundial. There's not much ready money to be made around here… except in drugs.' Deep Throat's words came back to me: 'Follow the money.' Figueroa and Arturo had raised the issue of where Lepan got his money from and how he funded his activism. Now I was convinced—drug money.

'You can't mean Ximena is involved in drug trafficking. That would be against all the principles she seems to stand for. She's sticking up for her people all the time.'

'Ximena, not directly, no. I'm not so sure about Jorge Soto. If Arturo is right about Lepan having contacts in Colombia who organise bringing drugs into Chile, he would have needed local contacts to handle deliveries. He's known Jorge since at least 2009 when they were both arrested at El Tatio.'

'But Lepan ignored him on the tour.'

'Or gave a good impression of ignoring him. But they were close, physically close. Lepan was sitting right up front alongside him…And Jorge could easily have passed something to Lepan when people were dozing on the way out to the geysers. Or he could have left it under his seat for Lepan to reach down and pick up. That's it. Remember, Lepan's big camera bag wasn't there when we found him. What if it wasn't missing? What if he had just delivered it full of drugs to a buyer at the geysers? That must be it.' My imagination was in overdrive. My pulse raced. 'Lepan arranges the deal in Colombia. The drugs make their way down through Peru and Bolivia. As a coach tour driver Jorge is well placed to have connections with other drivers, including some who take tours to and from Bolivia. In San Pedro he hands the drugs over to Lepan who makes the final contact with the buyer or distributor.'

'But the only other ones at the geysers were those in the Mundial ute,' Maria Paz pointed out.

'Exactly. No one was around because the tourist convoy was deliberately held up. Not to kill Lepan but to make the final handover easier for him.'

'But he wouldn't have been coming back here time and again to make future deliveries,' she argued.

'No, he would have been organising a new operation, a trial run to make sure it would work. Lepan was the brains behind it, he had to show he could arrange deliveries and that he could be trusted.'

'But then he died.'

'Or was killed once the delivery was made. The others were the ones who couldn't be trusted.'

'And they were Mundial's men?'

'Maybe.' I stood and paced around the table. 'Or, more likely, Mundial employees in it for themselves or working for a dealer.

Mundial wouldn't send men in company trucks if they were involved. Too obvious. However, Mundial's trucks and utes would be all over the Atacama and other parts of Chile if the company has a mining licence. That would make an ideal distribution network. Somebody is thinking ahead, Maria Paz.'

'But if Lepan is dead, who would arrange future deliveries? If this was a new operation, it doesn't make sense that those who had just received the drugs would kill him.'

'You're right, it doesn't. Unless Lepan didn't deliver what he should have. Or he was double crossed by the ute guys, drug traffickers who didn't want any competitors and duped Lepan into believing he was dealing with a new gang, they seized his drugs, then pushed him in the hot pool. Drug dealers aren't known for their scruples.'

Maria Paz reminded me that we had now accepted that Rico had bumped into Lepan.

'Maybe that photo doesn't tell us everything. Jorge looked distraught on the way back from the geysers. At the time it seemed a natural enough reaction to seeing the empty seat—Lepan had been sitting alongside him that morning and the day before. While everyone else thought Lepan had tripped, Jorge feared something had gone badly wrong. Maybe he did go to Santiago and has come back recently, or he was lying low all this time with his wife's folks out where Ramón and Ximena are now.'

'Why would Lepan get involved with drugs?'

'Some misguided sense of altruism—he used drug money to support indigenous people in different parts of the world, including the Atacameños. In his mind he was using bad money to do good. Makes sense in a way. Perhaps he wasn't so despicable after all.'

'And that's what Ximena is trying to reactivate, a drug running operation?'

'She's a determined young lady. I wouldn't put it past her to have a go if that was the only way she could find the funds to take on Mundial.'

'But surely Jorge knows the risks after what happened in April. And who would be supplying him with the drugs?'

I sat. Maria Paz's objections were sapping my confidence in my newly developed theory. 'I don't know. He could have held back some of what he should have passed on to Lepan. That might also explain why someone searched his hotel room that morning. They were expecting more and ransacked his room looking for any cocaine he might have hidden there.'

'What do we do now? Anything to do with drugs is trouble. What Ramón and Ximena are getting into is dangerous. You don't suppose Lucas and Miguel are also involved? I don't want anyone on our team hurt.'

'Well, Ramón had Miguel with him this afternoon, so Miguel at least knows about videoing Mundial, whatever they were doing on the salar. Miguel's a good guy, perhaps a bit naïve. Lucas, I doubt he's involved. He's a realist, got his head screwed on. What Ximena and Ramón might be trying is driven by idealism, not common sense. Ramón thought it would be a bit of an adventure flying drones in the Amazon for Lepan. Now he's doing it on the salar for Ximena. Getting involved with drugs is another step again. Those two could be in real danger.'

'Look, they're moving again. They seem to be coming back to San Pedro.' She pointed to the screen.

We watched the blinking light move along the road for another twenty minutes. 'They're turning off the road. Right in the middle of nowhere.' The light soon stopped moving.

'Maybe they've gone to pick up drugs. Jorge wouldn't have kept them where he is staying,' I said.

Half an hour later, still no movement. We hadn't spoken much and hadn't eaten anything except for a few biscuits. Worry lines wrinkled Maria Paz's face. I was also becoming concerned.

'Hi, guys. I told you there was no need to wait up for me.' Lucas was back.

'Grab a chair, Lucas, something has come up.'

'Hang on, let me check my texts first. One came in earlier when I was otherwise engaged.' Lucas reached into his pocket and pulled out his phone. He read the text, stared at his phone.

'Bad news?'

'It's Ramón. The text just says "help".'

# CHAPTER 24

'It just says "help", Lucas?'

'That's all, nothing else. Just "help".'

'No earlier messages?'

'Not a word. I'm texting him back. I don't even know where he is, let alone why he needs help.' He tapped his thumbs faster than the heels of a flamenco dancer.

'We have a fairly good idea where he is but not what he's doing. Have a look at this.' I showed him the trace of Ximena's Suzuki.

'You've been tracking her movements? How? Why?'

We gave him a rundown.

'What do you know about this, Lucas?' Maria Paz asked.

'Well…er… OK… I knew what Ramón and Miguel were up to this afternoon, videoing Mundial's mining site, that is. But nothing about drugs. You know me, Cliff, I wouldn't have anything to do with drugs.'

'We will discuss that later,' she said. 'Right now, what are we going to do, Cliff?'

'If we know where they are we need to go help them. C'mon,' Lucas said. He picked up the keys to the ute from the bowl on the kitchen bench.

'You stay here, Maria Paz,' I said. 'This could be dangerous.'

'No, Cliff, I'm coming. They might have had an accident. I'm the only one who knows how to use the tracker. They're part of my team. Let's go.'

We piled into the ute, Lucas at the wheel, Maria Paz beside him with her laptop.

'Take the road to the geysers, Lucas.'

He floored the accelerator.

'Any movement, Maria Paz?' I asked.

'None. What are they up to? I hope they haven't had an accident. Maybe someone's tried to run them off the road like they did to us.'

That's what came immediately to mind, but I didn't want to alarm her. 'They're probably waiting for somebody or something.'

'Or they're being held,' Lucas said.

We fell silent as we sped through the night. The stars were out; there's not much cloud cover in the desert.

'Watch for the turnoff for the B-159, Lucas. A gravel road, coming up shortly on our left... That's it. About ten ks from here... Start slowing down, another k or so to where they turned off the road.'

'We need to be careful from here,' I said. 'We don't know what's going on.'

'Look, there's a track coming up on our right,' Maria Paz said. 'That must be where they turned off.'

'I see it,' Lucas said. 'I'll pull over by that patch of scrub, it will give us a bit of cover. If I turn in they will see our lights and I'm not going down there with no lights. We'll have to carry on by foot. It can't be far.'

'No more than a few hundred metres, going by the trace,' Maria Paz said.

'Maria Paz, you stay here and keep monitoring with the laptop.' My real concern was keeping her out of harm's way.

'But I'm coming with you, I'm—'

'Cliff's right. You need to stay here.' Lucas checked his phone again, nothing more from Ramón. The two of us got out. He reached into the toolbox on the tray of the ute and handed me a hammer. He armed himself with a heavy wrench.

'Be careful. Maybe we should wait and call the carabineros,' she said.

'Too late for that,' I said.

Lucas and I crossed the road and followed the track. The pebbles and broken rock crunched under our feet. We looked at each other, realised we were amateurs and carried on paralleling the track fifteen metres to the left where it was sandy and we made little noise. The starlight was enough to see where we were going. It was also enough for somebody to see us. About four hundred metres in we could make out the outline of a small building. We crouched and crept forward. The building was an old adobe house, rundown and abandoned. A light came from one of the windows. Ximena's SUV was parked out front. They had not been in an accident. Alongside it was a ute. Had they come here voluntarily or were they forced to come? We moved closer. It was one of Mundial's utes. Not a good sign. I looked at Lucas, he nodded, and we crept to the side of the house. Through the broken window we could hear what was happening inside.

'I'll ask you just once more, you little bitch, where is the cocaine your uncle gave you?' Slap, slap.

'I keep telling you, we don't have any cocaine. We were just meeting my uncle. I wanted him to meet my new boyfriend.' Slap, slap.

'As if Jorge Soto would approve of this black bastard. Maybe he knows where the cocaine is. Your turn, Otto.'

'Let's see if his Portuguese is better than his Spanish.' Otto let out a string of louder and louder curses in a heavy nasal Portuguese, interspersed with a series of heavy thumps. Must be Brazilian. Ramón did not utter a word.

'Stop, stop. Stop hitting him,' Ximena cried. 'OK, OK. We didn't just go to see Jorge so he could meet Ramón.'

'Then, why?'

'To show him the video.'

'What video?'

'The video we shot this afternoon.'

'So, it was you two out on the salar. Did you hear that, Otto? These are the two that have been sticking their nose into business that doesn't concern them. You're the bitch who led the protest on Friday, aren't you?'

'Wait till the boss hears that, Luiz. What's keeping him?'

'He's coming from Calama. He shouldn't be long. How do we know you two are telling the truth? Show us the video.'

'It's in the Suzuki. On the laptop,' Ximena said.

'Go and get it, Otto. I can look after these two.'

'Where is it?' Otto demanded.

'Under the passenger's seat.'

The front door creaked open. I risked a quick look through the window. The light was coming from a large torch sitting on the table. Ximena and Ramón were tied to chairs on either side of the table. I couldn't see Ximena's face; her hair was dishevelled. Ramón's head hung low, blood streaming from his nose. The slaps and thumps we had heard would not have been the first. Standing between the two of them, his back towards me, was a beefy thug in a purple uniform, a holstered pistol by his side. I ducked and nudged Lucas. He stood and peeked. Otto returned with the laptop.

'Password locked, I see. C'mon, you two, we haven't got all night.' Thump, thump. 'No, still not speaking. We'll try this whore.' Slap, slap. 'No?' Thump, thump.

'Give it to them, Ramón.'

'What's the password, Ramón?' Thump, thump, thump.

'Give it to them, Ramón.'

'asteriskCoritibaelevenasterisk'

'That's better. He can talk, after all. A football fan, eh. Pity about that team, no firepower upfront, the defence leaks goals. Now, let's see.' Luiz's fat fingers circled the touchpad, but the screen stayed blank. He tapped it, each time more heavily. 'Goddamn, Otto, why didn't you bring the mouse as well.'

'Mouse?'

'You can't be that thick. That little black oblong thingy you use with a computer, about this big.' Palm up, he curled his fingers.

'But I never use a computer.'

'Right, requires a minimum of brains. Anything else under the seat?'

'I didn't see anything; it was dark.'

'Jesus wept... I'm no good with these touchpads. C'mon, you little whore, show us the video.'

'It's his computer, he has to do it. His system's different to mine.'

'OK Black Boy, show us the video.'

'I can't with my hands tied. I'll need both hands.'

'Otto, untie his hands but keep a close eye on him. I'm warning you, boy, don't try any tricks. Just show us the video.'

'All right, all right. It takes a minute or two for the program to warm up.'

I peeked again. Otto was a huge brute too, fat rather than muscled. He also wore a purple uniform and a side arm. Mundial security, the two of them. Otto had untied Ramón's hands and stepped back. Luiz was bent over, concentrating on the screen. Lucas inched up and peered through the window alongside me.

'Look at this, Otto. Little missy here and Black Boy have been filming out on the salar.'

'Let me see.' He moved in and peered over Ramón's shoulder at the aerial view of the Mundial site.

Lucas elbowed me gently. This was our chance. Adrenaline

flowing, we crept round to the front door. Otto had left it open while carrying the laptop in both hands. Lucas led the charge. In he rushed, wielding the wrench. Luiz looked up as he heard the noise. Lucas brought the wrench down squarely on his skull and Luiz slumped onto the laptop.

I was not as fast nor as agile. I raised the hammer to strike Otto … tripped on a loose floorboard and fell to the ground. Moving quickly for his bulk, Otto spun round, booted me in the ribs, reached for his pistol. Still bound around his body to the chair, Ramón sprang to his feet and cartwheeled his long limbs in a rapid arc, kicking Otto in the head. The Mundial thug collapsed in a heap on the floor beside me.

'Capoeira,' Ramón said.

For good measure, Lucas wielded the wrench once more. The two captors were out for the count. Not bad for a bunch of amateurs. Lucas stripped both of their handguns and freed Ramón from his remaining ropes. I got to my feet and gave a satisfying kick to Otto's inert body. My ribs hurt like hell as I bent over to untie Ximena. Lucas and Ramón tied the hands of Otto and Luiz

'Let's get out of here,' Ximena cried. 'My keys are in Luiz's pocket.'

Lucas grabbed the keys, Ramón picked up the laptop, Ximena the torch, and we rushed out the door. Into a blaze of light. We had been so focused on freeing Ximena and Ramón that we had not heard the other vehicle arrive. We were blinded by the full glare of the spotlight on the cab of a ute.

'Nobody moves,' shouted the driver who got out from behind the wheel brandishing a pistol. 'Search them, Franco. Then see what's happened to Luiz and Otto.'

Franco menaced us with his revolver as he patted us down with his free hand. 'Just the guns, boss.' Lucas and Ramón had dropped the guns taken from Luiz and Otto to the ground rather than try any heroics. This was not the OK Corral. Taking the torch from

Ximena, Franco edged to the door and looked inside. 'Both of them are tied up boss. They're not moving.'

'How fucking useless can they be. Couldn't even deal with a couple of amateurs.'

'Four of them actually.'

'I can count, dammit. Where's that Spanish broad we've seen with this lot?'

'You heard the man, speak up,' Franco said, poking Ximena with his gun. Silence. 'Maybe this old fellow knows, I've seen him with her a lot.' With that, he prodded me in the ribs, right where Otto's boot had landed. I doubled over in pain. 'Like that, do you?' he sneered and prodded me again.

'She's gone to fetch the cops,' I bluffed. Anything to spare my ribs. 'They will be here soon.'

'He's bluffing, boss.'

'Maybe, maybe not. She must know what this lot are up to and where they are. Hang on, where did those two come from? Luiz only mentioned he was following the SUV with the Indian and the Black, not the old guy and his mate. How did they get here?'

Franco targeted my ribs again to get an answer for his boss.

'We walked in.'

'Funny man, huh.' Franco poked me again.

'Our colleague dropped us off, then headed for San Pedro. There's no coverage here to make a call.'

'He's right boss. We've had that problem here before.'

'Another of Luiz's bright ideas. Fuck it. We can't stand around here all night. Check Otto and Luiz while I cover this lot.'

Franco darted inside.

'They're both out cold,' he reported back.

'We can't leave them here. You two, carry them out,' the boss said to Ramón and Lucas.

They came out grunting and heaving. Lucas held Luiz by his feet, Ramón had him by the armpits. With a lot of effort, they bundled him into Luiz's ute. Otto proved even more of a dead weight. They eventually humped him onto the tray of the ute.

'Now what, boss? What are we going to do with these four?'

'We've got to move. No time to tie them all up. Take your shoes off, all of you.' We did as we were told. Franco threw them into the darkness. 'Keys, who's got the keys to the Suzuki?' Lucas tossed them onto the ground. Franco picked them up and for added insurance hammered the electronics on the dashboard with the butt of his gun.

'Let's go. You take Luiz's ute.' As soon as Franco turned the ute around the boss got back into his. After a final admonition for us not to move, they took off along the track to the road. With the glare of the spotlight in our faces, we had not even caught a glimpse of the boss.

'Is everyone OK?' Lucas asked. Ximena rubbed her wrists, Ramón wiped his sleeve across his nose, both said they were OK. My ribs were giving me hell and I was shaking all over but said I was all right.

'What now?' Ximena asked.

Shots came from the direction of the road before anyone could answer.

'The Seventh Cavalry to our rescue,' I said and collapsed on the ground. The last thing I remember before passing out was Ximena saying, 'Just the drones.'

I must have been out for only a few minutes before the sound of sirens, blazing headlights and flashing blue lights brought me to my senses. It wasn't the Seventh Cavalry but the carabineros from Calama. We were soon surrounded by heavily armed policemen. The officer in charge wanted to know if there was anyone else in the building and if anyone was hurt. Lucas, who was in the best shape, said there wasn't but the rest of us needed medical attention.

A slight figure slipped past the carabineros. Maria Paz rushed over and hugged me.

'Cliff, are you all right? I was terrified when I heard the shooting, I dreaded to think what they might have done to you all if they were prepared to shoot at the carabineros.'

'Go easy on my ribs,' I groaned. 'I think I will pull through.'

'Sorry, sorry.' She stopped hugging me and gently propped me up against the wall.

'What happened?'

Instead of staying put, Maria Paz had driven further along the road until she got some cell phone coverage, called Miguel and explained we might be in danger. He woke his father who contacted his colleagues in Calama. She returned to keep watch from where she had been parked and soon after the ute turned down the track we had taken. She waited anxiously and did not know what to do when she saw the lights of two utes coming rapidly back up the track. They had just about reached the road when the carabineros arrived and blocked off the track. The leading ute swerved to evade the police vehicles and got stuck in the sand. Franco leapt out, started firing and was wounded in the exchange with the carabineros. His boss in the second ute realised he stood little chance of fleeing, stopped and waited for the carabineros to arrest him. When the shooting ceased, Maria Paz rushed over to the carabineros and urged them to go and see that we were all right.

'I'm so relieved to see you are all alive,' she said.

The carabinero who had been applying first aid to Ximena and Ramón came and checked me over.

'Bruised ribs,' he said. 'We will need to take you and your friends to the hospital in Calama for a proper examination and X-ray. Ambulances are on their way.'

'And we will need to take a statement from you later,' said the officer in charge who leaned in over his colleague who was taping me up. 'We will take yours now, ma'am,' he said to Maria Paz.

'But I need to stay with my colleague. Can't you see he's hurt?'

'You will be able to see him tomorrow. Well, later today in fact.'

I looked at my watch. Two in the morning.

'And we need to take yours too,' he said to Lucas who had come over to see how I was doing.

Maria Paz gave me a parting hug.

'My ribs,' I groaned.

# CHAPTER 25

At the hospital they checked me over and gave me some pain killers. I managed a few hours' sleep before being X-rayed mid-morning. I was taken back to my room and given some breakfast while waiting for the results. After the events of the previous night, I could have done with more than a roll, strawberry jam and lukewarm institutional coffee.

Arturo entered without knocking.

'So, Cliff, our paths cross once more. How's the body?' The detective sat on the visitor's chair and crossed his legs. He had not come to enquire about my health.

'Still sore but coming right, thank you, Arturo.'

'Thank *you*, Cliff. Your little hint about working in silos was correct. After our chat I did go and speak with Figueroa. He repeated your theory that Mundial Mining might have been involved in Lepan's death. And there I was believing the good professor was involved in drug trafficking. Was it too much of a stretch of the imagination to think that Mundial were also involved with drugs, that they were Lepan's local contacts, or his competitors?'

Our thoughts coincided.

'Competitors more likely, the drugs kept coming. Yesterday

afternoon we squeezed a couple of our informants in San Pedro and Calama. Two names cropped up: Luiz Moretti and Otto da Silva. Surprise, surprise, they are Brazilians employed as security guards by Mundial. So, yesterday evening my PDI colleagues in Calama tailed them. Moretti and da Silva turned out to be keeping tabs on your colleagues, the Atacameña and Macedo. Unfortunately, at some stage after leaving the place where your erstwhile tour coach driver, Jorge Soto, was staying, they lost the pair. That must have been when Moretti and da Silva forced your colleagues off the road and held them prisoner in that abandoned house. When they lost them, the PDI tail called in the carabineros to patrol the road between Calama and San Pedro.'

So that is how they got to the scene so quickly when Maria Paz alerted Miguel to the danger we might have been in.

'Are you with me so far?'

'I'm all ears, Arturo. I only came into the action towards the end.'

'How did you come to be at that house?'

'Dr Casals put a tracker in Ximena's Suzuki. The wonders of technology. Much more effective than a tail.'

'It would appear so. Why did she do that?'

I shifted in bed, trying to find a more comfortable position for my ribs.

'Maria Paz was concerned that members of our team were getting mixed up in the protest against Mundial's lithium mining project. Ramón had used one of his drones to video the site where they are proposing to mine. He and Ximena appear to have developed a close relationship—she has been facilitating our research as well as protesting Mundial's mining plans.'

'What did that have to do with Moretti and da Silva?'

'Like you said, they worked as security guards for Mundial.'

'So, Cliff, you are saying Moretti and da Silva followed and abducted Ramón and Ximena because they breached Mundial's security. That it had nothing to do with drugs?'

'What I saw was two guards in Mundial uniforms forcing Ramón to show them the video he had taken that afternoon.'

'Nothing more?'

'Not that I saw.'

'Wouldn't you say that was an extreme reaction by Moretti and da Silva?'

'I still haven't seen the video, I don't know what's on it, or how compromising it is.' I could only hope that the video was damning and that was why Ximena and Ramón had gone to see Jorge. 'Have you?' He did not answer but gave me a long hard look. I was right, the video exposed Mundial's activities on the salar. I met his eye. 'The guards were beating up Ramón and Ximena so they must have been desperate to lay their hands on the video. Lucas and I seized our chance while they were engrossed in it and charged in to rescue our colleagues.'

'Your loyalty is admirable, but taking on Moretti and da Silva was rather reckless. You were lucky to get away with it. And then?'

'We started to flee but were stopped by the other Mundial security men who had just driven up.'

'You knew they were Mundial?'

'The one called Franco who searched us was wearing a Mundial uniform.'

'And the other one?'

'I couldn't see him because he was behind the spotlight. The others called him 'boss' so I assume he was also with Mundial.'

'As it happens, he was.' Arturo leaned forward in his chair. 'So, to be clear, Cliff, you're sure last night's events were solely about members of Mundial Mining's security carrying out their company duties, not because they were moonlighting as muscle for a drug ring.'

'That's a fair summary.'

'And where does Jorge Soto fit into all of this? You implied yesterday that he might be one of the Chileans involved with drugs and Lepan.'

I sat up as straight as my ribs would allow, convinced they were broken. 'I was wrong about the drugs connection. It's all to do with the drones. As I'm sure Figueroa can tell you, Jorge Soto is an inveterate protestor. He and Lepan were involved in a protest at the geysers in 2009. He's Ximena's uncle. They went to show him the video, to show the evidence that Mundial had already been doing some exploratory work on the salar. The same video Moretti and da Silva were so desperate to lay their hands on.'

'That's all?' Doubt showed in his eyes. 'Nothing to add, Cliff?'

'That's all. Tell me about the shooting.'

'Franco in the lead ute panicked, tried to swerve around the police vehicles blocking the drive and started shooting. The carabineros shot out his tires and wounded him. He will survive. We don't know all the charges yet. The prosecutor will want to question him once he recovers some more. Last I heard he was having difficulty explaining what two bound Mundial security officers were doing in his ute. I don't think those two will be pressing any assault charges, so no worries there for you.'

'And the other driver? The one Franco called the boss.'

'Silveira, he was sharp enough to let Franco go first. He saw little chance of evasion and came quietly. Said he didn't know what Moretti, da Silva and Franco were up to. We're still working on him. He strikes me as the brains, the others were the muscle.' He put his notebook in his jacket pocket. 'That's all for now, I'll let you rest. I understand that you will be wrapping up your research in San Pedro by the end of the week and reporting back to Corfo in Santiago.'

'Correct. I've had enough excitement in the last twenty-four hours to last me for a long time. All I want to do is tidy up some loose ends and write up our research.'

'Right, back to being a researcher while I carry on as an investigator. Your cooperation is much appreciated, Cliff. I can see why Annie enjoys working with you Kiwis. Please let Figueroa know when you are leaving San Pedro.'

# CHAPTER 26

The X-ray showed my ribs were bruised not broken. I was told I would be sore for a few days, given some painkillers to take with me, and discharged. Ramón and Ximena had no fractures either and also left the hospital, probably feeling worse than me. The pair had been questioned at length by Arturo and the prosecutor before being told they were free to go. Keeping us in separate wards had reduced the opportunity for collusion.

The five of us would not fit comfortably in the ute. Maria Paz rented a car and Lucas drove Ramón and Ximena in the ute back to San Pedro later in the afternoon. Ximena's SUV would be towed there later to see if her cousin could repair the damage, an unlikely prospect.

On the way back, Maria Paz said she wanted to have a team meeting that evening to clear the air and make sure we could finish the project on time. I agreed. For me, completing the project was secondary. I wanted to check out my ideas about what had taken place the day before and how that related to Lepan's death.

Back at the house, Ximena, Ramón and I rested up while Maria Paz and Lucas picked up Miguel and bought pizzas and wine. When they returned, Miguel handed round slices of pizza and Lucas served the wine. It was not our usual round-the-table catch-up; those of us who were nursing our wounds got to sit in the armchairs. This also created a more relaxed atmosphere which Maria Paz and I hoped would encourage the whole team to speak more freely.

Maria Paz led off. 'We haven't got long to go on our project. A few things cropped up yesterday which were, to say the least, unexpected. It would be helpful if we shared our experiences so we all know where we are at and can focus on finishing up by Friday. Who would like to go first? … Ximena?'

This was a tactical call I suggested to Maria Paz. I wanted to see what tack Ximena would take and how much she would reveal. Her response was brief, diplomatic and gave nothing away.

'I just want to thank you three again for coming to our rescue,' she said and looked at Maria Paz, Lucas and me in turn. 'You came to help us even though what Ramón and I were doing was no concern of yours. God knows what would have happened if Cliff and Lucas hadn't rushed in when they did or you, Maria Paz, hadn't called the carabineros. You're more than a bunch of academics blindly focused on your research. I see that now. I can't thank you enough.'

'That goes for me too,' Ramón said. 'We weren't upfront with you about what Miguel and I were doing in the afternoon. And I also asked Lucas to lie to you. Sorry about that. But I'm not sorry about what we did,' he said, standing to emphasise his conviction. 'I share Ximena's opposition to Mundial. You would have stopped us if you knew we wanted to video on the salar, that we weren't afraid to confront those Brazilian bastards.'

'How did you get the video?' I asked. 'It's barren out here. Didn't they see you and try and stop you.'

'Of course they did. We planned on that. Ximena had spread the word around town that there would be trouble at Mundial's office in San Pedro on Monday afternoon and they posted all their security guys there. We knew they only had a heavy truck out on the salar site, one they used to transport their equipment. Ximena drove towards the site and Miguel sent up one of my drones as a decoy. They saw it and set off after the intruders. Ximena could easily outrun them in her Suzuki but stayed just far enough in front of them that they believed they could catch her. She headed in the opposite direction to San Pedro, luring the truck away. I was waiting nearby in the ute, drove down onto the salar, sent in my more powerful drone at a safe distance from the site and got the evidence I needed. It didn't take long. As soon as I was in the clear I texted Ximena, she put her foot down and the truck gave up the chase. There was no risk to us or the project.'

Not much.

'Why weren't you able to tell us what was going on later that night?' Maria Paz asked.

'When Luiz and Otto forced us off the road and drew their guns, I just managed to text 'help' before Otto grabbed my phone. I didn't know if you had got my message or not. I had given up all hope until Cliff and Lucas charged in armed only with a hammer and wrench. I couldn't have taken any more from Otto.' He put his hand to his bandaged head and winced.

'That was some cartwheeling capoeira that you did, bro,' Lucas said. 'Impressive.'

'Pure instinct, capoeira's supposed to be non-contact.'

'Whatever, Otto didn't see it coming.'

'OK, that's enough from the fight club,' Maria Paz said. 'Anything else to add, Lucas?'

He looked embarrassed. 'Yeah, I should have been honest with you when I came home by myself on Monday. Sorry. I didn't think Ramón and Miguel would come to any harm out on the salar or that they would compromise the project at all. This is my country too and I'm against lithium mining and Mundial. But not enough to protest directly, I'm ashamed to admit. I'm glad I was able to arrive for dessert, as we say in Spanish, and do my bit.'

Lucas eyed each of us in turn, stroked his beard. What was he about to reveal? Nothing. He grinned and said, 'Can I have the last slice of pepperoni?'

We all laughed. Nice one, Lucas, you're keeping everyone relaxed.

'Miguel, thanks for waking your dad,' Maria Paz said. 'If the carabineros hadn't arrived when they did, those Mundial thugs would have got away. I hope things are OK between you two.'

'Yeah, we're good. Dad got some of the credit for the arrests. I skipped the bit about helping with the drones. He wouldn't be thrilled about that. Can we keep that quiet?'

Thumbs up all around. Miguel sighed audibly. He was optimistic thinking his involvement would not come up as the carabineros continued their investigation.

'Cliff, your thoughts?' Maria Paz said.

All eyes were on me. 'We were extremely lucky to get away with just cuts, bruises and sore ribs. They're still painful but it could have been far worse. I didn't deliver with the hammer but—'

'Brilliant diversion, tripping on the floorboard. Gave me a chance to have a go at Otto,' Ramón said.

'—but I would like a few things cleared up.' I would not be diverted. 'Ximena, you said 'Just the drones.' That implies something else was going on. What was it?' I looked across at her.

She held my gaze. 'Just focus on the video, don't mention anything else to do with the protests against Mundial.'

'Nothing related to drugs?'

'No way. What makes you say that?' she asked with feigned surprise.

'Arturo, the PDI inspector, mentioned they were tailing Luiz and Otto because the pair were suspected of trafficking drugs.'

'What made him think—'

'Arturo, eh. So, now you're on first name terms with the cops,' Ramón interjected.

'Careful, Ramón,' Maria Paz said, 'Cliff is on your side. Continue, Cliff.'

'I had been questioned by the inspector before lunch yesterday in relation to his investigation of a possible connection between a drug ring and Lepan's death. One of Lepan's colleagues in Colombia has been arrested.'

'What did you say to that?' Ximena asked. She seemed unaware Ortiz was in custody.

'I already had a few ideas, some of which I outlined to Miguel's dad.' I summarised the possible connections between the Mundial ute, the convoy delay, Lepan's death, and drug trafficking. 'All of this required a local contact to pass on to Lepan the first lot of cocaine coming overland through Bolivia. It was only later that I figured out who this local contact was and how the transfer was done.'

Ximena had an inkling of what was coming and interrupted me. 'Cliff, remember Miguel is here.'

'Miguel has a right to know. You've involved him already, heavily, with the drones yesterday afternoon.'

Miguel looked at his shoes. Having a cop as a father wasn't always easy.

'But—'

I ignored Ximena's protest. Now to test my theory. 'That local contact was Ximena's uncle, Jorge Soto. Lepan knew Jorge from when they were both protesting at the geysers in 2009.' Ximena's jaw dropped—how did I know that? I did not mention the newspaper article. I wanted to keep her wondering what else I knew. The next bit was conjecture. I watched her closely to see how she reacted. She eyed me back. Old fellow versus young firebrand.

'Jorge transferred the cocaine to Lepan on our bus on the way to the geysers. It was stashed under the front seat which Lepan had commandeered. At the geysers, Lepan was to deliver the cocaine to a Mundial guy who had arrived before us in a ute. I figure they had chosen the geysers thinking that steamy environment might intimidate Lepan. They didn't know he had been there in 2009 and wasn't at all worried. Something went wrong, he handed over the cocaine, never got the money and ended up in the hot pool. Next day, Jorge was gone, fearing for his own safety. I don't believe Ximena knew any of this that afternoon she accompanied us up to the lagunas.'

Ximena nodded. 'I only found out a couple of days afterwards. Uncle Jorge was in danger and needed to lie low. Lepan had told him about Mundial's plans to mine for lithium. A few weeks later their plans became public. I had to take on Mundial as my uncle was still in hiding near my aunt's village.'

The others watched the two of us intently, switching from one to the other as if we were Nadal and Federer trading shots at Roland Garros. Miguel was wide-eyed. He would have heard a lot of stories about crime in San Pedro from his father, but this was the first time he had been close to any action himself.

'And, like your uncle,' I continued, 'you needed money to fight Mundial. You also knew, better than him, that you needed solid evidence of what they were up to. When you saw what Ramón could do with his drones you knew how you could prove what they were doing out on the salar.'

'I didn't need any persuasion,' Ramón said.

'I grew up in San Pedro and could see more mining on the salar was a bad thing,' Miguel said. 'I knew nothing about drugs and only learned last week who Mundial are and what they're doing.'

I focused on Ximena. 'Last night you drove out to see your uncle to show him you had proof of Mundial's illegal exploratory mining on the salar. You tried to persuade him to make another attempt at drug dealing to get the money to take on Mundial in an expensive court case. Using bad money to do good, Lepan's old rationale. Luiz and Otto were tailing you, they weren't after the video but the drugs they thought you had. They wanted to stop you from setting up a rival operation, same as they had done with Lepan. They weren't acting for Mundial, they were part of a rogue operation led by their boss, Silveira. Am I right, Ximena?'

'You don't have to answer that, Ximena,' Ramón said. He stood up, crossed his arms and glared down at me. 'It's all supposition, what you would expect from an ivory tower academic who reasons but doesn't act, who doesn't know what the real world is like, who writes papers on development but doesn't commit to the cause. I was ready to follow Lepan into the Amazon. I'm right behind you against Mundial in the Atacama.'

'Cliff was pretty engaged last night,' Lucas said. 'We saw Otto and Luiz were armed but he didn't hesitate to follow me. We saved your butts, remember.'

'Lucas is right, Ramón,' Ximena said. 'We owe Cliff much more than an explanation. He figured out what was going on and kept me talking while Maria Paz bugged my Suzuki. If he hadn't done that, we would be in much worse shape than we are.' She ran her fingers lightly over her bruised cheeks. Ramón slumped into his armchair. 'And you are right, Cliff, we did go to Uncle Jorge to persuade him to fund our fight against Mundial by trying to restart the operation Lepan initiated. We couldn't persuade him, though. Uncle Jorge had seen how dangerous drug dealing was. We didn't have any drugs to give them, that's why Luiz and Otto kept beating us. They wouldn't believe it. We'll have to find some other way of funding our fight now we've experienced first-hand how dangerous that is. How much of your theory did you tell the inspector, Cliff?'

'I assured him that Luiz and Otto were only interested in the drones, that you had breached Mundial's security and all they wanted was the video. He was sceptical but accepted my account. It's satisfying to know I was right. There's no reason for my theory about the drugs to go any further.'

'Thank you,' Ximena said. 'I can see you understand what we're up against and what we've been trying to do.'

'That's a good place to wind things up,' Maria Paz said. 'For my part, I am disappointed that members of the team put our project at risk. You may think it is only academic, Ramón, but I'm sure our findings will help Ximena's folk manage their resources better. That's important even if it's not as dramatic as taking on the bad guys. I couldn't be prouder of the way the team came together last night. Cliff and Lucas, your heroics—and that's what they were—amaze me. You were right to insist I stay in the ute. Miguel, you too played a key part by acting as soon as I called. We should be grateful we're all still in one piece. And, Ximena, your cause isn't lost. The politicians and public will soon learn about last night. Even if those involved were not sanctioned by the company, all the bad publicity surrounding Mundial now will reduce their chances of being granted a lithium mining licence. The video will show that what Mundial has been doing is illegal. It won't be buried. I'm sure Ramón has made copies that will be circulating on social media before long, if they aren't already.' He nodded. 'As for the project, we have enough data. I suggest we all take a break tomorrow and on Thursday collate everything and work on the presentation. I wish we had more time for you to recover but the budget won't hold up any longer and I know Ramón needs to return home. Meanwhile, Lucas, could you please refill my glass, I can sure do with another wine.'

# CHAPTER 27

I should have slept well despite my aching ribs providing a constant reminder of Otto's boot. I was now confident I had a plausible alternative explanation which would exonerate Rico—Lepan's death was the result of his drug smuggling activities. I could sell that to the boy and his parents.

Sound sleep did not come readily. A kaleidoscope of images and ideas, of events real and imagined, kept swirling through my mind as I lay half awake: drones and data loggers, Lepan and Rico, hammers and spanners, Maria Paz and Ximena, *pataska* and pizza, Otto and Arturo, El Tatio and Easter Island, Mundial Mining and Adventures Atacama, Valle de la Luna and the Tropic of Capricorn.

I staggered into the kitchen at 10am. Lucas handed me a juice and brewed us coffee.

'Get much sleep, Cliff?'

'Not a lot. Too many confused ideas running through my head. Tell me, does the Tropic of Capricorn run through Easter Island?'

'Comes close if I remember right. Geography's not my strong point. Why?' Lucas looked puzzled.

'I'm not sure, it seemed important during the night.'

'Too much red wine and too many painkillers. How are the ribs?'

'Still bloody sore but gradually coming right. I'm too old for that sort of caper. You seemed to be having fun though.'

'Fun!' Lucas laughed. 'No way. I was shit-scared when we ran into that room. But it was the only way to stop them beating Ramón and Ximena. It was pure adrenaline that got me through. I wondered what the hell we were up against when we ran out into that dude's spotlight.'

'Good morning, Cliff. Hi, Lucas. Look what I have,' Maria Paz said. The smell of freshly baked rolls and pastries got our attention. 'But they're only for those who stop talking about the last few days. Who would like one?'

'Yes, please,' Lucas and I answered in unison.

'Ramón not up yet?'

'Up and away,' Lucas said. 'He and Ximena are nursing their wounds together.'

'As long as that's all they're doing. OK, quiet time now. You both need to rest up.'

Rest up we did. We ate a late lunch in town, had a long siesta, Maria Paz made a salad for dinner, and we all turned in early. The Tropic of Capricorn and Easter Island continued to intrude on my thoughts throughout the day but their significance, if any, remained unclear.

•••

We got back to work on Thursday, splitting into two groups after a general catch-up. Maria Paz, Ramón and Miguel focused on the technical challenges of monitoring visitor movements from GPS data and drone video, one of our key deliverables. Lucas and I worked on the application component, on how the combined results could be used to manage natural attractions better and enhance the visitor experience. Provided an effective stakeholder network could be developed. I enjoyed working with Lucas on this, seeing how far he had come since completing his PhD thesis with me. We were working as equals: I had decades of experience as a researcher; he had insider knowledge of Chilean society and institutions, knowledge essential to getting our recommendations implemented. We were all aware of the dangers of working in silos. Maria Paz now appreciated the value of traditional participant observation and called me over for some input on that. I reciprocated by seeking clarity when the GPS data and the video stills did not align or were open to different interpretations. Our immediate goal was to make a convincing presentation to the funding agency on Tuesday. After that we would work on the journal articles and on the final report which had a Christmas deadline. We would do this by Skyping each other and sharing drafts online.

Despite the drama with the Mundial thugs which could have derailed us, the project team had come together as I had hoped. Maria Paz was developing into a strong team leader and her academic future was bright. She would need to be careful not to go down the same road I had and focus solely on her work, on publishing another paper to the exclusion of all else. Ramón appeared to have relaxed his nascent activism and relished the nerdy debates with Maria Paz over the merits of their respective technologies. Miguel hung on his every word and was absorbing it all like the drone disciple he had become. His enthusiasm and intellect needed to be channelled into further study.

I sensed though that for me the curtain was coming down. It was time to make way for a new generation of scholars with all their technology. However, I still had an itch to scratch—Lepan and Rico.

'Cliff, you still with us? How are we going to get all the tour operators on board? San Pedro is still pretty much a frontier destination, like the Old West, where new arrivals battle it out for a share of the market with the older hands without being too particular about their methods.'

'Sorry, Lucas, I wandered off there for a moment.'

'Still wondering if Easter Island is on the Tropic of Capricorn?'

'No, just how well the team has done. What were you saying about the Wild West?'

'There are a few cowboy operators here, always ready to cut corners to make a quick buck rather than work collectively in the interests of the destination.'

'Whoever broke into the house trying to scare us off didn't have the interests of the destination at heart.'

'San Pedro needs more responsible operators like Marisela's company.'

'Not Marisela's company, Adventures Atacama… That's it, the missing link. It's Adventures Atacama, or rather Carlos and his photos, and the Tropic of Capricorn that's the connection. Sorry, Lucas, I've got to check something out.' I clicked through my picture files.

'No worries, about time we called it a day. We can sort the remainder tomorrow. Are you lot finished, Maria Paz?' Lucas asked.

'Almost done. You can sign out.'

In the excitement which followed, I had forgotten what I was doing on Monday afternoon when Maria Paz came in to tell me about tracking our ute. I was looking for the photo Carlos had taken of our group under the Tropic of Capricorn sign. I eventually found it and stared at the screen. A stock standard photo, taken before Carlos's marketing epiphany, of a group of tourists standing under a sign capturing their visit to a supposedly significant place.

'What are you looking for, Cliff?' Maria Paz asked.

'I'm not sure, exactly. It seemed important on Monday, but now I can't remember why.'

'When on Monday?'

'Right before you came to tell me about Ramón and Miguel being out on the salar.'

'If it helps, I saw you and Maria Paz coming out of your bedroom, Cliff,' butted in Lucas who was packing up his laptop. 'I'm not sure what you were doing in there.'

'Not what you think,' Maria Paz retorted.

'But when you came in,' I said, 'I had just found out that Ana Rojas had been to the Easter Island conference where Lepan was the keynote speaker. That's why I wanted the Tropic of Capricorn photo; it's the only one I've got with Ana in it. Look, there she is in the front, on your right, Maria Paz.'

'What does that tell you?' Lucas asked.

'Nothing.' I stared at the photo.

'I must have a similar one,' Maria Paz said. 'Let me check.'

Maria Paz was more organised than me and quickly produced her photo. The three of us peered at the screen.

'Still looking for red dots?' Ramón asked from the other end of the table.

'Found it,' I cried jubilantly. 'See, Maria Paz, in your photo she's wearing a hat, a bright red hat. She didn't have it on when Carlos took the photo for me.'

'So?' She failed to grasp the significance.

'It means the red dot behind Lepan at the geysers might not be Rico's scarf after all. It could be Ana's hat. Ramón, have you still got that enhancement you did for us? Send him this photo, Maria Paz, so we can compare the two.'

Ramón sighed. He could not understand my excitement or my obsession with Lepan's death. He was willing to help, though, to show he was still one of the team. He soon had the photos of Lepan and a headshot of Ana and her red hat side by side on the screen. The red in the two photos was identical. And by the shape of it, the dot resembled a hat more than a scarf. The others agreed. Ana had been right behind Lepan moments before he died.

'You're not suggesting Ana's a drug smuggler, are you?' Lucas asked.

'No. I'm beginning to think Lepan's death has nothing at all to do with Mundial or with drugs. I need to go and see her.'

'Not until after our presentation on Tuesday, Cliff. We need you there,' Maria Paz reminded me.

'Sure, it can wait a few more days.' First, I needed one more piece of information. I sent a quick email to Marisela and a fuller one to Ana Rojas.

•••

We spent Friday morning on our presentations. The technical expertise of my younger colleagues produced much slicker presentations than the PowerPoints I used to make. They had incorporated aerial views of visitors taken from the drones with detailed multi-coloured maps of changing visitor movements and photos that Lucas and I had taken highlighting associated management problems.

We wanted to make sure everything would run smoothly for Tuesday and held a trial run after lunch in front of Ximena, Marisela, Alvarez and Sergeant Figueroa. Miguel had been excited to show his father what the project had produced. Alvarez and Figueroa chatted while we were setting up.

Other than a couple of minor glitches when changing from one presenter to another, our presentation came over well. Our select audience applauded. Alvarez made a couple of useful comments from a tour operator's perspective which we would incorporate. Ximena now understood more clearly what we had been trying to achieve and asked if we could make a public presentation in San Pedro. We agreed that Lucas would come back later in the year and do that once the report was finalised. Miguel would assist him. The good sergeant beamed with pride. Maria Paz thanked everyone for their contribution and ordered the wine be opened. Marisela had laid her hands on some *vino del desierto* for the occasion.

Miguel's father was about to go on duty and could not stay for drinks. He said farewell to the others and asked me to step outside.

'Professor West, thank you once again for inviting Miguel to be part of this project. I never knew what he was capable of before. He wants to carry on with his studies, but we will have difficulty supporting him. His sister starts university in Antofagasta next year. If you hear of any opportunities for Miguel, do let us know.'

'Miguel has the makings of a fine researcher. We will all keep an eye out for any scholarships he can apply for. I would be pleased to write a reference for him.'

'Thank you. We would appreciate that. You were right about the convoy of vehicles to the geysers being deliberately held up the morning Professor Lepan died. The two Australians are long gone but Silveira, the boss, has started talking to play down his own part in the whole affair by incriminating Moretti and da Silva. Silveira says the two isolated Lepan at the geysers as part of a drug deal he swears he knew nothing about. That's hard to credit. Those two thugs don't have the brains to have organised that by themselves. Without eyewitnesses we may never be certain how Professor Lepan was involved and how he died.'

So, I was right about the drugs. And now I thought I knew how Lepan had died. I kept that to myself.

'And this is yours, I believe.' Figueroa handed me one of the missing maps of visitor movements at the geysers. 'My colleagues in Calama found it under the seat of the ute they shot up but didn't know what it was. Even though it was screwed up and dirty, I recognised it right away from what you showed me on the computer the other week. That impressed them.' He allowed himself a tight grin. 'Those city folk always think they're smarter than us. They then applied a bit more pressure on the driver, Franco. Seems he's also been working on the side for one of the new tour operators who has been giving us some trouble. It was Franco who broke into your house, trying to scare you off. The operator was the one spreading the rumours of more restrictions once the authorities got your recommendations. Pity he didn't hear your presentation first and understand your project better. I've assured Alvarez he won't be having any more problems from him.'

So that's what the two of them were discussing.

'I don't think you and your international colleagues will be required any further,' the sergeant added. 'Ximena Lopez lives in San Pedro, and Lucas Marchena can come up from Valparaíso and provide additional testimony for the prosecutor's office if required. Inspector Eterovic said to tell you that he didn't find any local experts in probability statistics. I don't know what he meant by that. Those PDI fellows keep everything to themselves. Anyway, he passed your advice on to his Interpol colleagues and yesterday the Irish garda arrested one of those Irishmen who was on that tour of yours. Not the big red-headed chap, the other one, O'Connor.'

It had been a shot in the dark when I had mentioned stats and trafficking to Arturo, but it had hit a target. I am glad it was Rory, not Pat, who was involved. Or maybe Pat was just the smarter of the two.

Back inside I poured myself a wine. Ramón clinked his glass against mine.

'Cheers, Cliff, great project. Seeing how you used that video from the drones to feed into visitor management has given me a bunch of ideas for using them in other projects. That should keep the head of department out of my hair for a while.'

'Just make sure you stick to tourists or wildlife and stay out of trouble.'

'I'll try, but no promises. I've also learned a lot from Ximena.' He picked up a bottle to refill her glass and the two huddled together in an intense conversation. No promises.

Maria Paz stepped outside to take a phone call and announced on her return that the Tuesday meeting had been rescheduled for Wednesday afternoon as an urgent issue had cropped up at Corfo.

Marisela gave me the information I had requested. Ana had been a late addition to the tour in April.

I now had everything that I had come to San Pedro for. Bill Broughton had been right all along. *'Cherchez la femme,'* he had suggested that night in the Wairarapa. My quest for an alternative explanation was no longer quixotic. As soon as we finished our drinks, I booked a Sunday morning flight from Santiago to Coyhaique.

In the evening, we went for one last drive in our trusty ute, out to the viewpoint where tourists flock to watch the sun go down on the Licancabur volcano.

# CHAPTER 28

Coyhaique is not my favourite city in Chile. It is promoted as the gateway to Patagonia, the region whose very name evokes images of mountains, glaciers and fiords, of condors soaring in vast open spaces, of whales spouting in the chilly waters of the southern Pacific. The city itself has little going for it. A statue of a shepherd and his flock is Coyhaique's main tourist attraction. For much of the year Coyhaique is cold and damp. In winter it is reputed to be the most polluted city in South America. The locals still use wood fires for much of their heating and an inversion layer traps the smoke so that it lingers all day. This was one of those days, raw and gloomy.

I had arranged to have a late lunch with Ana Rojas in the restaurant of the hotel where I was staying the night, El Reloj. Ana was waiting for me in the lobby. I studied her closely. She was short, had long black hair and a brownish complexion, darker than the average Chilean but lighter than most Malays. I knew the reason for that. If my calculations were right, she was forty-one years old.

It was only when the light caught her face from a certain angle that the likeness was there. I should have seen the resemblance earlier, but I hadn't had much contact with the Chileans on the tour or at the conference. Except for showing solidarity the morning Lepan died, they had largely kept to themselves. I had spent most of my time with Maria Paz, Viviana and Pat. And once you pigeon-hole someone—Ana was part of the Chilean group—it takes a lot to shift that image.

After exchanging greetings, we were shown to the restaurant and seated at a window table overlooking the surrounding woods.

I had a lot at stake in meeting with Ana. Only she could substantiate my theory about what had happened to Lepan. Would she speak freely or clam up, fearing she might incriminate herself? Was I sitting down for lunch with a patricide? I looked outside at the dreary day and opened my case with the weather.

'It must have taken you a while to become acclimatised to this place.'

'What do you mean?'

'After growing up in Malaysia it can't have been easy adapting to all this cold and damp.'

Ana did not miss a beat. 'I see you've been talking to Lucas, Professor West. How is he?'

'He's doing well. It was great working with him up in San Pedro. The Atacama is an interesting place.'

'Quite different from Coyhaique, that's for sure. Lucas was lucky to have you as his supervisor.' Was she being polite or deliberately shifting the topic away from Malaysia and the Atacama?

The opening niceties were interrupted by the waiter who had come to take our orders. We opted for a sharing platter of raw lamb ham, small pork sausages, venison pâté, lamb pâté and onion marmalade. Ana said the platter was one of the restaurant's specialties. I hoped sharing it would make it easier to exchange confidences. I suggested a wine. She preferred a sparkling water.

Ana put down the menu and came straight to the point.

'Professor West, why have you come to Coyhaique? Why do

you want to talk to me? You don't appear to have a particular interest in cultural tourism or in the Mapuche.'

'You are quite right, Ana. I'm sorry if I misled you. I wasn't sure you would believe me if I gave you the real reason.'

'Which is?'

'I was a friend of your mother.'

'You knew my mother?' Ana gaped at me.

'Zubaida and I were good friends when we were students in Aix-en-Provence. Unfortunately, I lost touch with her when I returned to New Zealand. That was at the end of 1975.'

I put the cropped Pont d'Avignon photo on the table. Ana stared at the photo, wide-eyed and open-mouthed. Then at me. And back at the photo. Despite the ravages of more than forty years, I was still recognisable as the smiling moustachioed young man with a mop of Seventies' hair standing beside Zu. Ana could not believe her eyes.

I looked at her and at the photo. In person, Ana more closely resembled her mother than when I had earlier compared Maria Paz's group photo at the Tropic of Capricorn and the Pont d'Avignon snap. No resemblance at all to her father.

'But, but...how do you know Zubaida was my mother if you were no longer in contact with her?' she asked once she had recovered her composure.

'I only realised you could be Zubaida's daughter a couple of days ago, when I emailed you. I wasn't one hundred per cent certain until just now.'

'What made you think that? she asked, eyebrows raised. 'We hardly spoke in San Pedro or afterwards in Santiago.'

'I made the connection through your father, Antoine Lepan.' I was not completely sure of that either. I had stunned her into silence once more. I had connected the dots correctly. I waited while she recovered from this second revelation and decided how best to continue. Ana sipped her water. What else might this relative stranger reveal? What can I safely say to someone who knows who my parents were?

'You must have been shocked, discovering that you were Antoine Lepan's daughter.'

Ana sat back in her chair and shook her head slowly. 'Shocked is putting it mildly. Imagine discovering after all this time that the famous Professor Lepan was my father.' She was alert and cautious, not wanting to give anything away. 'How did you work that out?'

'I've spent a lot of time since the conference in Santiago researching Lepan.'

'Ah, I see, you were one of the contributors to the famous festschrift.' She was quick on the uptake.

'That's what got me started. The festschrift has been canned but I became intrigued by him and carried on finding out what I could.' It was too soon to tell her what clarifying Lepan's death meant to me—a possible path to redemption.

I explained how I had found out, through seeing Esperanza's slide of the Bastille Day party, that Zubaida and Lepan knew each other. I had that photo with me but judged it too painful for Ana to see and left it in my pocket. How Carmen confirmed that Zubaida had been in Borneo researching tourism in longhouses earlier that year and not long after the party she had to go home without completing her thesis. How I had made the connection to Lepan's longhouse paper, knowing he plagiarised graduate students' research. I left out the bit about his habit of sleeping with students to gain their confidence and access their material. I explained how he had been elsewhere when the fieldwork for 'his' seminal longhouse paper in Portuguese had been done. How on my recent trip to the Atacama I had learnt from Lucas that Ana was from Malaysia, not Chilean as I had assumed. How she and Lepan had been at the Easter Island conference where his address alluded to his pioneering work many years ago on longhouses in Borneo. How they were the only people both at that conference and on the Atacama tour.

'On Friday,' I concluded, 'I learned from Marisela that you only signed up for the tour right before it began, a couple of days after the Easter Island conference finished. I figured you had worked out that Lepan might be your father and that you would have a better chance of talking to him on the tour. Right?'

'I can see why you have such an international reputation as a researcher, being able to dig out all those details and piece them together. Very impressive.' Was she flattering me hoping that I would go no further?

'That's as far I got. I was sure there's more to the story, so I contacted you and here I am. I don't want to upset you in anyway, and I will understand if you tell me it's none of my business, but I would like to hear more about your mother.'

'It's OK. It's a few months now since I worked out who my father was, or at least who I believe he was. We will never know for certain, but how you have come to the same conclusion seems to confirm it. Antoine Lepan must have been my father. But before I tell you what I know of my mother, please tell me about her, about your friend Zubaida.' She picked up the photo. 'Other than my family, and they never said much, I've never met anyone who knew my mother.' Ana put her elbows on the table, steepled her fingers and rested her chin on her hands. She wanted to hear what I had to say, not eat lunch.

I realised that I had something to offer Ana, a means of gaining her confidence. I was not Machiavellian enough to have considered this angle before. Zubaida had been a good friend. I spoke of her with genuine warmth.

'I used to call her Zu.' I smiled at the recollection. 'Your mother was a wonderful person, always cheerful and smiling, got on well with everyone.' Ana's face lit up. 'We met at a function for international students. She looked gorgeous in her national dress, stood out from all the others.'

Ana's eyes moistened. 'That dress, the only thing I have of hers. I've never worn it, though.' She wiped away a tear.

I paused but she waved me on.

'We immediately hit it off, common ties between our two countries, both far from home, English speaking, members of the Commonwealth. She was the only Malaysian in Aix; I didn't know any other New Zealanders there. She spoke better French than me. We were in different halls of residence. I used to go over and see her there. Zu didn't eat in the university cafeterias often. She used to make these delicious curries. Laksa sometimes. Other dishes too whose names I can't remember. All very exotic to me.'

Ana did not hesitate to probe the depth of our relationship. 'Did you date?' she asked. Fair question, I was asking a lot of her.

'Not much as such. We hung out a lot, usually with other friends. I remember one night the two of us went to see *La Nuit américaine*. Typical French movie, I lost track of all the relationships, who was connected to who. Zu raved about it; she was a huge fan of François Truffaut. She told me later that some of her African friends gave her a hard time for going out with a White. When I asked her how she had responded, Zu said she laughed and told them that she wasn't racist. That was your mother.'

Ana laughed too, grateful for the anecdote.

'I don't know how we lost touch. I suppose it was partly me going back to New Zealand and getting wrapped up in my new job, then Zu going back to Malaysia for her fieldwork. I always wondered what had become of her. Now I know a little more.'

Our lunch was served, a timely pause for Ana to begin her side of the narrative. I picked at the platter and let her tell her story her way without interrupting.

'I don't remember my mother at all. She died when I was barely twelve months old. All I know is what the woman who brought me up—my mother's sister—has told me. What you said about her time in France, about doing research in Sarawak and not completing her thesis confirms what my aunt told me. Returning home without graduating made life hard for my mother. Her family were not well off; her father was a village postmaster in Kedah. She had nothing to show for the sacrifices they had made to support her in France—she had a scholarship but that wasn't enough to live on. What's more, she had nothing for her father's brother in Kuching, the tour operator who had arranged her visits to the longhouses and who had been boasting about the research his niece in France was doing. That meant a huge loss of face for her uncle amongst the other operators and strained relations within the family. She humiliated them even more when they learned that she was pregnant and unmarried. My grandparents were strict Muslims and kicked her out. Her elder sister who lived in southern Malaysia and was much more liberal in her views took her in. Apparently, my mother suffered a lot giving birth to me and her health never recovered. She died a year later, of shame and humiliation as much as from the difficult childbirth. My aunt and her husband were kind people and raised me as one of their own. Their four children treated me as their sister, not their cousin. I often wondered as a child why my complexion was much lighter than theirs. It was not until I was a teenager that I learnt from my aunt who I was. All she told me about my father was that he was a lecturer my mother knew in France.

'I had a happy childhood, did well at high school, attended university in Penang, got a scholarship to James Cook in Townsville for my master's. I met and married Fernando there. My aunt and uncle came to the wedding, we keep in touch, but I've never been back to Malaysia. After we graduated, we came here—Fernando is originally from Puerto Aisén—and we were both lucky enough to land good jobs in Coyhaique. So, now I consider myself as Ana Rojas, a Chilean.

'I wanted to talk to Lepan, to let him know he had a daughter and to ask why he treated my mother so badly. I didn't get the chance on Easter Island because he wasn't around the conference after he gave his address; the organisers had arranged special visits to the *moais* and other sites for the distinguished professor as well as some high-level meetings before he flew back to Santiago. I had planned a few days with Fernando's sister in Viña del Mar before the TADSAI conference. Instead, I joined the Atacama tour at the last minute. The first day there wasn't a real chance to speak to him. It was harder than I thought to summon up the nerve to approach him, he came across as cold and arrogant. He didn't acknowledge that we had both been at the Easter Island conference. He spoke above his audience, literally and figuratively, and wouldn't have noticed me amongst all the Pasifika participants. Next morning... he died up at the geysers.'

She chewed on a mouthful of lamb ham and looked at me. She knew that she had arrived at the reason for my visit. It was my turn to be direct.

'Ana, you were there when it happened, weren't you?'

'What makes you say that?'

I moved the platter to one side and laid down another photo.

'That green spot is Lepan and that red dot is you. Maria Paz took it just before Rico cried out.'

'Not exactly distinct, is it?'

It wasn't, but we were not in a court of law. 'Lepan was the only one with a green jacket and you were the only one with a red hat.' I showed her the group photo which Carlos had taken at the Tropic of Capricorn.

She continued to cast doubt on my case. 'Rico's scarf was also red.'

'That was on the ground, you wouldn't see it in this shot.' I could see her resolve weakening in the face of evidence I had produced.

'That hat didn't do me much good at the geysers. It was a sun hat. Going that far north, I was mainly prepared for stinking hot weather, like what we had at the Valle de la Luna and the lagunas. I bought it on Easter Island.'

Another diversion. Enough of that. 'Why don't you tell me what happened, Ana?'

She again countered with questions of her own.

'You are taking Lepan's death very personally, Professor West. Why is it so important to you? How has it impinged on your life? I don't understand what it's got to do with you.' All good questions I had to agree.

'It is personal. You were the first on the spot with Rico and saw how upset he was. That was only natural. It was a horrible sight. Rico is still unsettled by the experience. He cries a lot, wakes in the night, his schooling has suffered. Rico believes he was responsible for Lepan's death, that your father tripped on his scarf. He is convinced he's to blame even though his parents keep telling him that it was an accident. Alba blames Pablo for letting Rico run loose. Pablo accepts responsibility. It's all put a lot of strain on the household. Now Alba has taken Rico to live with her mother in Mendoza, leaving Pablo in Rosario.'

'That's terrible, I had no idea. Of course, at the time he was understandably upset but I thought he would soon get over it. I still don't see why that should concern you, Professor West.'

'Something similar happened to me in New Zealand. My son Rod blamed himself for a mountain bike accident that left his best friend paralysed from the neck down. Two years later Rod took his own life. His mother blamed me, with good reason. Soon after, we split up and later divorced.'

'I'm sorry to hear that.'

'So now I'm seeing parallels between what happened to Rod and what is happening to Rico. I don't want to see the same ending for him and his parents. We need to be able to convince Rico that it wasn't his fault, that something other than tripping on his scarf or bumping into him caused Lepan to fall. I've persuaded myself that being able to do that—saving Rico, Alba and Pablo—would go some way to providing redemption for me, relieving me of some of the guilt I've been feeling all these years for Rod's death. When Rod's friend had his accident I was correcting the proofs of one of my books, not biking with them as promised. I compounded that by letting Rod go mountain biking by himself when he wanted to go out again, the day he died. That's what is driving me on, finding some other explanation for how Lepan died.'

Ana nodded her understanding and waited to see where I was going next.

'On this last trip to San Pedro, we heard that Lepan was involved in smuggling drugs, that a handover was to be made at the geysers that morning, that something went wrong, and he was killed. Maybe that's what did happen, but the evidence is circumstantial. The coroner reported that he either had a heart attack or tripped and fell. Either way, that doesn't help the Toledos. Heart attacks are difficult to explain to a young boy. Rico understands tripping over, only he's convinced he's responsible. Then I came across that photo which suggests you were present and can tell me what happened.'

Time to close my case. 'Do you have any children, Ana?' I had already seen their smiling faces on Facebook and wanted to draw on her maternal feelings.

'Two, Rafael, he's a year older than Rico, and Teresita, who is six.'

'As a mother you will understand what Alba is going through and what my ex-wife, Wendy, had to deal with. Perhaps you will now appreciate what I'm trying to do to redeem myself and why.'

'What do you want me to do?'

'Tell me what you know, Ana. What happened to Lepan?'

Ana had little to gain by telling me. She could incriminate herself. Get up and leave. She hesitated. I waited. She drank half a glass of water. I spread some venison pâté on a cracker. At last, she continued.

'Well, I was determined to talk to Lepan up at the geysers.

He was first off the bus and got ahead of me. I had a hard job catching up and following him in the dark with all that steam around. Eventually I heard his voice up ahead of me. I don't know who he was talking to and only caught fragments of the conversation when the others raised their voices. Something about "where's the rest of it", "we're keeping the money". Then silence, except for the geysers. You might be right about the drugs. I waited a couple of minutes then walked towards where I had heard the voices. Lepan was standing on the edge of the path, staring across the pool. I just walked up behind him. I hadn't worked out beforehand what to say. I greeted him with *'Bonjour, père'* a little bit of French I remembered from the year of it I did at high school. You wouldn't know I had French blood in my veins. He turned round in surprise, stunned at seeing and hearing me, tripped and fell into the pool. My aunt says I look like my mother, so the ghost of Zubaida coming out of the steam could have given him a heart attack. I just stood there, emotionless, as he flailed around in the water. This man meant nothing to me, he had not been in my life for forty-one years. He was responsible for my mother's death. I don't feel any guilt at all. How was I to know how he would react when I greeted him? Anyway, I couldn't do anything to help. I'm too short to have reached over and pulled him out. I just stood back. Then Rico came running by looking for his scarf, saw the dead man in the pool, his red scarf at the water's edge, and burst into tears. I went over to comfort him. That Irishman arrived. Then you and Maria Paz rushed up. You know the rest.'

The truth at last. I had my alternative explanation. Relief and elation flooded through me.

Followed by a flash of anger at the realisation that the Toledos' distress could have been avoided if Ana had corrected Rico's belief that Lepan had tripped on his scarf. Instead, when I had handed her a sugar-laden coffee back at the bus she was ready to pass the blame to Rico, saying Lepan had tripped on his scarf. Ana reinforced that account by glaring at Rodrigo for spreading the idea and upsetting Rico even more. The succour she had given the boy had only been temporary. If she felt any guilt for prolonging the needless suffering of Rico and his parents, it did not show.

The role of on-the-spot comforter of Rico, I now realised, had also served her well in directing attention away from any other part she might have played, intentionally or otherwise, in the events of that morning. Getting the boy away from the hot pool and returning him to his parents as quickly possible was seen as a natural reaction, a motherly response we appreciated at the time. It also took Ana out of the picture. Maria Paz's arrival was a bonus; two kind-hearted women caring for a small boy, anxious to get him away from the scene of a dreadful accident. Ana had acted instinctively in assisting the boy— she could not have foreseen Rico would come running by when she stepped out to confront her father. But had she also taken full advantage of the situation to remove herself as a possible suspect in the event Lepan's death was not deemed accidental?

As doubt and anger welled up inside, another thought struck me. Had Ana come forward that morning with the account she had just related, I would not have spent countless hours trying to ascertain how Lepan had died. But she hadn't. Her silence had given me the opportunity to unravel the truth and to redeem myself. If not the whole truth, then enough for a plausible alternative explanation. That was sufficient for me.

'How much of this did you tell that sergeant who interviewed us that afternoon?'

'Very little. Just that I heard Rico crying and ran to him. I was afraid that if I mentioned anything else the carabineros might suspect that I had pushed Lepan, taking revenge on an absent unfeeling father if our relationship ever became known. The sergeant was more interested in what you foreigners were doing. To him, I was one of the Chileans, the others had gone down one of those side tracks and didn't see anything. They didn't know what I had discovered about Lepan. His death didn't affect me at all. I carried on as normal on the tour, attended the conference in Santiago. I couldn't understand all that praise that Brazilian fellow heaped on Lepan. When Carvalho mentioned the seminal Borneo paper, I had to force myself to stay in my seat and not stand and shout out it was all my mother's work. No one would have believed me. I'm so glad there will be no festschrift. I went home to Coyhaique and told Fernando all about it. He was completely supportive and told me to forget Lepan and carry on as usual, as if my father never existed. Which for me was true. That's what I've done. You're the only other one who knows what happened at the geysers.'

Did Lepan's indifference to the feelings of others run deep in Ana's veins too? Was she completely unmoved by witnessing the death of her father? Or was it all a façade—going up to the lagunas, attending the conference, presenting her paper, dancing the *cueca*? A deliberate attempt to avoid any show of emotion or change in behaviour that might have revealed her relationship to the dead anthropologist and raised doubts about his accident.

'What else can I tell you, Professor West?'

'Did you see his camera bag, that big one that he had been lugging around?'

'No. I was looking at him. I do remember seeing Rico's scarf on the ground, but he was so upset when he saw the body that I ran to him right away and didn't pick it up.'

'The missing bag suggests whoever he was talking to snatched it from him. The bag probably did contain drugs.'

'Does that make a difference to anything?'

'No, but it firms up my theory about what Lepan was up to.' It was good to know I was right. 'If it was the two thugs who grabbed the bag, then he would have already been shaken up when you approached him.' Lepan would have stood no chance against Otto and Luiz.

'Will you tell this to anyone?' Ana looked unsure of herself for a moment. Had she told me too much?

I hesitated before answering. 'No. A few people know I was curious about Lepan's death, even suggested that I had become obsessed with it. A couple know about the photo at the geysers, but nobody is aware of all the connections I have made except you, Ana. And nobody needs to.'

Nothing would change the fact that Lepan was dead. He had died a horrible death. Had he got what he deserved? Had justice been done? That was too cynical, even given the long shadow he had cast over so many lives. I was furious with Ana but took her at her word that his death was accidental. She could not have anticipated her father's reaction to his unknown daughter's sudden appearance. I had no reason to pass on Ana's account to Figueroa.

'Thank you.' Ana breathed a sigh of relief. 'What do you want me to do?'

She needed to make amends to the Toledos.

'You must go to Mendoza and talk to Rico and Alba; he will remember you and believe what you tell him. That should stop him blaming himself and allow Pablo and Alba to get back together and resume their lives as a family. They're suffering, you don't appear to be. Talking to them would spare them any more heartbreak. Relieving them of that would also help lift some of the guilt that I've felt ever since Rod died and Wendy left me. Can you do that, Ana, for them and for me?'

She gazed out the window, reflecting on what I had said.

'I can go with you to Mendoza if it would be easier,' I added.

Ana turned back to me. 'I don't know Alba. We only spoke that morning. I didn't see her at the conference.'

'She had to return home early because Rico was so upset. Surely you knew that. Remember, they didn't come with us to the lagunas.' I clenched my fists under the table but didn't want to play the guilt card too hard. I did not say outright that their sudden departure was because she had not spoken up at the time, but the message was getting through.

'Do we need to go all the way to Mendoza? Wouldn't a phone call do? Or we could Skype. Then there's the cost. Last month the bank increased the interest on our mortgage; Fernando and I have to watch our pesos.'

'Rico needs to hear it from you in person, Ana. He's met you but may not be able to place you over the phone. Alba will rest easy hearing first-hand what happened and how Rico isn't to blame. And don't worry about the cost, I can cover that. You will be doing me a favour too.'

I spread some onion marmalade on a cracker, allowing Ana more time to think over my proposition. I was relieved when she agreed for the family's sake. 'And I've learnt a lot more about my mother and Lepan from you, Zu's friend,' she added. That seemed to weigh heavily in her decision. 'When do you propose?'

'I have a meeting in Santiago on Wednesday afternoon. If we're lucky and can get seats, we could fly to Santiago tomorrow, then on to Mendoza to see Rico and Alba on Tuesday We would be back in Santiago on Wednesday morning. Short notice, I know. Would that work for you?'

She reached for her phone and checked her diary. I held my breath.

'Should do. This week I don't have any lectures until Thursday. I can skip the library committee meeting on Tuesday and re-schedule the one with my research group. I will have to check with Fernando. He's got an aunt in town who should be able to help look after the kids.'

We finished the meal and I accompanied Ana to the door. I looked up at the sky and saw the sun breaking through.

With a lighter heart I went back inside and searched for flights online. We would have to overnight at an airport hotel in Santiago as there was no connecting flight on to Mendoza that evening.

Seats on the Tuesday morning flight were not cheap and would exhaust my project fee and the per diems I had saved. I had no choice, getting to Mendoza as soon as possible was critical in case Ana changed her mind. I was not looking forward to doing more flying, my ribs kept reminding me of my encounter with Otto.

Before booking I had called Alba. She was not as confident as I was that talking with Ana would help. She agreed to meet us because she was at the end of her tether coping with Rico and was anxious to work things out with Pablo. On Monday, while waiting at the Coyhaique airport, I sent Maria Paz a quick text saying I would not be back in Santiago until late morning on Wednesday and would go directly to the meeting. I did not explain the delay.

# CHAPTER 29

Ana and I had plenty of time to talk while we were travelling. She wanted to learn more about Zu's time in Aix and pumped me for more information about Lepan. I answered out of respect for my late friend, not sympathy for her daughter.

'How could my mother have fallen for him? He wasn't good looking. Did she, you know... er...? You hear stories about the French... and being students...'

'Zu had lots of friends, male and female. But if you mean, did she sleep around, I'm sure she didn't. I never even got a *bisou* from her. Lepan was by all accounts a real charmer, smooth and seductive. He flattered students by asking lots of questions and offering advice on their research. He was interested, not to help them but to use their hard work himself.'

'I suppose I have half siblings all round the world,' she mused, shaking her head. 'What was my mother like as a student?'

I handed her a copy of the longhouse paper.

'I can't read Portuguese.'

'I can't either, but from what Esperanza told me it's an amazing piece of original research, far ahead of its time. The empirical research in the Iban longhouses is detailed and insightful, full of astute observations. That's what your mother did. She was gifted, she would have become an outstanding researcher. OK, Lepan wrote the paper and some of the interpretation is his, but it is all based on Zu's ideas and on her fieldwork. You can be extremely proud of your mother.'

'I am,' she said, with a lump in her throat. 'But not of my father.'

I told her what I had learnt about him, how he had rapidly established an outstanding publication record by lifting other people's work. How he had become an activist, whether by conviction to the causes he championed, or because the chances of his plagiarism being detected increased significantly when cross-referencing sources became easier in the digital era. Without mentioning names, I told her about Montse and her friend, Begoña Pi. We talked about the protest at El Tatio and how he was planning to help Ximena and her uncle fight more lithium mining in the Salar de Atacama.

'So, he wasn't a bad man in the end, was he, Professor West?' I noted some grudging acceptance in her voice.

'Antoine Lepan was a complex man, Ana. As a scholar I can't forgive the way he built his reputation on plagiarism, how he destroyed your mother and hurt others. He didn't need to do that; he had a brilliant if flawed mind. His early work shows he was an extremely capable researcher. He had a massive ego, though, and his academic ambitions exceeded those of mere mortals like us. He wanted much more than he could achieve by himself and ruthlessly exploited the work of others. As for his activism, it's not for me to judge. I don't know much more than what I found out in the Atacama. As an academic activist, the image he cultivated of himself, he did appear to be helping the poor and oppressed but it also gave him the notoriety he craved. If he was involved in drug trafficking, then he had little sympathy for those further down the line, the users and addicts, their families, and the victims of crimes to support their habits.'

That was as fair a picture as I could paint.

'You're right, I hadn't thought of those people. Lepan doesn't have any redeeming features after all, does he?'

I had no answer for that. Instead, I told Ana she could keep the longhouse paper. 'It's a tangible link to your parents, produced by the two of them.'

'But my mother was an unknowing partner. He stole her work. This paper helped establish Lepan's reputation but led to my mother's death.'

Ana slowly and purposefully tore the paper to shreds and handed the remains of her parents' legacy to the flight attendant who was collecting used paper cups, serviettes and other rubbish in a plastic bag.

I felt Ana was being unduly harsh. Later, I decided she was right. Shredding Lepan's plagiarised article was a much more fitting end to his scholarship than a festschrift.

There was nothing else to say and we fell silent until we arrived in Mendoza. We took a taxi directly to Alba's mother's house. Rico was still not attending school and Alba had let him know we were coming.

'Good morning, Professor Cliff,' he said politely when he answered the door.

'How are you, Rico? I see you've still got your New Zealand cap.'

'He wears it everywhere,' Alba said.

'It's the only cap like it in Rosario, and in Mendoza too,' Rico said with evident pride.

'You remember Dr Ana, don't you?'

'Hello,' he said without looking at her.

Was he just shy? What if seeing her again brought back and amplified his experience at the geysers? Had I miscalculated his reaction? Would our visit only make things worse?

'Rico, why don't you go and get your book on animals and

show it to Dr Ana. She has a boy your age and would like to see it. I've got to talk to Professor Cliff.'

This was the strategy we had agreed on; Ana would explain what had happened at the geysers to Rico, I would tell Alba what I knew about Lepan and how Rico had nothing to do with his death. If necessary, we would swap over and reinforce the message. Or messages.

Rico was a much happier boy when he and Ana came back into the kitchen where I had been talking to Alba.

'Professor Cliff, come with me, I've got a secret I need to tell you,' Rico said.

'Plan B,' Ana whispered as I passed her.

'Plan A,' I said. We had two different versions for mother and son. I had told Alba that Ana had seen Lepan trip on the stones not Rico's scarf and that she had not realised they weren't aware of that. This with my fingers crossed behind my back. Ana must have known.

In the lounge I knelt beside the boy. 'What is it, Rico?'

'It's a secret, Dr Ana just told me. She said not to tell anyone. I can trust you though because you gave me this cap and the Tintin book.' He took the cap off, inspected it, looked at me and put the cap back on, reassured of my trustworthiness.

'OK, I promise I won't tell.'

'You remember when we were in Chile and visited the geysers, that place with all the steam and spooky stuff.'

'I remember.'

'And there was that old Frenchman who fell into the hot pool and died.'

'Professor Lepan.'

'Well, he didn't really trip.'

'No?'

'No. Two baddies did it, they pushed him in. They were drug smugglers and stole some money from the old guy. He had a lot of it in his camera bag. Dr Ana saw it all but couldn't help him. She's a tiny lady and they were real big bad men.'

'Wow! Imagine that.' I was tempted to ask the boy what he had seen when he had arrived on the scene. Nobody ever appeared to have asked Rico that for the same reason I refrained now, fear of causing him any further distress.

'Have the police caught them, Professor Cliff?'

'They nabbed them when I was there last week. The baddies are all in jail.'

'I'm glad. I didn't like the Frenchman. He told me off for scaring the flamingos. But they shouldn't have pushed him in the pool, should they?'

'No, they were very bad men. They deserve to be in jail.'

'Don't tell Mum, she would be scared to know those baddies were there when we were.'

We rejoined Ana and Alba. Alba picked up her son. Both were full of smiles now.

'It was so good of you to come,' a greatly relieved mother said. 'Thank you so much. I will let Pablo know you were here. He will be so pleased to hear your news. Won't you stay for lunch?'

'Thank you, but I'm sure you've got a lot to be going on with,' I said.

Alba and Rico hugged us both and we left.

'That went well,' I said to Ana in the taxi to the hotel.

'I could see when I started talking about the geysers to Rico that simply saying I had seen Lepan trip and fall into the pool would not convince him. So, I switched to Plan B, the drug smuggling version. The best stories always have an element of truth.' She gave me a Mona Lisa smile.

Which story and which elements of truth had she told me? Could I ever be sure about how Lepan had died and Ana's part in it? Did it matter anymore? Not to me. What I had set out to do was show Rico and his parents that he was not to blame for Lepan's death. Job done.

# CHAPTER 30

The visit to Alba and Rico had lightened my burden. I was now confident I had put Lepan behind me. Ironically, however much I had come to despise the man, Lepan had left me a positive legacy—he had provided a path to my redemption. I could move on.

And try to move on I did. I switched to my second mission in Mendoza—a surprise visit to Viviana. I needed to see her before heading back to New Zealand, to find out how she felt about me. And how I felt about her. Maria Paz had dropped enough hints to suggest Viviana viewed me as more than just a friend and colleague. In the few days since I had pieced together a credible alternative explanation, I had begun to see the world differently. I dared to believe I could leave the past behind and it was not too late to find someone with whom I could share my remaining years. Was that person Viviana?

I had not contacted her beforehand in case the visit to Alba and Rico failed and redemption eluded me. Big mistake. Back at the hotel I could not reach Viviana on her cell phone or landline. I left messages but got no reply. She was not online. My ribs were playing up because of all the travelling, making me even more miserable.

Ana spent the afternoon shopping. Mendoza had much more to offer consumers than Coyhaique. Judging by the overweight suitcase she bought for her purchases, increased mortgage rates had not dampened her spending.

The flight back to Santiago next morning was delayed. Ana rushed to make her connecting flight to Coyhaique. I grabbed a cab to join Maria Paz and Lucas for the debriefing with Corfo. Ramón had returned to Brazil during the weekend. Miguel had stayed behind in San Pedro. Our trial run on Friday served us well. Maria Paz and Lucas's polished presentation made me proud and impressed those who had financed the project. We had completed the stated deliverables. The meeting ended with talk of future collaboration applying the dual drone/GPS methodology in other parts of Chile where growing visitor numbers were creating a need for better destination management.

We celebrated with a pisco sour at the nearest bar. Maria Paz buzzed with the reaction from Corfo, over the moon with what her team had achieved. She and Lucas were certain they would collaborate on some future project and would stay in touch with Ramón. Maria Paz reckoned Miguel had a good chance of obtaining a master's scholarship in Barcelona. I would not be drawn on my plans once I was back in New Zealand. It was time for me to take my retirement more seriously, I said, time to do some creative writing. Lucas hugged Maria Paz. He shook my hand, laughed, and gave me a bear hug before catching his bus to Valparaíso.

Maria Paz and I took a taxi to the Vegas. I was travelling light because of my sore ribs and had left my suitcase at the hotel before going to Coyhaique. The receptionist handed me my key and said my suitcase had already been taken up to my room. I trudged up the stairs to another night alone in a foreign city. I opened the door. An unfamiliar suitcase on the luggage rack caught my eye. I checked my key, yes, this was my room. There must be a mistake.

I was about to call reception to sort it out when the phone by the bed rang. The receptionist was half a step ahead of me. I picked up the phone.

'How's the room, Cliff?' Maria Paz asked.

'It's nice but it looks as though somebody is already here. Must be a mix-up.'

'Mix-up, no, I don't think so. Check the name tag on the suitcase.'

I did. *Viviana Arévalo, Mendoza*. I could hear Maria Paz's chuckle from where I stood. Followed by a polite knock on the door. I opened it.

'Good evening, Cliff.'

'Viviana,' I managed to say as I hugged her tightly. 'Looks like there has been some mix-up in our rooms.'

'No mix-up, Cliff. You can leave your suitcase there.'

# REFERENCES

Cliff found the following publications useful in his background reading about the Atacama.

Babidge, S. (2016) Contested value and an ethics of resources: water, mining and indigenous people in the Atacama Desert, Chile, *The Australian Journal of Anthropology*, 27, 84–103.

Bolados García, P. (2014) Los conflictos etnoambientales de 'Pampa Colorada' y 'El Tatio' en el salar de Atacama, norte de Chile. Procesos étnicos en un contexto minero y turístico transnacional, *Estudios Atacameños Arqueología y Antropología Surandina*, 48, 229 – 248.

de la Maza, F. (2017): Tourism in indigenous territories: the impact of public policies and tourism value of indigenous culture, *Latin American and Caribbean Ethnic Studies*, 13 (1) 94-111.

Glennon, J.A. and Pfaff, R.M (2003) The extraordinary thermal activity of El Tatio Geyser Field, Antofagasta Region, Chile, *The GOSA Transactions: a special report*, 31-78.

Liu, Wenjuan; Agusdinata, B. and Myint, S.E. (2019) Spatiotemporal patterns of lithium mining and environmental degradation in the Atacama Salt Flat, Chile, *International Journal of Applied Earth Observation and Geoinformation,* 80, August, 145-156.

Montero, C. and Parra, C. (2001) El cluster del ecoturismo en San Pedro. In: Buitelaar, R. and Gómez, J.J. (Eds) *Serie Seminarios y Conferencias.* CEPAL, Santiago, 17, 93-114.

Pierce, S.A., Malin, R.A. and Figueroa, E. (2012) Sustained dialogue for ground water and energy resources in Chile, *Journal of Contemporary Water Research & Education,* 149, 76-87.

# ACKNOWLEDGEMENTS

Manuscript assessors Sue Reidy and Geoff Walker each provided valuable candid advice for improving initial drafts.

Many thanks to my readers for their helpful feedback and encouragement to see Cliff's adventures through to publication: Paul Kleinman who was there from the first draft, Sergio Cruz, Marcela Correa, Caê Silveira and Carol Perwick.

I enjoyed bouncing ideas off my son Rémi as Cliff's story unfolded and found his observations insightful. He and Rowena Cumming also provided technical assistance.

Above all, very special thanks to my wife Chantal. She has been there every step along the way, encouraging me to realise my youthful ambition to write a novel. Chantal was a willing listener as I outlined Cliff's deeds over the dinner table. Her keen eye as a reader helped me avoid inconsistencies in the plot and errors in the text; any that remain are mine. This book is dedicated to her.

Douglas Pearce is an emeritus professor of tourism management at Victoria University of Wellington, New Zealand. His teaching, research and consulting projects have taken him to Europe, Asia, South America and the Pacific. He has written numerous academic papers and five scholarly books on tourism. His books have been translated into French, Spanish, Portuguese, Italian and Japanese. *Lepan's Shadow* is his debut novel. Douglas lives in Wellington with his wife Chantal.

www.ingramcontent.com/pod-product-compliance
Lightning Source LLC
Chambersburg PA
CBHW020051180626
46812CB00006B/2276